FALSE HORIZONS

By the Author

An Intimate Deception

New Horizons Series:

Unknown Horizons

Savage Horizons

False Horizons

FALSE HORIZONS

by

CJ Birch

2019

CREDITS
EDITOR: ASHLEY BARTLETT AND SHELLEY THRASHER
PRODUCTION DESIGN: STACIA SEAMAN
COVER DESIGN BY W.E. PERCIVAL

Acknowledgments

Science fiction is always a lot of fun to write because you're able to take your imagination on a journey of what-ifs.

What if humans no longer lived on Earth? That's the question that started this whole series. This led to so many more questions, some simple: where would we go? And some difficult: how do you make living on the asteroid belt possible? To the inane: what would you snack on late at night?

I truly believe the human species is resilient. We have the great ability (to our own detriment) to adapt our environment to our needs, and I wanted more than anything to showcase how that could be used for good in this series. What started as one book grew to three and became more than just a journey of what-ifs. It became an optimistic fantasy of what could happen if we worked together as a species instead of against each other as nations.

As much fun as it's been to write, this series wouldn't exist without all the amazing people behind the scenes at Bold Strokes. I couldn't ask for a more supportive publishing family and I'm honored to work with such talented people.

And as always, I'd like to thank my readers. It wouldn't be nearly as much fun without you, and not just because these stories would still be locked in my imagination. Thank you for coming along with me on this adventure.

CHAPTER ONE

Ash

There are worse ways to die than an explosion in space. At least it's quick and painless.

I have the crew scouring every millimeter of the *Persephone* looking for Sarka's bombs. Before he took Jordan and fled the ship in an escape pod, he hinted he'd left bombs around the ship. Everyone's grumbling that it's a waste of time. But I know Davis Sarka. He's crazy enough to do it.

I may have an entire ship of crew giving me cut eye, but that's not new. I don't give a shit what they think. I'd rather waste several hours on the off chance I'm right than assume I'm wrong and get everyone killed.

It's a heady thought. My decisions are going to affect life and death.

I'm in charge.

That's a horrible thought. It's a lie to say that all first officers have ambitions to command their own ship. I've never wanted to captain a ship. There's nothing worse than facing the isolation of being at the top of the command structure. No one wants to play mahjong with someone who has the final say in whether they get promoted or not. And here I am, thrust to the top, not by ambition or choice, but because that prick took Jordan.

I swear my heart stopped when they disappeared. No trace, nothing. Our sensors are still undergoing repairs after the explosion on the *Posterus*.

I'm still not sure how I survived that. I should've exploded when

Hartley pulled me away before I fell into the core pit. That is according to Dr. Prashad, and I have no reason to doubt him. Thanks to the Burrs I'd become one half of a walking, talking bomb. Ben Hartley, our civilian engineer, was the other half. Touching was supposed to be the trigger.

And yet, here we are thousands, possibly millions of light-years from the Milky Way, with no real explanation of how we got here. I guess I should be thankful, except I'm not.

When I was being laced with carcinogens, the Burrs also implanted a mind knot, an old military device used to control soldiers. Meant to control me. I still have that creepy mind knot floating in my head like a dead body drifting in a pool. It can't do anything to me now because we're too far from the Burrs and their control. But it's still off-putting to have this thing inside me, some foreign intruder that was never meant to be there in the first place.

Yet I haven't felt anything since the engine core exploded. I've even been sleeping better. Well, better for me. I only ever get about four or five hours a night, unless I'm sleeping in caves next to Jordan.

"Ash." Hartley barrels down the corridor, his arms outpacing his body by at least half a meter. "We found something."

I'm both elated and pissed. "Is it a bomb?"

"Pretty sure. Come take a look." He motions where he's come from.

"Did you disarm it already?"

He shakes his head. His shaggy red hair sweeps across his freckled forehead.

"Oh, please, by all means. Let's go take a look at the bomb that could blow us to smithereens."

He gives me a withering look. "It's lodged under the console of the manual guidance station. If that thing goes, half the ship is gone, including the bridge. It's not going to matter where you are when it detonates. You'll still be dead."

"Good point. You think we can actually disarm this thing?"

He shrugs. So like Hartley. Only two things freak him out—not being relevant and being wrong. Hartley's the engineer who invented the engine for the *Posterus*. He's the reason it's possible for the first ever generational ship to take a small section of what's left of the human species to go find another planet to fuck up.

If we hadn't ended up here, we'd be on our merry way toward a planet in a galaxy far away with forty-five thousand humans who would all be dead by the time we got there.

The first time I met Hartley he had this cocky bravado, but after getting to know him, I realize it's an act. He's worried that if he's not acting like an ass, he'll fade into the background. I suspect he's spent a good chunk of his life in the background and now is determined to be front and center.

When we reach the manual docking bay, half the engineering crew is crowded around a tiny container the size of my fist. It's improvised, to say the least, wedged into the space with some rigging tape and good old-fashioned friction.

"Is that a can of tofuloaf he's used to encase the innards?"

"Yeah," Hartley says as he pushes people out of the way to get us closer.

"And we're sure it's a bomb?"

"If it's not, I worry about what they're feeding us on this ship," someone in the back says. A few of the crew laugh.

"Why are you all standing around? It doesn't take," I do a quick head count, "nine people to defuse a bomb." The joking subsides and everyone sobers up. The moment becomes awkward, and I remember all of a sudden that no one likes me.

And now I'm in charge.

"Keep looking for bombs."

"But—"

"I don't care what excuse you're going to give me. Just do it."

After everyone leaves, Hartley turns to me from under the console. "Yelling at them like that is not helping matters."

"I'm not here to make friends. I'm here to keep this ship in one piece so that when Jordan—the captain—comes back, it's here for her."

Hartley grabs a flashlight and slides over for me to crawl under the console next to him. "You think she'll be back? I saw it. The pod just blinked out of existence. What if it exploded? What if she's dead?"

I yank the flashlight out of Hartley's hand. "She's not dead. As soon as we defuse this bomb and secure the rest of the ship, we're going to find her."

"Okay. But what if—"

"Hartley. Focus." I direct the light at the tofuloaf can. The circuitry is beyond confusing. It looks like the inside of a computer, which means Sarka programmed it. Without the software to disarm it, we're shit out of luck. Even if someone could recode it, there's no way we have that kind of time.

Hartley looks at me and I see we have the same thought. We're screwed.

"Uh, Lieutenant?" a reluctant voice calls out. I almost smack my head on the console. Towering over us is Dan Foer, one of Hartley's engineers. He has that gangly look teenagers get before they grow into their skin. "We've found two more bombs," he says.

Three? What are the odds we find more? Sarka was a very busy man. If there are more, it'll take weeks to search the entire ship. The *Persephone* isn't huge, it can only carry a max of a hundred and fifty crew, but it contains millions of tiny spaces, especially considering the size of these bombs. "Hartley? Can we scan these bombs and find a common signature and use that to search the ship?"

"Sure. If the sensors were working at full capacity, but we haven't gotten everything up and running yet."

"Why not?" My question comes out harsher than it should.

"Because we've been a little busy with other things. Foer and I spent almost a week on the planet. And then we got highjacked by Sarka. Fixing sensors wasn't a priority."

"Well, I'm making it a priority." I pause and rethink that statement. "After we sort out this bomb issue." It's dark under the console, but I swear Hartley rolls his eyes at me. Jesus, I need to get my shit together.

I push myself out from under the console and sit up. "Where were the other bombs found?"

"Behind the central computer and another in the aft cargo hold."

"So what do all those places have in common?"

"On their own, they're all places that will cripple us, almost fatally. If they all go off, we're toast."

"We need to look at places that can cripple us."

"That's stupid. Almost any bulkhead on the exterior corridors of the ship will devastate us if a bomb blows."

"The emergency airlocks will prevent that problem." In fact, that's exactly what happened when the explosion on the *Posterus* cut us loose. We lost eight crew members, but the ship survived. And thanks to the way it's designed, we were able to patch the hole pretty quickly.

"That's the first place I'd put a bomb then, the airlock system," Foer says.

"Good. Go check there. We need to start thinking strategically." Foer looks relieved as he bolts from the room.

"And while we're doing that, a little bomb in a toilet is going to be the end of us," Hartley says.

"Let's not worry about what we can't fix. Right now we have to figure out how to prevent them from going off. Any chance they're dormant? Maybe Sarka didn't arm them before he left."

Hartley gives me another withering look.

I duck back under the console and examine the device. "What if we just remove them and blow them out a hatch into space?"

Hartley takes the flashlight and checks around the rigging tape. "I'm guessing he's got a trip wire for that."

"A what?"

"Something that'll set the bomb off if you remove it. It could even have a gyrometer. If it's moved at all, the thing will go off. Hell, that might even be the trigger."

"I'm going to hope that's not the trigger, because that gives me an idea of how to get them off the ship. What if we remove the part of the console it's attached to and send that out a hatch?"

"Well?" Hartley runs his hand along the underside of the console. It's like a caress. I can see his brain turning through all the possibilities. "That could work in here. This system is a fail-safe. If something happens to the bridge, we can still dock if we need to. Right now that's not a priority. The one in the cargo hold isn't attached to anything important, but the central computer is a problem. Without looking at it I can't say for sure."

"Then let's go take a look."

By the time we make it to engineering, we have received reports of two more bombs, which brings our total to five. At least we're running out of places they can be.

We enter through a side corridor, which is much less impressive than coming through the main entrance. From there you're immediately intimidated by the towering computers and servers flanking much of the room. It's the only room on the ship where you could have an all-out game of basketball and not worry about the ball hitting the ceiling.

The main computer is surprisingly small compared to the rest of the equipment in the department. Most of that is for storage. Each server represents a system and holds about a hundred zettabytes. The last thing you want to do is run out of storage when you're in deep space. A lot of this was upgraded for our mission with the *Posterus*. But the main computer isn't for storage. It's a quantum computer that controls all the tasks for each system so it can afford to be smaller. I'm unprepared for how small. I enter the room and my heart sinks. It won't be like removing a section of console in the manual guidance station. The bomb is so tiny it's almost the same size as the main computer.

Hartley examines it. In this case, Sarka's used a tin of lentils to encase the bomb, attached to one whole side of the computer. He makes a noise like *hmm*, and I'm struck by how calm he is. I'm about to freak the fuck out, and he's standing there like he's examining what's for dinner. This is why Jordan should be here. She'd have this problem solved in an instant.

I focus on calming myself while Hartley pivots around the main computer. The panic I thought I'd gotten under control is back in a big way. It's only when Hartley looks up at me that I realize he has no idea what to do either and that everyone is counting on me to come up with a brilliant idea.

I take a deep breath and turn away. Hartley's puppy-dog eyes aren't helping me think. But this is it. I have no choice but to pull my shit together and figure something out, or everyone's dead.

"What happens if we lift this component and jettison it out a hatch?"

Hartley's eyes widen like I've suggested the galaxy is just a big bowl of pudding. "It's the main computer, Ash."

I give him a so-what look.

"It controls every system on board. That includes life support."

"We don't have backup for that?"

He rubs his hand through his hair. The sweat makes it stay up for a few seconds before it flops back down. "We do. But that's not the only system affected."

"And we don't have a spare on board?"

"A spare main computer? Are you fucking nuts? It's a quantum computer. Do you know the resources that go into making one of these? Holy Christ, Ash. That's like asking me if we have a spare *Persephone* in the hold. It's worse. This thing is probably worth three of this ship put together."

"A simple *no* would've done it."

"No. No, we don't have a spare main computer."

I roll my eyes. "Calm down. I'm only asking questions. We need to get this off the ship. We may not have a main computer, but if we let this bomb blow up, it won't matter because we won't have a ship for it to be a main computer of. Can we function without it?"

He huffs and kicks his boot into the floor. I can almost see his brain working. "Geez, Ash. I don't know. I think so. But we'd lose the ability to do everything."

"Let's talk this out. What do we need to function? Realistically. Life support." I hold up one finger and motion for Hartley to keep the ball going.

"Artificial gravity. It's not essential, but it'd be a bitch without it. It'd take us twice as long to get everything done."

"Speed is essential, so that makes artificial gravity essential." I hold up another finger and count two. "Power. At least emergency power." He nods and I hold up another finger. "That's three things. Is anything else essential to survival?"

"In space? Yes. Everything is essential."

"Breathe, eat, sleep, shit. Those are the only requirements at their base form. Life support, power, gravity. The only thing missing is the toilets. Are they on backup systems?"

"Of course. Could you imagine a day without them?"

"Okay. Do we absolutely need the main computer for any of these systems?"

He scrunches up his face and scrubs his hand over it, scratching at his patchy beard. "No. We have backup systems for all of those."

"Then we have to jettison."

I can almost hear the expletive on the tip of Hartley's tongue. But he doesn't say it. Instead, I get those puppy-dog eyes.

CHAPTER TWO

Jordan

There are worse ways to die than a blaster to the face. It's quick and painless. At least I hope it is.

This particular blaster is silver with a pulsing yellow strip down the length. And even though it's less than four inches from my nose, I can still see what must be the charge indicator. It's full. Not that I was worried.

Fuck.

I've had better days, which is a nice way of saying this has turned into a real shit show. There's a low grunt beside me. And that would be the reason I'm in this predicament. I guess not *that* but who.

I risk a glance at my periphery and see the asshole isn't even going to be awake to see me shot point-blank in the face.

I'm on my knees with my hands tied behind my back. I woke up this way and have no idea how I arrived here. The bulky creature in front of me has all my attention. The darkness in the room makes it difficult to tell who or what is shoving their blaster in my face, only that they smell. It's like being in the middle of a cow pasture back on Delta, where I grew up.

Delta's where we kept the farms for the Belt. Cow manure and fertilizer is a hard smell to get rid of. Eventually you can't remember any other smell. And they say only when you leave it do you realize you miss it. I've never missed this odor. To me it smells like defeat. It smells like starvation. You spend all your waking hours growing and harvesting and caring for all this food, and by the time it leaves on the maglevs, you're left with just enough to watch your family starve to death. And that's if the backbreaking work doesn't kill you first. But I guess it's better than Eps. Working in the mines is worse. Much worse. And if I hadn't grown up on Delta, if my mom hadn't sacrificed herself, I'd have grown up with the asshole next to me. A Burr. A space pirate. My father. The man who used me as a hostage and then shot us out of my own damn ship in an escape pod.

I'd never been so afraid in my life, watching the *Persephone* shrink and then disappear in the blink of an eye. I don't remember much after that. And now I'm here, wherever the fuck *here* is.

Maybe it's for the best. But then I think of Ash. She'll never know what happened, and I don't think I can live with that. She better come get us. But a more logical part of me hopes she stays far away. Chances are their fate will be the same as ours. As I stare into the darkness I worry about what will happen to the *Posterus*. Forty-five thousand humans on board are waiting to start a journey to their new home. They may not end up where they intended since we ended up in this unknown solar system. But as we've already discovered, there are inhabitable planets. They just have to find one that isn't occupied and settle down.

The bulky creature in front of me shifts the blaster to his other hand as he speaks into the sky above him. At first I think he's talking to us, but he's turned away, and then I realize I can understand what he's saying. How do they speak English? I take advantage of the break in his attention to look down at Sarka, still sprawled on—is that grass?— still unconscious. I'd head-butt him, but I'm sure that would return the attention to me. I don't want someone with a weapon aimed at my head worried I'm becoming violent.

The lights snap on. I actually hear the crackle as they illuminate, and my breath grinds to a halt. The room is cavernous, the ceiling's a couple kilometers high. And I thought the *Posterus* was big. It's a minnow compared to this thing. You could fit ten of the *Posterus* in this room alone, never mind the rest of the ship. If it wasn't for the telltale hum—something no good ship's captain could miss—I'd have thought we were on a planet.

This must be where they grow their food. It's humid, and that is definitely some sort of grass covering the floor. Each side has towers of panels, similar to our living walls on the *Posterus*, but the vegetation is strange, and it's organized better. Each crop has its own tower.

The smell is beginning to make sense, and not only because we're in a pasture. The figure in front of me looks like a cow, if they could stand on two legs. His nose is large, taking over almost a third of his lower face, and his nostrils flare as he breathes. He's still speaking to some unknown I can't hear or see, his attention drawn to the ceiling. His arms sport dark, luscious hair.

I shift, testing my bonds, but his attention isn't as diverted as I thought. His eyes swing back to me in an instant, and the blaster gets closer to my nose, if possible.

His squat form—he's only about an inch or so taller, and I'm on my knees—nears, like he's trying to loom over me. He might not have me in height, but there's nothing weak about his body. He's like a thick, heavy brick—if bricks were made of fur and muscle.

He's agreeing reluctantly with someone on the other end of his communications. He snorts and turns to me. "You with the illya?"

My mouth drops open like a landed fish. I understood what he said, which is surprising in itself, but not what it meant. "I don't…I'm with the Union fleet."

"The what?" His voice is deep, almost like I can feel it instead of hear it. "She said Union fleet. That mean anything to you?" He waits, and I realize he's not talking to me anymore. "I'll give 'em this. They don't look like illya. They're like nothing I've ever seen before. You want me to toss 'em, roast 'em, initiate, or what?"

None of those options sounds promising. I risk another look down at Sarka. Still unconscious, which means I'm on my own, but what else is new? I twist my fingers around, feeling for some way to release my hands. If I can get free, I can even the odds a bit. Whatever has me tied is fluid. It's slippery, and every time I try to feel for some sort of edge, it slips out of my grasp.

And then just like that, I find myself in the unlikely position of asking what Ash would do in this situation. She'd probably charge the guy when he was looking away. And for some reason, it would work. But I'll be dead before I even get up my nerve.

"All right. If that's the way you want to do it." He taps something on his neck, and his focus is back on me. My heart hammers so fast and loud I'm surprised Sarka hasn't woken up.

"So," he says to me. "What the flip is Union fleet? You guys military of some sort?" He jabs a large boot in Sarka's ribs. "Looks like a dud if he is." He turns back to me, all teeth. They're big and shiny and could probably take a chunk of my arm off.

"How is it I can understand you? You speak English?"

He frowns, bringing large bushy eyebrows together. "English? No." He taps the side of his head. "We got translators. They analyze your speech and then project the correct language in your head. To me, it sounds like you're speaking Varb."

"Like a Babel fish?"

His eyes go wide. "A what?"

I shake my head. "Never mind. It's something from...It's a yellow fish you stick in your ear that translates for you."

"You have talking fish? Why would you stick them in your ears?"

"No." I shake my head again. "It's from a story." I wonder if they even have stories, which is silly. What culture doesn't have its own stories? "It's not real."

He levels his blaster at my forehead. "So. Union fleet."

My mind goes blank. I have no idea how to explain us, our mission, how we managed to get God knows how many trillions of miles from our own solar system. I don't even know where the fuck we are, let alone how to explain it to this guy. Should I mention Sarka taking me hostage, or will that complicate matters more? I need to get back to the *Persephone*, and I need this guy on my side to do it.

"If I had to categorize us, I'd say we are the exploration division of a generational ship on its way to find a new home for our species." There. That's mostly true. When the *Persephone* joined this mission, it ceased being a part of Union fleet since we left the fleet along with the Union behind on the Belt—the asteroid belt humans call home. The less this guy thinks we're military, the better.

"And who's this guy?" He nudges Sarka, who turns over. I notice he's also bound at his wrists.

"My pilot."

The guy snorts. "Some pilot. He almost rammed into our aft engine. If we hadn't picked you up when we did, you'd be ash floating through the stars." He waves his blaster, indicating our surroundings. "Lucky you ended up here." He toes the grass at his feet. "Emergency extraction can be tricky. We once had a guy end up in the waste system. Knee-deep in other people's shit. Not exactly a hard landing, but whoo-eee. I'd rather land anywhere but there."

"We were in an escape pod. There's no navigation, only propulsion."

"An escape pod?" Those bushy eyebrows do another dance. "Who you escaping?"

"It was a mistake. I need to get back to my ship. It can't be far. It's orbiting the nearby planet."

A booming laugh escapes from him. "A planet? Is this like your Babel fish? Another story? This system doesn't have any planets."

I'm speechless. What the fuck were we stuck on for the last four days? I flash to a group of avians sprinting toward Ash and me as we run toward an impossible cliff. I didn't imagine jumping off and crashing through a kilometer of tree branches. My shoulder where the avian pierced me with his claw definitely remembers. There's no way the pod could make it out of the system. We'd have died a million times over before that happened.

I have more than an urge to kick Sarka awake now.

"Look, I don't know how else to explain it. One minute my ship was there, the next it wasn't. But I swear, there is a planet not far from here. How else do you explain an escape pod in the middle of nowhere? Those things have the range to help you leave an exploding ship, but that's about it." I readjust myself so I'm looking in his eyes. My knees are starting to hurt. "We just need help getting back to our ship."

He snorts. A small dribble of snot rolls out of his nostril. He wipes it with his forearm, smearing snot into his hair. "The one orbiting that planet no one can see but you swear is around here somewhere? What do you take us for? If you're not working for the illya, then you've escaped from one of their ships, and there is no way, honey, I'm going to let you go blabbing about our setup."

It's the second time he's mentioned that word. "The illya? I don't know what that is."

"Doesn't matter anyway. I've been instructed to pull you into intake. I really hope you like it here 'cause you ain't going nowheres anytime fast."

"You haven't even mentioned where we are."

"Any rule says I have to?" He jiggles the blaster. "I'm the one with the weapon pointed at your head. Means I make the rules." He kicks Sarka in the ribs. "Rise and shine, sweetheart. Time to go." Sarka grunts but doesn't move. The man hooks his boot under Sarka and flips him over. A large black burn mark covers his lower abdomen.

"You shot him." I try to scoot closer and assess the damage but lose my balance and fall sideways. The man grips my arm and hauls me to my feet.

"Relax. He'll be fine. The worst he'll get is a bruise that takes a while to go away."

Standing at my full height, I tower over him. His glance roams the length of my body. "You looked tall. But wow, I've never actually seen anyone as tall as you. Are all your people like that?"

He's obviously never met the avians who inhabit our mysterious planet. They're two feet taller than me. The man with the blaster reaches below my shoulders, but I have no illusions about his strength. He might not be tall, but he could take even the strongest of our species, even without a blaster.

"Where the fuck are we?" Sarka's eyes are finally open. He still looks out of it. His black hair, which is usually slicked back, is a mess, and his pale skin is even more taut than usual.

"You're in luck, good sir." The man helps Sarka sit up. "We pulled you from your crash course into our engines, and you are now about to be recruited into the Varbaja." His voice is chipper, like this is good news. I have a feeling it's more like being drafted into a war you had no intention of ever fighting. "Your day could not be going any better."

Sarka looks up at me as if I have a better answer for him. I shrug. He's lucky I don't kick him. If he hadn't taken me hostage on his suicide mission, I'd be back on the *Persephone* preparing to head back to the *Posterus*. I keep my lips shut. Now is not the time to get into it. If we're going to make it off this ship alive, we have to keep our heads.

Sarka grunts like an old man as he raises himself to a standing position. The recruiter's eyes go big as he looks at the mountain of a man standing in front of him. Sarka is at least five inches taller than I am.

"Wow. They really do make 'em big where you guys come from. That can come in handy." He pokes Sarka in the ribs. "Now come on. They want to turn the lights back off so the npua can go back to sleep." He waves to several small animals grazing by a stack of pink flowers.

They're covered in dark-gray hair matted at the end, and their ears are long and thin, hanging over their eyes.

A thought occurs to me. I turn to Sarka. "You didn't really plant bombs on my ship, did you?"

He looks at me and shrugs. "Oops."

CHAPTER THREE

Ash

I've been in charge of the *Persephone* for less than a day, and already I have a potential mutiny on my hands.

I'm sitting alone in the dark on the bridge. Everyone else is restricted to their cabins until we can figure out how to get some of our more crucial systems back online. Hartley assures me it's possible, but it'll take time.

I should be thinking about how to get this ship back in working order, but my mind is full of Jordan. Those last fifteen minutes have been looping in my brain for hours. Could I have done anything so she was here now?

Those escape pods have only so much oxygen, enough to last two days at most. Less with Sarka. And instead of getting out there and looking, we're stuck here with no way to move this damn ship.

Less than a day in charge and I've crippled the ship, doomed the crew, and lost their captain.

We've removed all the bombs on the ship. The only critical bomb was the one attached to the main computer. The rest were distractions. I've got to hand it to Sarka—he knows how to make a getaway. With the ship crippled, we won't be going anywhere until Hartley can rig a new computer to replace the previous one. A quantum computer that can handle trillions of simultaneous functions at the same time. As Hartley explained it, that's like asking third-graders to build a fifty-foot bridge with pipe cleaners and ribbon. It can be done, but it'll take a hell of a lot of time. Probably years, which we don't have.

In the right corner of the main observation port, a tiny burst of light ignites. Here and gone in a flash. And that's the end of our main computer. I lean my head back against the headrest and stare up at the ceiling. It's eerie in the dark. The only light comes from a far-off sun through the bow porthole, which takes up most of the front wall. All the consoles stand dark and silent. The silence gets to me most, though. You don't realize how accustomed, how reliant you are on those sounds until they're gone. With nothing to fill the empty space, my head overflows with dark thoughts.

What if they do mutiny? Maybe it would be better. Anyone in charge would be better than me, especially after what Dr. Prashad told me.

I fiddle with the tablet wedged between my leg and the command seat. I haven't had the guts to read Dr. Prashad's diagnosis all the way through. He presented it to me earlier, and I still have no idea what to think.

I'd gone down to the med center to discuss any casualties we'd suffered. Besides Yakovich's leg and a few other minor injuries, the crew was in pretty good shape.

"I wanted to speak with you about something else too." The doctor passes me a tablet and crosses his arms. "There never seems a good time for this." I swear he's frightened. I've never seen him so nervous to share information.

"What is it?" I stare at the tablet in my hand, afraid to swipe it on.

He runs his hand over the tablet I'm holding. I read the first few lines but am not sure what I'm reading.

He points to the tablet. "I encourage you to pay attention to everything I've collected. The information will be helpful for treatment."

I look down at the first paragraph, and one word jumps out at me. "Bipolar?"

"Over the last two months I've observed behavior in you I believe is consistent with—"

"You're saying I'm bipolar?"

He guides me to a chair and nudges me to sit. I sink into the cushion, still clutching the tablet.

My mouth opens but I'm stunned. I sit there for a few seconds, mute, thinking over what he's said. The word bipolar conjures up all sorts of negative things. Crazy. He thinks I'm crazy.

He takes a seat on the bed next to me and rests a hand on my forearm. "You're not crazy." It's uncanny how he can read me sometimes. "This is nothing to be ashamed of or worried about. It's a lot to digest, I know. I want you to take your time with it and not jump to conclusions." He points to the tablet gripped in my hand. "You'll find information about your condition as well as the medication I'm putting you on. Before you judge anything, I want you to ask yourself how you dealt with stress this past week. I want you to assess your sleeping patterns over the last few days." He stands. "And in a few weeks I want you to reassess. I think you'll find a big difference. If you have any questions, come see me."

"Why is this coming up now? Why hasn't anyone figured this out before?" How did it go unnoticed for so long?

He shrugs. "This isn't an exact science. There's no blood test. Every case is a little different. The dose I'll put you on is very mild, and I'm sure we'll see an improvement."

I've been on the medication for half a day. He said it will take a while to see changes, but I'm worried what kind of changes. This is me, this is who I've always been, and I'm afraid whatever he has me on will fundamentally change me and maybe not for the better.

Hearing a loud screech behind me, I turn to see Hartley manually pumping the bridge door open. He locks the door in the open position, and we stare at each other from across the bridge. He's outlined by the green emergency lights lining the hall. I feel like he's caught me sneaking pudding from the mess after hours.

"Why'd you turn the emergency lights off?" He stomps onto the bridge. I like the guy, but sometimes Hartley is too much Hartley for my liking. He's loud, arrogant, and obnoxious, not to mention the slowest eater I've ever encountered. Not that eating slow impugns someone's character, but it grates on my nerves to watch him slow-chew through his tofuloaf.

I shrug.

He slaps me on the side of my head. "Stop feeling sorry for yourself."

"I'm not." I sink lower in the command chair. "I'm regrouping and coming up with a killer plan to get us moving again."

Hartley sucks on his lips, staring out at the expanse of stars before us. I hope he's about to say he has an idea. But he shrugs and walks toward the observation port. "The main computer is gone."

"I know. I saw." I bite the cuticle of my thumb, debating if I want to ask my next question. I've never been one to shy away from bad news, but the longer I hold off from knowing, the longer the panic will take to dock. I sigh and ask. It's better to know. "How long do we have until we run out of emergency systems?"

Hartley rests his forehead against the thick metallic glass. "Depends on a lot of variables. Each system uses a different amount of power, and on top of that, each system is taxed different. For instance—"

"Hartley?"

"Yeah?" He turns, a slump in his shoulders not normally there. And I know if I could see him better, I'd spot stress lines along his forehead.

"Give me the worst-case scenario. I want to have a solution in place before that happens."

He doesn't hesitate. "Two days."

Shit.

"What if we send out a team to unfurl the sails manually? Can we pull in more energy, buy us some time?"

"The energy-conversion system isn't essential. Even if we could get the sails open, we can't convert that energy to power our systems."

"What about rigging something from the escape pods? They're built to be self-contained."

He shakes his head. "Ash, that's like trying to squeeze a soccer ball through a gray-water pipe."

"Women do it every day. It's called giving birth."

He rolls his eyes. "We'd blow the converter in two seconds."

I bolt out of the command chair. There has to be something. "Work with me, Hartley. I'm bouncing ideas back and forth, only you keep dropping the pass."

"All right. We should take the escape pods and land on the planet."

I'm shaking my head before he even finishes. "No. We're not abandoning the *Persephone*. We'd have no way of getting back up here. We'd be stranding the crew on the planet for the rest of their lives."

He laughs. It sounds strange in the silence and dark of the bridge, like it came from somewhere else—another time when things weren't so shitty. "That was the whole idea of this mission. To find a planet and settle there."

"Not as a last resort. We'd have nothing. You were on the planet. We are so not prepared to live the hunter-gatherer life." I do a brief tally in my head of the number of times I almost died on the planet in a few days. I'm close to double digits. "That's a suicide mission."

"Our ship is sinking. If we don't abandon it, we'll go down with it. And we wouldn't have nothing. We can take systems with us to convert solar power to energy. We have brains and each other. We'll survive."

"Not all of us." It's a sobering thought, but true. Inevitably, as we learn how to live in a totally different environment than any of us are used to, casualties will occur. That's what happens when you take a group of people, most of whom have never even been on a planet, and drop them into a foreign world.

"No. Not all of us. But most of us would survive. We'd find a place as far away as possible from the avians and start a new life," Hartley says.

"And the avians? Are our lives more important than theirs? You know what will happen. We'll force them into extinction. Jordan didn't want this."

"The captain's not here. You are. It's your decision."

It may be my decision, but what would Jordan do in this situation? She wouldn't let the crew die. And then I have an idea. "Is it possible to put the ship into hibernation? We could take supplies with us to build a new quantum computer and rig the escape pods to get us back to the ship."

"That could take years."

Jordan doesn't have years. But maybe I could rig an escape pod to navigate and go in search of her myself. Before I have a chance to expand this plan, the ship lists.

I seize the armrest of the command chair and hang on as we tilt, and keep tilting until we're almost standing on the ceiling. Hartley slides along the wall and hits the navigation console with a dull thud.

"What the hell was that?" I ask.

"We lost stabilizers."

"You said two days was worst-case scenario until we started losing backup emergency systems."

"I also said we couldn't know for sure. The stabilizers must have needed more energy than the others. These systems are not meant to be used at the same time."

"I also want to send out an emergency probe to alert the *Posterus* of our location and situation."

Hartley bites his lip.

"We have the ability to do that, don't we?"

He shakes his head. "We can drop a probe, but we don't have the power to program it to do what we want."

"Aren't they under their own power?"

"Their propulsion, yes. But not their function. The main computer has to program that."

My heart sinks. Why didn't we do that before we jettisoned the main computer? "Okay. Go see if you can bring the stabilizers back online. I'll prepare us for evacuation to the planet. We need to take everything we'll need to survive, plus equipment to make it back here and get the *Persephone* up and running again."

Hartley nods and scrambles along the ceiling, holding on to different stations, to get off the bridge.

It's only a matter of minutes before he reports back to me. It wasn't the emergency stabilizers. Sure, they went offline. That's what caused us to list. That's why we're still adrift, alternating between upside down and leaning to port. But they were only a side effect.

We missed a bomb.

Sarka planted a bomb in the waste-management system. You don't realize how important that system is until it's spewing gray water through vacuum tubes. It's also got a fail-safe that opens vents to divert that water off the ship because too much water is dangerous on a ship. That's why we listed. We didn't have enough power for the ship's stabilizers to compensate for all that extra strain as the water rushed through the corridors, pooling against the port-side bulkheads.

I hope to God Jordan never sees her ship like this. I've turned it into a foul, useless heap of junk.

Right now, we need to prepare for evacuation. I expected the crew to be upset, to demand we do everything we could to save the *Persephone* and go after Jordan, but most have realized what I refuse to admit. We have to think about saving ourselves. We're in no position to rescue Jordan. I don't want to believe that, so I'm making my own preparations. I'm going after her myself. The crew will be fine on their own. In fact, they'll be better off without me to fuck everything up.

As I'm stocking my escape pod, I feel someone hovering behind me. I assume it's Hartley, but when I turn around, I find Quinn Yakovich leaning against the wall watching me. Her leg is still in a heavy-duty brace from when she broke it on the planet.

"Going a little overboard on that one, aren't you?" She points to several large bins strapped to the cargo hooks in back of the pod. They're filled with a bunch of tins of tofuloaf—the food the crew felt wasn't worth bringing—and backup oxygen and a small generator to keep the pod going.

"You've been on the planet. What would you consider overboard?" Things have been frosty with Yakovich since we left her behind to die on the planet. That's how I feel about it. Jordan would say we had no choice. The avians captured us and left her with a broken leg and no way to defend herself in a harsh jungle. She apparently wasn't worth the effort. I can understand how she feels. She should be pissed.

Sarka found her and brought her back on board. That should endear the man to me a little. But it doesn't. Not even a little. He only did it because he thought she'd be on his side. But she turned on him, so now I'm left wondering where her loyalties lay.

"Listen, Quinn. About what happened—"

She waves my words away with her hand. "I know you guys would've taken me if you could. I'm not an idiot. I don't blame you for leaving me." She scrubs at her shaved head. "I'm sure as shit happy I didn't end up dead in a humid fucking jungle, but I know it wasn't your fault if I had."

I nod but don't say anything. We've lost too many people in the past month, so I should be numb to it by now. But if anything, those losses make me appreciate how fragile everything really is. And also how crazy we are to be doing this. Anything can happen. One tiny mistake and all of us could die. Humans have been testing the boundaries of space for hundreds of years. The casualties are high. Since humans first started exploring space in the mid-twentieth century, thousands have died. In the first hundred, not many, even though it seems more dangerous, but that was only because the science was young. But as we started colonizing the moon and building stations around other planets and their satellites, the casualties grew. Since we've migrated to the Belt, the numbers have become unacceptable.

"Do you need help?" She points to the rest of the bins I'm trying to stuff into the tiny escape pod. "I'm assuming you're going after the captain."

I freeze. Have I been that obvious? Do other crew members know?

"If I was in your place, I'd be doing the same thing. It's not really the *Persephone* without the captain here." She pauses for a second. "That is, if we ever make it back."

"We'll make it back. We have to."

"How will you know? You'll be floating dead somewhere in space in this piece of shit." She points to my escape pod.

"You just said this is exactly what you'd do."

"I didn't say it was the smart thing. But the fact is, we'll be on the planet, and you'll be out there somewhere. What if you do find her? Is she still alive? The escape pod she left in has already run out of air by now."

I've been trying desperately not to think about that probability.

"But of course one of the many, many ships in this system must have picked her up."

"Are you trying to talk me out of going?"

"Of course not. I think it's great. I mean, it's not like they create contingency plans for things like that. The crew will be fine without you. I'm sure Hartley will have no problem keeping everyone in line."

"I see what you're doing. You're trying to make me doubt this plan."

She holds up her hands and backs away. "Not at all. Knowing you, you've thought this through and made up your mind. I wouldn't dream of changing it." She turns to leave and even makes it a few feet before she stops. "Although I thought you'd like to know that Hartley put Vasa in charge of packing our communications gear."

"What?" Vasa has been confined to his cabin since we discovered that he was behind the last attack on me. Why would Hartley trust him with something so important?

"Just thought you should know," she says and walks away.

Goddamn it.

As I set my manifest down on a container to go look for Hartley and kick some sense into that thick head, the ship shudders. This isn't like before. It's much more subtle, like passing through a tunnel on one of the maglevs back home. But then another shudder, much more serious than the last, stops me from going for Hartley. Instead I'm heading in the opposite direction, looking for a porthole.

I climb down two decks to the running track. The three-hundred-and-sixty-window span will give me the best view. I stop frozen at the doorway. Instead of stars and a green and blue planet with purple haze, I see darkness. At first, I think everything's vanished, like Jordan and Sarka. But as I run to the window, patterns and lights come into focus. I see windows and decks, and if I crane my neck up, I spy two green fluid arms connected to us.

We're inside another ship.

CHAPTER FOUR

Jordan

I could kill Sarka. He's strolling through the pasture, chatting up our captor as if we're on a tour of a friend's new crop field.

"And how much yield do you get from one field?"

The cow man, who introduced himself to Sarka as Tup, ambles behind us. He may be a powerhouse, but those legs don't allow him to go very fast. "Don't know," he says. "I'm not one of the agriculturalists. All I know is that when I sit down in the mess there's always a nice big bowl of chowder like my mom used to make. They feed us, we protect them. That's how it's always been." He hikes a thumb at me. "Your missus here might get assigned to the cafeteria. She might be able to tell you then. If you're still interested."

"Is everyone in this goddamn galaxy sexist?" I say. Sarka turns and grins.

Tup laughs. "That was a joke. I doubt they'd waste you in the kitchen, which is lucky. We got about fifty thousand mouths to feed. That's not an easy job."

"So you boys are prepping for war?" Sarka winks at me as he says "boys."

Tup stops and scratches the side of his head with his blaster. "Just exactly how far away do you guys come from? The Varbaja have been at war for hundreds of years. For as long as any of our elders can remember." In this light his eyes look massive, two big black holes positioned under bushy caterpillar eyebrows. He looks us over a little more carefully. "Where are you from?"

"We come from a place called Earth. It's in a galaxy far away." Sarka chuckles to himself.

"You may be from Earth. But I grew up on the Belt," I say.

He bulks up like I've spit in his face. It's not easy to do with your hands bound behind your back, but he manages to make himself imposing all the same. "You grew up on the station orbiting Earth. Same thing."

"It is not the same thing. I grew up breathing artificial air, a prisoner looking at something I could never have."

"Oh, spare me the theatrics. You had a wonderful childhood."

I step back like he's slapped me.

Tup waves the blaster in between us like a white flag of surrender. "I'm sensing some unresolved issues here. And as nice as it would be to sit around and talk about our feelings…" The way he says it makes me think that's the last thing he thinks would be nice. "I don't give a hoo-ha's ass what your issues are." He flicks his blaster in the direction he wants us to walk. "Keep moving. Believe me, you'll have all the time in the world to hash through your childhood traumas as we make it through intake. The whole thing takes a few days, and it involves a lot of sitting around doing nothing."

I step forward, distancing myself as much as possible from Sarka. I can't tell if he's trying to get a rise out of me or he truly believes my childhood was something to reminisce about. I spent the first twelve years of my life a prisoner of the Burrs. Sarka's pirates raided Union ships for cargo and weapons and sometimes people. My mom was one of those people, and I doubt she thought my childhood was as idyllic as Sarka believes.

We come to a field at the far end of the colossal farming structure, where several crew are waiting by a large control panel, presumably to turn the lights back off when we leave. A few of them look like Tup— short and stocky, cow-like. But a few are much smaller, thin and bluish gray. They remind me of smaller versions of the avians we encountered on the planet. Only these creatures are not as sharp as the avians. They have noses instead of hard facial structures that resemble beaks.

After what feels like more than an hour, we come to the end of the farming. I look back and can't see the other side, only crops and pastures with small herds of animals that resemble nothing even my imagination could come up with.

In one of the pens we pass, a group of hairy red balls of fur bound over a small incline and head toward a large structure with troughs of water lines along the outside.

In another field, small dog creatures lie about soaking up heat from a set of panels hanging from the rafters.

And I thought the *Posterus* was an achievement. It took thousands of our greatest minds, even more workers, and over twenty years to complete, and it doesn't even come close to this place. I have a feeling this is only the beginning.

Tup grabs my arm and shoves me through a door. I have to duck. I'm getting the impression we're a lot taller than the other species on this ship. It's so large I'm starting to doubt it's a ship, although he doesn't think this system has any planets, so it can't be a planet. An asteroid? But then they'd be at the mercy of the asteroid's trajectory.

"Is this a ship? Where are we?"

"This," he pats the wall of the lift we've stuffed ourselves into, "is the *Avokaado*. The greatest warship of all time. We can deploy twenty thousand fighters in under a minute on this beauty."

"Avocado?" Sarka smirks. "Let me guess, Pineapple was taken?" He keeps his head at an angle so it doesn't bang into the ceiling of the lift.

"It was named after the umquashi god of war. Avokaado defeated two hundred thousand enemies with only a rock and a shield."

Sarka laughs out loud. The man has the tact of a five-year-old. The last thing we should be doing is insulting the religions of armed strangers.

I try to explain. "Where we're from, an avocado is a fruit that grows on trees."

But the little man doesn't get mad. Instead he shrugs his broad shoulders and presses a code into the lift. "And where I am from, Avokaado is a great warrior who died a hero's death defending the people he loved." He pats the bulkhead like a beloved pet. "It fits, the name."

"And what exactly are you fighting for?"

"Fighting for? Nothing except to be left alone." We reach our destination, and he waves his blaster toward the door. Sarka ducks into a smaller corridor with large windows on each side of a hallway that seems to stretch into infinity. From here we can see the bulk of the ship.

It's shaped like two bulbous rumps. Each section must have hundreds of levels, each with its own ring of windows and circling passages. This corridor connects us between the two sections. Beyond the ship, the stars dot the expanse of space, the pattern so different than what I'm used to. It's like we're trapped in the dark with only pinpricks of light to show our way.

And as he leads us through the stars, he recounts how his people have been fighting a war for over two hundred years.

The illya, we learn, procreate by harvesting the essence of other species and blending them with their own. It's the result of a deadly disease that wiped out most of their people thousands of years ago. The harvesting is fatal and coerced. I'm not exactly sure what he means by essence. Blood? And for almost a thousand years the species of this galaxy suffered unspeakable losses. They banded together to stop the illya and formed the Varbaja—the recruiters.

We're about halfway across the walkway by this point, and I want to ask how the war's going, but that seems a little rude.

But I don't need to worry about being rude when Sarka's around. He asks the question instead. "You guys close to defeating them yet?"

Tup stops. His face has taken on that look people get when they're about to barf propaganda. "We have right on our side. That's all that matters. With the help of people like you, the war will be won. Maybe not today or even tomorrow. But someday."

So this righteous army depends on reluctant recruits? Sounds a little like getting your essence harvested without permission.

When we make it to the other side of the walkway, I'm struck by the difference. It's hard to explain, but everything seems harsher. The lights, the colors. It's almost like stepping from a daycare center with its warm, welcoming colors into a morgue and all its sterility. The other section must house the living compartments—the side that focuses on keeping all these soldiers alive. There is no doubt we've reached the military side.

Several soldiers jog past chanting something that refers to shoving their weapons somewhere indecent. My anxiety ratchets up several notches while Sarka calms. He's spent most of his life in one army or another, so that makes sense. He's come home.

As much as I don't want to fight someone else's war, I would rather not leave Sarka alone in a place like this. I don't trust him. Knowing him, he'll have his own army and a ship if you give him a few days. Sarka's always been good at recruiting people to his cause. When I was a kid, I used to watch him talk to his men. Before a big raid or maneuver he would gather everyone in the main dining hall and rally the troops. He was hypnotic.

As an adult I recognize him for what he is, charismatic. But at the time, I was as swept away as everyone else. It helped that he was my father and I worshipped him. But even then I could tell that he was different, that he was somehow better than his men because of how he could rouse their courage and loyalty.

My mom tried to keep me away from all that. I get it now. Back then I would have to sneak out to watch, and it always felt worth it.

Tup directs us around a corner and into a large empty room. A man dressed in black is standing near a small computer station. He's taller than Tup, but we still dwarf him by at least a foot. His hair is so white it's translucent in places. Next to his rich brown skin, the effect is even more jarring.

"Welcome, friends." He spreads his arms wide. I take a step back. Nothing good ever came of being welcomed by a stranger unless they wanted something from you. And like a sudden sharp jab I realize Sarka told me this. I was ten and wanted to know why we weren't friends with anyone who flew Union ships. It's not the most cynical statement I've carried with me all these years, but certainly the most memorable.

Growing up I'd always heard talk of the Union fleet, Union officers. Everything bad was always about the Union. At the time I didn't know it was bad, but it was a word I'd come to recognize as other. As in, not us. Naturally that made me curious about anything Union. After I pestered Sarka enough about it, he finally told me the story of when he first encountered the Union after humans migrated to the Belt.

After the wars, the final disputes over the dregs of resources left on Earth, humans embarked on the Great Migration. As far as important in our species' history goes, the only other migrations as great were when humans crossed the Bering Strait and when they left Africa.

Each migration would change our species forever. No longer were we encased in the protective electromagnetic field of our planet. Instead we'd been cast out like disgraced house guests who took advantage of our host's hospitality.

Sarka had been part of those last armies, and as he told it, their welcome was not that of returning soldiers. The Union didn't offer them a place among the ordinary population. They could either work in the mines on Epsilon or start their own colony on Zeta. Currently Zeta houses the prisons and a few rogue outposts of those who don't want anything to do with the Union.

They had been heroes on Earth. But as soon as they weren't needed, they were outsiders, pariahs, reminders of everything humans had lost. Sarka chose a third option. He formed his own army, which became known as the Burrs.

The Union has a very different version of events. They said the soldiers revolted and refused their invitation to join the Union. I suspect the truth is somewhere in between. It's interesting that I've never heard of any ex-Earth soldiers living on the Belt. Surely some would have taken the offer.

Ash once told me her grandfather led the migration, back when he was a young man. It's strange to think of my father as a contemporary of someone long dead. But that's also the curse of the Burrs. Their programming during the war had a nasty side effect. They don't age as quickly as most people, if at all. My father is over a hundred and sixty-five years old and doesn't look much more than sixty. Some may see it as a blessing, but if the life you're living is shit, why would you want to live forever?

"Welcome," the man in black says again. The word echoes through the chamber.

Tup pushes us into the room with the blaster. "This is Rowlf. He'll guide you through intake. Listen to him and everything'll go okay."

"That doesn't sound like a glowing endorsement," Sarka says, low so only I can hear.

As soon as we step into the room, the door behind us snaps shut. Great. We've entered crazy land and there's no way out. I feel a little like I've fallen down the rabbit hole and the guy standing in front of me is the Mad Hatter about to serve tea made of strychnine.

"This way." He beckons us to come closer, and more than anything that gesture sends a creepy shiver down my spine.

Whatever's about to happen is not going to be good.

Sarka swings his giant fist toward Rowlf's head. Instead of hearing the crunch of bone and flesh, something unexpected happens. Sarka's fist goes straight through the man's head, and he staggers forward from the momentum.

Rowlf keeps that calm smile plastered on his face, hands still folded under his bowling-ball stomach. "This isn't our first time recruiting unknown species. We find it easier to process your intake remotely."

Sarka's breathing so loud it's drowning out Rowlf, who is taking way too much pleasure in this. He must encounter people like Sarka a lot—the overly proud full of anger, frustration, and uncontrolled aggression. I put a hand on his arm to calm him down. He's looking around like he might find some way to make Rowlf appear in person or possibly something harder than his fist, as if that's going to help.

I personally don't care if Sarka hyperventilates to death, but I'm not going to make us look like idiots. "Slow and steady wins the race," I say.

He turns to me with eyes so blue they look like two crystals sitting on his pale face. He looks ready to beat me. His fists are still clenched, and he sounds like a lion huffing paint. Slow and steady wins the race. He used to tell me that. It's from a book my grandmother read him as a kid. He didn't have the book anymore, but it's something about a rabbit and a turtle racing. The turtle, who shouldn't win because he's much slower than the rabbit, does win, only because the rabbit gets cocky. The turtle wins because he keeps going, slow and steady, never giving up.

It was no secret to me or those I grew up with that I inherited Sarka's temper. When I would get angry or frustrated, he would pull me aside and tell me, "You don't win by rushing or getting angry. You win by remaining calm and biding your time. It will come, and if you're too wrapped up in your own anger, you'll never catch your moment."

With a spark of recognition, he visibly cools. And like that, the arrogant veneer is back in place.

"Shall I repeat the procedure?" Rowlf asks.

Sarka folds his arms. "No. We heard you the first time. What's the option if we refuse?"

Rowlf smiles, showing a line of gums where teeth would usually sit. He must eat a lot of soup. "We didn't give you an option. This tracker is for your protection. It lets us know if you're in trouble. It can monitor your vital signs and dietary requirements. Since we began using the Isims, we have cut down on our fatality rate by twenty percent."

If it was possible to eye-roll with your whole body, Sarka would have been the first person to achieve it. His fingers dig into his arms and his eyes dart around the room. There is no way to escape. I checked as soon as we walked in and saw only two doors, one on each side of the room, with no handles, which is only one of the reasons I suspect they lock from the outside.

We're not going to find a way out of here. If Sarka refuses, this won't end badly for just him. It'll be bad for both of us.

"Suck it up, buttercup. Let them inject it and we can remove it later," I say.

He leans over and, with a venom I've never seen, points to the back of his neck and whispers, "Oh, yeah? The last time someone 'injected' me with something for my own good, it programmed me to kill, and as you're probably aware, they only come out of corpses." The large pink scar on the back of his neck isn't from when the military inserted the mind knot. It's from trying to remove it.

A few months ago, they implanted one in Ash. Dr. Prashad said she'd never survive its removal. The mind knot, created to help control soldiers, entangles itself in a person's central nervous system. Removing it would be like detaching their spinal cord from their brain stem and severing all functions.

"You have no idea what they're going to put in us. It could very well be benign."

"Exactly. We have no idea what they're going to put in us."

"What do you think will happen? If we refuse, they'll pump some sort of knockout gas in here, put it in anyway, along with who knows what, and then all of a sudden we're labeled troublemakers."

"Oh, boo-fucking-hoo to that. Who gives a shit?"

I'm astounded this man has evaded the Union fleet for as long as he has. "Do you want to spend the rest of your life fighting other people's wars?" He doesn't answer, but he's at least quiet. "We want to get out of here, and the only way to do that is to stay on their good side. If we cause problems, we'll never escape. I for one want to get back to my ship." And Ash.

"I…" He looks over at Rowlf, who's been watching this entire hushed exchange with that same creepy toothless smile from before. "What if whatever they put inside me reacts badly with the mind knot?"

"Your mind knot's still active?"

"Of course it's still active. It'll always be, until the host dies. Only it's dormant because it's not within range of any central computer."

Rowlf waves a small tablet at us. "How's it coming? We need this room for a decontamination soon."

I nudge Sarka toward Rowlf. "Okay." He gives me a death look but still manages to say, "We're ready when you are."

"Good. Please step over to the station in front of you." From the floor, two metallic pedestals rise. "Please place your bare arms, wrist down, on the top."

I roll up my sleeve and rest my wrist on the cold metal.

"Thank you. This will hurt."

Holy mother of Christ. I pull my wrist away and stare at a crescent-shaped scar on the underside. Below it is a faint purple glow. It reminds me of branding cows. We used to do it to our cattle on Delta to make sure no one stole any of our herd. I'd like to think we were a little more humane about it. Kate always said they didn't feel a thing. Now I'm not so sure. Sarka rolls down his sleeve and gives me another death stare.

"When this goes tits up, I'm blaming you."

I do my own fair impression of a full-body eye roll.

"This way, please." Rowlf is nothing but sunshine now as he motions us to step through the opposite door of the room.

We spend the rest of the morning? afternoon? several hours at least, making our way through what everyone calls intake. After the branding, they separate us to go through something resembling twentieth-century delousing. First they make you strip down to nothing. A strange robotic arm extends an orange thong. My modesty is an odd thing for slave masters to concern themselves with. After I decline the thong, they paint me from the neck down in foul-smelling purple stuff that burns away after a few minutes. I'm guessing it's supposed to kill anything living on me. Incidentally, it also removes my body hair. People pay good money for this service on Alpha. The experience, I'm sure, is better on Alpha.

After the foul purple stuff, I'm coated from head to toe in a clear gel that pours from spouts in the ceiling. It smells antiseptic and does a good job of stinging the back of my throat. I try not to breathe it in. The shoulder where the avian gouged me is especially painful. Before I'm herded to the next section, a second, fatter robotic arm drops from the ceiling and straps my arm in place before poking me with a syringe. A third drops and rolls liquid on the injury, which hardens. I'm told the cost for this medical procedure will come out of my first paycheck. I haven't even joined their army and am already in debt. Great.

After delousing, I'm taken to a stall. The back shuts and a dark-green beam scans my body. After a few minutes a small slot near the front slides open, and I'm presented with clothes. It's a variation on Tup's uniform. This is all too prison-ward for my liking. I feel like I've been charged with an offence I didn't even know I'd committed. The material is darker than any I've ever seen, hard in all the right places, and I suspect it doubles as armor. When it shifts between my fingers it almost shimmers. What other capabilities does it have? Hartley would kill to get ahold of this stuff. When I slide it on, the fabric fits like a second skin and breathes surprisingly well.

After I'm clothed again, Sarka and I reunite in a small room with two rows of desks facing a large screen. His new uniform is an improvement of the ragtag outfit he's been sporting. This one doesn't have any patches, nor does it smell like cabbage and dust. His face is even more taut than usual, which isn't a good sign. It means he's stressed, and a stressed Sarka is a dangerous Sarka.

"Calm down."

"What?" His voice is gruff and hard. "These people are strange."

"I know. Very contradictory."

"Why bother with all the pleasantries? It's not like they're asking our permission." He runs his hands down his sleeves, admiring the fabric. If they had asked, I get the feeling he'd say yes.

"I was thinking more about the orange thong," I say.

"I figured that was to protect your junk."

"Huh. It didn't seem like enough fabric to offer protection." I'm now wishing I hadn't refused the thong. Who knows what that purple stuff actually was.

"How much fabric do you need?"

The screen in front of us lights up, and a small, and I mean tiny—
like the size of a teapot—woman flashes on screen. Her hair is green
and sweeps into a spiral bun on top of her head. Her pale white skin is
smooth and flawless. The four teeth I can see in her mouth taper into
sharp points that make her smile, which has most of the real estate on
her face, appear sinister.

I lean over to Sarka and whisper, "Why do I keep feeling like I'm
Alice in Wonderland."

"Did you think all aliens would look like you?"

"No. Of course not." Yes. A little.

He points to the screen. "At least they're not flesh-eating
octopuses."

"Gee, thanks for that nightmare."

"Please be seated," the tiny woman says. She introduces herself as
Veera and directs us to turn on the tablet sitting at each desk.

A logo pulses blue and then fades. I think we're about to be
indoctrinated.

"Welcome to basic training," Veera says.

My screen glows blue for a moment. A small dot blinks on and off,
followed by a short diagram of how to sit in a chair and pull it up to a
desk. When they say basic, they mean it.

Sarka points to his tablet. "That was helpful. I was worried I was
doing it wrong."

"Over the next few days you will both be assessed and placed in
the division best suited to your talents. In order to make this process
as smooth as possible, we request that when asked questions, you
answer as truthfully as possible. We understand how disorienting this
procedure can be, but for the good of everyone, it's in your best interest
to cooperate."

"Where have I heard that before?" Sarka pushes his tablet on his
desk and leans back in his chair, folding his arms over his chest.

"For thousands of years the illya have poached this system, taking
what isn't theirs. The Varbaja have dedicated themselves and their
resources to purge this system of the illya for good."

The screen fades to white and a diorama appears. Over the next
forty minutes the history of this war unfolds. It's not pretty. And it isn't
going to end well. Our lives will be sacrificed for a war that will likely
go on for another couple of centuries.

The illya invade colonies and attack ships, taking prisoners. No one knows where their home world is, or if they even have one. Nor do they know how many are left. But they are deadly, and they won't stop coming until they're wiped out.

As much as that sounds awful, I can't say I'm moved to help fight the illya for the Varbaja. I need to get back to my ship and help my own people.

By the end of the ordeal I feel like I've just been purchased by a new farm on Delta. The system is set up to process many bodies at once. My mind swims with images of the *Persephone*'s crew filtering through here, terrified, angry, confused. How many ships have they conscripted to this army? Thousands? Millions? Billions?

This question is somewhat answered when we're brought to the mess. The room is gigantic and must feed over a thousand people at once. This isn't the only one on the ship either. Several more are scattered throughout each section.

The familiar face of Tup greets us as we exit the indoctrination room. He waves us to follow and we set off down white, sterile halls. This area is so clean it's like being on a different ship. Our reflections follow us down the corridor, matching our stride. I don't recognize myself. I feel like I'm playing soldier. Sarka, of course, is at home in the menacing uniform. I don't think it's my imagination that he's walking with his chest puffed out slightly, and every so often he checks himself out in the wall reflection. Yeah, they probably wet themselves over people like Sarka. He's ten times the soldier I'll ever be.

Despite what some people think, Union fleet is not a space version of the army. We aren't military. We're more like officers of a corporation. Our first mission is to protect the Belt's assets. Only if it's absolutely necessary will we take up arms. I was trained for combat at the Delta Academy, but fighting never came naturally to me.

Not like Sarka, who's been a soldier since he was a teenager. When he holds a weapon it's more than natural. It's expected.

Tup takes us in through a door that leads us to a meandering line of soldiers queuing for food. He takes a tray and begins pointing out stuff we should try and what to avoid.

He places a plate of what looks like moldy rocks on my tray. "These are cornu. A specialty from my planet. We grow them here in huge tubs of seawater, but they're originally from home."

"What are they?"

"They're very good."

I decide to let that one go. He puts what looks like black spaghetti on Sarka's plate and some brown peas on mine. He loads himself up with leafy greens and dishes with different-colored sauces. As we reach the end of the line, everyone receives plates with a heap of brown meat.

We find a free spot near the back just as a siren goes off.

"What's that?"

"New recruits." Tup slathers his meat in an orange sauce and shoves it into his mouth.

CHAPTER FIVE

Ash

Yakovich and Hartley join me on the track. The green beams have brought us to a halt in the center of a large bay that looks very much like a dry dock. Figures crisscross the walkways above us, but they're too far away to see any details.

"We are so fucked," Yakovich says.

"Calm down." If they were going to kill us, they wouldn't be pulling us in. They would've just shot at us. Although, if they want the ship intact, then they may secure it safely first. I turn to Yakovich. "Get your team together. Arm everyone you can. But tell them to shoot only if they're attacked. We don't know for sure if these people are hostile. Hartley, get your guys together. Do you have any more of those Jackies?"

"Tons."

"Good. Get a bunch and secure your team in the cargo hold. I'll come find you. If anything bad happens to Yakovich's team, we'll be the resistance."

Nobody moves. They're both staring at the giant ship that's swallowed us, mesmerized.

"Go," I shout.

The medical center is several decks up. When I arrive, Dr. Prashad has his face in a tablet. He projects an air of calm competence, as usual, so he must not know what's happened. But that's not a given. I've seen him keep his cool in pretty stressful situations.

"Doctor, I need you to load some syringes that will knock people out."

His bushy brows come together, causing the lines of his forehead to deepen. "What's happening?"

"We're about to be boarded, and if our first line of defense fails, I want to be ready with an alternative. You should be happy we're not planning to kill, only sedate."

"Who's trying to board us?" He looks around as if any second they'll storm through the med-center doors.

"I'm not sure. But I want you to come with me to the cargo hold. Hartley and his team are there. That's where I'm directing the rest of the crew."

"Have you thought about surrendering peacefully? It could mean a lot less casualties. What if they're only here to offer assistance?" He leans back on the counter and folds his arms.

That question sounds even more crazy when he says it. It's a nice thing to hope for, but I just can't see that being the case. What if they're here to pillage the ship? Maybe they're this solar system's version of the Burrs. We're adrift in space with little more than bottle rockets as weapons. How effective can we be?

Dr. Prashad places a calming hand on my wrist. "We'll make it through this. If they were here to kill us, we wouldn't know it. We'd be dead already." He leads me to the console and begins mixing a syringe. He places a tube into an oblong computer and presses a few buttons. The tube fills with liquid. When the computer chimes, he hands me the syringe. "I want you to take this with you."

"What is it?"

"Backup if you lose your medication. I don't want you to miss taking it, even during this turmoil."

The syringe is filled with a white, creamy liquid that coats the sides as I turn it. "And do I just take it when I miss a dose?"

"If you miss more than three days, take it."

"What happens if I don't?" I hate putting stuff in my body, especially when I'm not a hundred percent sure what it is.

"It would be very harmful to stop the treatment once started. There are side effects. Not many, but if you have any issues, you come see me." He puts a hand on my arm, grabbing my attention. His brown eyes are full of concern. "Ash, this is important."

I believe him. Dr. Prashad has always been kind and honest. He's helped me more than most would be willing to do. And he puts up with only so much of my shit. Sometimes I think of him as the father of the ship. He's older than everyone by at least twenty years. Even on the *Posterus* few are older than thirty-five. When we started this mission we believed we'd be traveling to our new home hundreds of light-years away. We wanted viable procreators so we could expand the population and keep the ship staffed.

Dr. Prashad has aged well. For over fifty, he doesn't look it. That's the benefit of not living under a sun. Nothing dries out your skin and causes premature wrinkles.

"You said there weren't many side effects, but that doesn't mean there aren't any."

"No, you're right. You might suffer nausea, headaches, fatigue. Nothing too outrageous." He hands me five syringes, which I shove into my pocket, making sure to keep my medication separate.

I lead him out of the medical center toward the cargo hold. The ship is scary quiet without the engines. The corridors are empty. We don't encounter any crew or hostile aliens. Maybe they haven't boarded us yet.

Our footsteps clank along the corridor as we move through the silent ship. Any minute I expect to hear a loud bang or explosion as the intruders find a way to enter the ship. So when I do encounter one of them for the first time, it's so quiet and unexpected, I almost trip over my own feet.

We round the final corner before the chute to the cargo hold, and I bump into a small, thin man. He's using a small computer as a shield, holding it in front of his chest. My momentum knocks him to the ground, and his computer scatters down the hall, ricocheting off the walls and coming to a teetering standstill on the edge of the chute opening. We all watch, mesmerized, as it tilts and plummets, echoing off the chute's ladder and walls with cringeworthy loudness. The sound of it shattering at the bottom is all the catalyst the little man needs. He jumps to his feet and runs to the chute, where he peers over the edge. He jabbers something at us and points down the chute, angry about his broken computer. He's not hostile about it, more concerned. No one else is with him, so if he does become hostile, I'm sure I can take him. If he wasn't so short, I'd think he was an avian, although he's without wings, from what I can see. There's not much room under his brown and green uniform to hide wings, even folded.

But his face comes to a sharp point like the avians, and his skin is the same pasty gray.

It's possible they're related. Hartley said the avians probably get their height from the low gravity of the planet, which makes their bones grow longer. So if these creatures don't live on the planet anymore, it's possible their height was reduced. I'm sure Hartley could explain it better.

The man is on his hands and knees now, pointing down the chute. Does he want one of us to go get the computer? It's probably smashed to bits by now.

I nudge the doctor. "Do you mind getting it? I'll keep an eye on this guy."

"You'll be okay?"

I nod, and he looks relieved to be the one to go. The man calms as soon as Dr. Prashad begins his descent. And now we're left in that awkward position of what to do while we wait. The little beak man stands next to the chute staring at me. His dark eyes are reminiscent of the avians, and the resemblance gives me chills. They have a way of boring through me as if I'm less important than my surroundings.

After a few minutes the doctor emerges from the chute and places several pieces of electronics on the ground in front of the man. I wouldn't say he scurries back to me, because I can't ever imagine Dr. Prashad scurrying, but it's close enough.

The alien squats and busies himself fitting the pieces back together. The edge of his bottom lip curls up around the beak protrusion, and I realize this must be his smile, because when he stands he points the computer at us, and suddenly his jabber makes sense.

"I am Vonn. Why are you orbiting our planet?"

I'm speechless for a second. The device somehow manages to translate languages. My mouth opens, and all I can think to say is, "Your planet?"

"We protect the nishga."

"The nishga?" I mime wings and he nods. "Why do they need protection?"

"If people discover the planet, they will come for resources and threaten the nishga's habitat. They are primitive but special." He steps forward, pointing the translator closer, as if it's something threatening. "Why are you here?"

I don't think sharing our predicament is a good idea. Telling strangers we're crippled isn't the best way to stay alive. "We're making repairs to our ship, and as soon as we've done that we'll be leaving to join our main ship." I hope by main ship he knows we're not alone, and from that he assumes they know where we are and are much deadlier than we appear.

"Your ship is very broken. And from our scans it doesn't look like you have the necessary equipment to repair it. You are adrift," Vonn says.

No such luck. "We have a plan in place and will be able to get the ship going again."

"Not before you run out of emergency reserves. We can help. We have resources that you don't."

My heart soars, but only for a millisecond. Something my father always used to say runs through my head—there's no such thing as pure altruism. My dad is a very cynical man, but that doesn't mean he's wrong. I'm not sure what these people want in payment, but we don't have it. We have nothing to spare.

"That's very kind. But we don't have anything to offer in return."

"We don't want anything. We want you to leave the planet." His face scrunches into a tight ball. Is that a frown? I feel like I've demanded he share his lunch after he'd already offered to give me half. Obviously diplomacy is not a strong point for these people.

"We have no intention of staying. We need to join our ship as soon as we're ready."

"We'll take you to your ship. You have no need to wait."

A loud bang sounds, and the ship shudders. Vonn's eyes widen, and he peers down the chute, the source of the loud bang.

"What the hell was that? Are your people attacking?" I ask.

He's frozen. Then the hand holding the translator shakes. He doesn't look like the head of an invasion army. But I could be wrong. It's happened a few times before. He looks back at the doctor and me and shakes his head. "That wasn't us. We don't use force. It's not our way."

I run to the chute and prepare to descend. "Doctor, will you keep an eye on our guest, please? Make sure he doesn't wander. I have a few more questions." More like a million. I grip the sides of the ladder and use the sides of my boots to put pressure on the edge and slide down fast. A few feet from the bottom I let go and land with a teeth-jarring thud. I don't see anyone in this corridor, but the cargo hold isn't far from here. I wish I'd thought to grab a weapon from the armory before finding the doctor. Now I'm unarmed and running toward trouble. What else is new?

I like to think of this as bravery. Jordan would say it's rash, a nicer word than my dad would've used. I do have a habit of acting on impulse, though it always works out in the end. And if it's not me, then who? What if Vonn is lying and they are invading the ship? What if Yakovich mistook a welcome for something less friendly? Or one of Hartley's Jackies discharged?

I round the corner and stop dead. Yakovich's whole team is lying prone on the floor in front of me, their weapons dropped where they fell. I kneel at the first body, Wyatt Fossick, my least-favorite person on this ship. He's got a grudge because I elbowed him in the jaw once. I was so sure he was the one behind the attacks on me. But he wasn't. Instead it was someone I thought was my friend. I have no idea why Vasa attacked me. He still won't talk.

I poke Fossick in the ribs, but he doesn't move. I check his pulse. He's still alive, only unconscious. I pick my way through the bodies and find a standoff in the cargo hold. Hartley is brandishing a large spanner, while several of the beak people stand at the back of the hold.

"What's going on?" I demand in my take-no-shit voice.

One of the beak people steps away from his group and bows before me. "I am Bragga, leader of the illya."

"The illya?" I look at Hartley, who shrugs. He's still got the spanner cocked as if he's going to bash the guy's head in. I motion for him to lower it. He does, but keeps a firm grip. "What are you doing here?" I ask.

Bragga spreads his arms. Like the man we encountered earlier, he's wearing a brown and green uniform, only his has a deep-green stripe down the center. A rank? Department? "We noticed your ship is without power. We wanted to assist you."

I jab a thumb behind me. "And the unconscious people outside? Was that your hello?"

He heaves a sigh. "That was a misunderstanding. They're not damaged. They had weapons pointed at us when we entered."

"What did you do to them?"

"We projected sound waves that encouraged them to sleep. They will wake up in a few minutes refreshed."

Hartley snorts.

"Is this possible?" I ask him.

"Maybe." He shrugs. "Deep sleep produces delta waves, and it's been theorized, although never actually proven, that if you project delta waves at someone it could induce sleep. I don't believe it's possible. But theoretically someone could use other sound frequencies we haven't discovered." He says the whole thing without taking a breath. I've never met a faster talker than Hartley. It drives Jordan mad.

"Jesus, Hartley. A yes or no next time." He takes a deep breath, preparing for another onslaught of words, but I hold up my hand. "Go get the doctor. I want him to check on the crew outside. He's a few decks up. And have him bring that other illya with him. I don't want any of them wandering the ship unattended."

Hartley closes his mouth and nods, leaving his geeklings.

I turn back to Bragga. "As I explained to your colleague up a few decks, we don't have anything to pay you with. What few resources we have are needed."

"We don't ask for anything in return. Meeting new people and learning their stories is payment enough for us."

"You want our stories?" There's an old Earth saying: if it sounds too good to be true, it usually is. These guys sound too good to be true. They come at the exact moment we need them, and they want to help us without any payment in return. What's the catch? "Are you sure you can fix our ship? We require a quantum computer to run most of our systems." And that's only one of many issues.

"This is no problem. We scanned your ship before guiding you into our ship bay. In fact, we will be able to help restock some of your depleted resources."

I almost groan. This is becoming way too good. For the millionth time I wish Jordan was here. She'd know exactly how to handle this situation. I don't want to reject it outright because we really need the help. Hell, we were minutes away from abandoning ship. But taking their help feels like making a deal with the devil.

After the doctor attends to the crew—turns out they were asleep—and everyone wakes up, I usher the senior crew into the officers' mess for a meeting. This is a big decision that I don't want to make alone.

We don't have enough room for all of us to fit around one of the tables, so Yakovich and Mani push two tables together. I squeeze in beside Hartley and the doctor, while Mani takes a seat on the opposite side.

"Okay. What do you guys think?"

"I think they're great," says Hartley at the same time Yakovich says, "I don't trust them."

"I'm with Yakovich." I look around the table. Foer and Mani share a look. Dr. Prashad, as always, keeps to himself, choosing to keep his opinion off his face.

"Why do you always have to assume the worst?" Hartley asks. "What if they are here to help us? Good does exist, you know, though maybe not in your world." He frowns at me. It's the angriest I've ever seen him. And I know he's afraid he won't get a chance to check out their ship. Hartley's that kid who would go with a stranger if he had a cool toy to show him. Hartley's very lucky he grew up on Beta and not some Earth city. He wouldn't have made it past puberty.

Yakovich and I are very similar in our views. Everyone's an enemy out to get us until proved otherwise.

Mani raises his hand. "Hartley's right." He keeps it raised even after he's spoken. When no one argues with him, he lowers it. "If they wanted to poach our ship like a Burr, they would've already. Why make friends with us?"

"Mani has a point," says Dr. Prashad. "If you want my opinion, we should be cautious, but I see no reason why we shouldn't take their help."

"It beats the alternative." Foer looks around the table for confirmation.

Mani nods vigorously. "The last thing we want is to be stuck on that planet."

Yakovich sighs. She's starting to relent. I know she'd much rather stay on the ship. I would too. But I hate having debts. And letting them help us without payment is a debt. It's a bad way to start in this galaxy. Who's to say they won't come calling for a return someday?

"How long will it take the ship to get up and running, Hartley?"

He exchanges a grim look with Foer. "At least four weeks. And that's if everything goes to plan. We don't even know if their parts will be compatible with the *Persephone*. Every system that is working has been running on emergency power for a day. We need to do an entire overhaul and diagnostic run, and that alone takes two weeks to do properly." He takes a breath. "And we want to do it thoroughly, or else what's the point in getting help? We could be halfway back to the *Posterus* and lose a major system, and then we won't have any help."

"I realize we need help. That's not the problem."

"Why are you so against them?" asks Mani.

"I'm not against them." I'm against help in general. I know this about myself. It's not a very attractive trait in a first officer. In fact, it could be considered downright disastrous for my rank. "I'm worried about owing a debt we can't repay." True, but not the whole truth. When I was growing up, my grandfather used to use an expression, all that glitters isn't gold. And right now I'm worried about how glittery the illya look to everyone.

I adjourn the meeting to think. After all, the decision rests with me. I'm in charge now. As much as I hate it, I'm going to have to suck it up.

I end up on the track. I'd be running if we still had showers, but they aren't essential as much as they should be for some of the crew. So I stand with my head against the glass, looking out at the ship bay. I know what I have to do. I just don't like it. If I say no, then I strand my crew on a hostile planet. Vonn didn't sound so thrilled to see us here. Who's to say they'll even let us land? What if they take the *Persephone* and imprison us?

But if I do say yes, what happens if things go wrong? What if they aren't what they appear? Is this what Jordan feels like when she has to make a tough decision? She makes it look so easy. And she always makes the right one.

I nearly jump a meter when I hear a throat clear behind me. It's Hartley. He shrugs and joins me at the window. He doesn't say anything. As the silence spreads between us, it makes me happy to have the company. It's rare for Hartley to keep his thoughts to himself, and I appreciate that he sees that I need it.

After a few more minutes he nudges me. "Vonn offered to show us around their ship." It's both an invitation and a request for permission. With this possibility on the line, I'm even more surprised Hartley kept quiet as long as he did. His first chance to examine alien technology up close is making him almost explode from excitement. His eyes are bright and eager even in this light. He's radiating anticipation. "It might help you get a better feel for them. Make an informed decision?"

"Plus you really want to see what makes their ship go."

His head bobs up and down. "More than you'll ever know."

I look back out at the ship. I remember standing at this window with Jordan right before we embarked for the *Posterus*. It was the last time we'd ever see Alpha, and she asked me why I'd signed up for the mission. I certainly got my wish; I'll never have to worry about being a shadow. My grandfather may have commanded the ships that brought us to the Belt, but in the last two weeks I've been part of the most important discoveries in our species' history. The only problem is, no one back home will ever know it.

"Hey, Hartley, why'd you decide to come on the mission? You could've stayed back on the Belt and lived with fame and glory."

He rests his hands on the rail and peers up through the window. "True. And I thought about it. How great would it be to run the physics department at the Alpha Academy? They offered, you know?" His smile is shy. "But I knew if I stayed I'd be the same person I always was. I grew up on Beta. My parents worked in the factories, and we all knew I could do more than that. School came really easy to me, so I worked as hard as I could so I wouldn't end up like my mom and dad. Dead at age fifty-two and forty-five. And it worked." He shrugs. "I made it out. But I never got a chance for a normal life. That's why I came out here—to redefine who I am."

"Yeah, out here you get to be the guy who saves my life." He blushes when I say it. I've never seen him blush. "I never thanked you for that. If you hadn't reached for my hand, I'd have fallen into the pit and been ejected with the core." I'm not the crying type. I can get angry and react in an instant, but positive emotions? I'm really good at burying those deep. But I can feel myself tearing up, and I don't want it to come out in my voice, so I nudge him and walk toward the chute. As we're climbing, it finally feels safe to use my voice. "Thanks, Hartley."

"You're welcome, Ash."

❖

The illya's ship is the strangest place I've ever seen. It's like walking into a living thing. The walls seem to breathe, and the floors yield with each footstep. I'm with Hartley, Yakovich, and the doctor. They invited us to tour some nonessential areas of their ship. I wouldn't trust guests on our bridge either. But we won't be seeing engineering, which has Hartley bummed out. Not for long. The first place Vonn shows us is the main throughway, which is similar to the concourse on the *Posterus,* but ten times bigger. It's like stepping into one of the jungles on the planet. Vegetation is everywhere. Trees tower above us, probably from the planet, because they're as tall as the ceiling, which must be several kilometers up. Plants and vines fill out receptacles lining the avenue. Some climb the trees, others the walls. If you'd told me I was on a planet I might actually believe you.

The place is deserted. If it weren't for the vegetation our voices would echo throughout the great room.

"This is our common space where we meet and converse with each other." Vonn points to the balconies above us with benches covered in colorful cushions. We sometimes even take our meals here. It was built because it reminded our people of home."

"Where is everyone?" Yakovich asks.

Vonn smiles, but the way he looks around, catching all the emptiness with his eyes, it's not a happy smile. "We all work during this hour."

Yakovich nods, but like me, she doesn't appear convinced.

Then Vonn perks up. "Why don't I show you where we prepare our meals? We are celebrated for our food." Vonn leads us off to the side. Between two trees is a hidden corridor. As we meander through the halls, we don't meet a single person. Not until we reach their kitchens do we encounter any illya.

Two are standing behind a giant stone in the middle of the room. The top surface is flat, but the sides round into the floor, where a sort of moat allows for food and water runoff.

The two chefs have their heads bent together. They're quietly working and chatting, and one looks like he's laughing. They could even be gossiping, but I can't understand what they're saying. The computer Vonn uses to translate needs to be pointed toward the speaker. They don't sound anything like the avians from the planet—no harsh or guttural tones. This is more like the birdsong we heard up in the trees. It's almost like they're singing to each other.

Vonn stops in front of the stone and expands his arms. "This is where we prepare our food. And these are our chefs." The two chefs don't even bother looking up from what they're doing. They carry on as if we weren't even here. "They're preparing our evening meal." Before he can go any further, Hartley is peppering him with questions.

"What's the stone do? Is it conductive? Does it have its own heat source, or do you heat it some other way?"

Vonn blinks for a moment, digesting all those queries. It's a side effect of dealing with Hartley. I'm convinced his mind works ten times faster than everyone else's. "The stone is a superconductor, heated by water from beneath. The steam off our cooking in turn heats much of the ship." He points to the exhaust above the stone. "It takes very little energy to heat the stone, and it stays hot evenly across its surface."

And we've lost Hartley as he asks more and more questions about the process. I hadn't thought about how much we can learn from these people. They've been space travelers much longer than we have, and it's obvious their technology is centuries ahead of ours. Perhaps it isn't such a bad idea to say yes.

CHAPTER SIX

Jordan

"New recruits?" I ask Tup as I pick my way through the food in front of me. Buckets with utensils are placed every few feet along the table, but they're not like anything I've ever seen before. There's a small wooden mallet and a sheath of metal.

Tup picks up one of the mallets and smashes the moldy rock. Inside is a bright-red hairball. He turns the mallet around and uses the top of the handle to pry the hairball out, then rolls it in the bright-yellow sauce and pops it into his mouth. He hums and smacks his thick lips together. Sarka and I share a look of revulsion.

"A siren means we've picked up a ship and they're about to go through intake."

A ship. God, I hope it's not the *Persephone*. Although if it is, we'll have allies to help us get out of here. Then a thought occurs to me. "What happens to the people who resist intake?"

His mouth is full as he says, "Try the cornu. They're especially good today." He pushes one of the moldy rocks toward me.

I push it toward Sarka. "You first. I double-dog dare you."

"You're such a baby." He rummages through the pile of rocks like he's choosing which oyster has the pearl. His fingers pluck a medium-sized rock, and I watch in disgust as he smashes the top off with the mallet and pries the hairball out. "Does it matter which sauce?"

Tup nods and points to the yellow sauce. "You eat cornu only with beva."

Sarka nods, his expression grave. He slathers the thing in beva and, without hesitating, shoves the whole thing into his mouth. He chews, nodding a little, then in a more exaggerated manner. "You're right. That is good." He also hums as he sifts through the rocks again, looking for his next choice. "Jordan, don't be a baby. Try it."

Heat fills my cheeks. It's been years since I was this embarrassed. "Excuse me?"

"You heard me. When did you become such a picky eater? When you were a kid your mother and I could get you to try anything. It's that bland diet the Union forces on you."

"As I recall, the only adventurous stuff to eat was borscht in a tube."

"And you loved it." He squishes the cornu between his fingers, offering it once again.

I throw him the dirtiest look I can. No way am I going to let him goad me into trying that thing. It looks like that pink fungus Ash and I encountered on the planet.

Tup squints at me. "You don't look young enough to be his daughter."

I scowl. "He's like a hundred and thirty years older than me."

Tup's eyes bug out. "Seriously?" My scowl deepens. "I wasn't even sure you were the same species." He circles a hand around his face. "It's the face."

I laugh, because the look on Sarka's face must mirror my own from earlier.

"He's had work done."

"Work? What does that mean?"

I shake my head. "Never mind."

Sarka drops a cornu into his mouth. "You know what these remind me of? Back home on Earth, we had these things called chocolate truffles." He licks his fingers and reaches for another one, then pauses before cracking it open. "You sure you don't want to try one, Jordan?"

"I'm not falling for that."

He shrugs.

"I don't blame you for being wary," Tup says. "Only one percent of our new recruits ever get up the nerve to try 'em. They look strange, and people tend to be afraid of strange."

"Fine." I grab the rock and crack it open. The smell puts me off a little. It's very salty. I pry it out and roll it around in the yellow sauce, then pause to psych myself up. "Fuck." I place it in my mouth and chew as fast as I can. They taste like someone went swimming in salty hot sauce and then stuck their head in my mouth, only so much dirtier than that. I glare accusingly at Sarka, who's got the biggest grin on his face. I notice the second cornu he took is sitting on his plate untouched. "You bastard." I don't know why I'm so mad. I knew he was teasing.

It's not until later I remember Tup never answered my question. What happens if someone refuses to go through intake?

After dinner Tup takes us to sleeping quarters. Quarters is a loose term. They're coffins lining several walls. They reach five high and at least fifteen or twenty across each wall. Ladders are built into the bulkheads that connect to the top bunk.

Tup consults his tablet before leading us to a row halfway down the room. He points to the top two. "Doesn't matter which of you takes the top, but remember what room you're in. Some of us don't like finding strangers in our beds." He stuffs the tablet into one of his many cargo pockets. "When you hear two loud siren bursts, it means lights out shortly. Make sure you're not caught out of bed when that happens."

"Why?"

"Anyone caught out of bed gets the stocks."

"Stocks?"

"The next rotation they're in charge of keeping the latrines clean." Tup points to a few of the coffins. "Some of the species we have on board haven't mastered how to use them properly. Makes it the perfect punishment." He gives Sarka a hearty punch on the arm and walks back the way we came.

I risk opening one of the low coffins. It's empty and not much bigger than the single mattress sitting on the floor. As the door opens, a cool purple light emanates from a ring above the bed, illuminating the tiny space. On one side is a thin shelf piled with mementos and what look like souvenirs from past battles. There's even a necklace of strange-shaped fingers threaded on a string hanging by a hook at the top of the bed. I close the door before the owner comes back.

I stare at the tiny stepladder leading to our new home. I thought the *Persephone* was small. Sure, I was proud of her because she was sleek and fast, but not big. You would never describe her as a luxury liner. But even the tiniest cabin would be a five-star hotel compared to this.

"How do people live like this?" I ask.

"Because they have no choice." Sarka grabs my arm and pulls me toward the opposite end of the hall, keeping us moving. "This isn't the Belt. Keep your head down and become invisible. The less you're noticed, the better."

"You're giving me advice now?"

"Good advice. If you want to survive, you need to listen to me." He gives me the once-over. "Maybe we should cut your hair. I haven't seen a lot of women. Maybe we'll get lucky and you'll get transferred tomorrow to somewhere more suitable. You don't belong here."

"Excuse me?" I know I'm not army material. I would never in a million years choose to join this war, but hearing it from Sarka is insulting. "I belong wherever the hell I say I belong."

We've reached a loud open room filled with off-duty soldiers. It must be the lounge where they unwind after a day of killing people. A loud roar comes from a back table. They're throwing stones at a wall and watching them bounce back onto a chalked grid on the table.

The room is semidark, with red lights hanging every few feet. One of the men begins to argue with the last stone thrower, and chaos erupts. Sarka pulls me farther down the hall. "When you live in a world where all you have to fight over is garbage, that garbage becomes treasure. Don't underestimate these people. They have nothing to lose, which makes them more dangerous than the best-trained army in the universe."

The noise from the clubhouse follows us down the corridor. Something shatters. I take another step. A thought occurs to me, and I feel stupid for not figuring it out earlier. Of course Sarka probably realized it the second we woke up on the artificial farm. At some point they'll separate us, and I'll be at the mercy of every piece of shit who thinks I owe them something. We call it human nature, but I have a feeling that several traits are universal.

I'll just have to make sure we don't get separated, and the only way to do that is to be better than him. We reach the end of the hall, which has two windows on either side looking out at the rest of the bulbous section of the ship. A small cargo ship is attached to the side, and I hope it's the ship they just recruited from. I'm not sure who I'd feel sorrier for, the Varbaja or Ash if they captured the *Persephone*. If

Sarka couldn't break her, and I know only half the things he's capable of, then no one can. She'll die letting them try.

The next morning I look for any of my crew at breakfast. Tup isn't with us so we're fending for ourselves. Sarka sticks with an all-meat diet. I'm tempted to do the same. At least it tastes similar to beef. I've had it only once—the day I graduated from Delta Academy. Kate got it special for us. It's strange having grown up on a cattle farm and only ever eaten beef once. It's expensive, as is all meat back on the Belt. It was only for special occasions, unless you lived on Alpha.

Sarka and I pick a table in the back with fewer people. It's almost quiet. Sarka uses his hands to rip into his breakfast, tearing off a piece of meat and packing it into his mouth. The sight puts me off my meal. Not a hard thing to do. I place a green stick in my mouth and tentatively bite down. Then again, maybe I should just stick to meat.

"We need to find a way off this heap," Sarka says through a mouthful.

"I agree. But how?"

"Leave that to me. I'll have a plan before the end of the day."

"Oh no. We aren't following any of your plans. We need to lay low for a while, let them forget about us."

"That's stupid. We need to get out as soon as possible. If we're not out of here in two days, we'll never leave."

"Two days?" How has this man commanded an army for the better part of a century? I'm starting to think either the Union fleet isn't as good as we claim to be or the Burrs have been very lucky. I lean back and fold my arms. We're going to have one hell of a fight, two captains used to taking charge. I already know it would be stupid to get separated from him, but he's going to make this so much harder.

"Listen, Jordan. I've been doing this a hell of a lot longer than you, so for once you should just trust me."

"I'm here because you took me hostage. On my own ship." My voice is beginning to rise above the din. A few tables down we get a couple of looks. Right now I don't care. "If you'd wanted to leave on your own you could have asked. I would've let you take an escape pod."

Sarka throws a piece of gristle on his plate. "Staying on that ship probably wasn't the best idea for anyone."

"Why? Because you planted bombs? I don't believe you. Why would you plant bombs on a ship you were on? You didn't know Ash and I would make it off the planet. No thanks to you, by the way."

"Those bombs would go off only if I detonated them or something went wrong. The ship is fine."

"Why would you even plant them in the first place?" My voice is deafening. I lower it as two men in uniform saunter over to us. "Over a hundred people are on that ship."

Sarka shrugs. "You never know when a bomb will come in handy. Or several." He waves a hand at me. "Relax, will you? Hartley probably had them all disarmed in a few minutes. They weren't very sophisticated."

"If anything happens to my ship, I will kill you." I keep my voice low this time but slap the table for emphasis.

The two soldiers stop on either side of Sarka. "You have a problem?"

"No problem. We're done. Where do I go from here?" I ask.

One of them nods to someone behind me. When I turn, Tup is making his way through the crowd. I pick up my tray to dump it.

"You're going to waste all that food?" Tup asks.

"I lost my appetite."

"Shame. You're going to need it today."

Sarka stands as well, but Tup waves him down. "I'll be back for you once I drop her off."

Sarka frowns. It's not always easy to tell. His face tends to hold its shape. "Where are you taking her?"

"Don't worry. You'll see each other again at the halfway meal." A quick battle rages behind Sarka's eyes as he decides whether to back off or make a fuss. We're outnumbered, even without the two soldiers still flanking him. He drops back into his seat and gives me a tiny wave with his fingers.

I turn to follow Tup, but all my bravado has disappeared. I had one goal, stick close to Sarka, and I've already screwed that up. I dump my tray at the exit. "Where are we going? Why aren't Sarka and I training together?"

"We're assessing your strengths and weaknesses today. Your only opponent is yourself, so you don't need to do it together. Also, we find people perform better if they know their shipmates aren't watching them. It takes some of the pressure off."

That's a strange thing to say. I'd rather my crew mates watch me than these people. If I felt like cattle yesterday, I have a feeling today it'll be a lab rat. What's the best-case scenario? They think I'm great, hand me a weapon, and put me in the front line? No, thanks. If I fail every test, will they have me cleaning toilets?

"What sorts of things are they going to make me do?"

We stop at the end of a hall. He taps in a code and a lift door opens. "It's different for everyone. They don't want to keep the tests the same, in case the soldiers start sharing with new recruits."

"And what happens if we fail?" I follow him into the lift. This one has windows running the circumference.

"There's no pass or fail. It's not that kind of test."

We're both silent as the lift descends with a soft hum. Once we're free of the upper section of the ship, the lift shaft becomes transparent and we're sinking into space. We've moved a large distance in the short amount of time we've been on the ship because their sun is much closer. Not far off the starboard bow an asteroid, trailing debris, travels through the system.

"The recruits you brought aboard yesterday, were they the same species as Sarka and I?"

Tup drags his eyes from the stars and looks me up and down as if he hasn't noticed me before. "No. We've never seen your species before."

We soon sink back into the ship and reach our deck. He motions me across the hall and opens a door opposite the lift.

I enter and stare, and then I blink, hoping it's an illusion. It's not.

"You've got to be shitting me."

CHAPTER SEVEN

Ash

Over the next couple of days, we work to get the *Persephone* at least able to sustain life for more than a day. We keep losing emergency systems. Hartley constantly reminds me that they weren't designed to work like this, but we don't have a choice. The illya offered to let us stay on their ship, but I won't give up that much control. I can't pin down anything sinister about them, and that's what bothers me the most. They're too perfect.

Yesterday I was on the bridge with one of them—a young woman, as far as I could tell. There's not much difference between the sexes. Not like the avians—or nishga, as the illya call them—who amputate the wings of their females. That was an easy indicator. This woman was explaining how they care for the nishga by keeping the planet hidden from the rest of the system. The next system has a few habitable planets, but a group the illya call the Varbaja control them. If the Varbaja were to learn of this planet, they would immediately kill the nishga. So the illya wander the galaxy harvesting asteroids for resources and keeping an eye on the planet. That whole story smacks of pretty wrapping, like one of those stories they tell you as a kid that sounds too perfect until you get older. Once the glossed-over details come out, suddenly the truth doesn't look so great.

Hartley thinks I'm being too cynical. He almost swooned when he saw their engine room. They use dark matter for propulsion—don't ask me to explain it because the whole thing sounded like they were talking gibberish. I swear, Hartley almost pissed himself. Now they can do no wrong. He wants us to adapt some of their technologies for the *Persephone*. I know Jordan wouldn't approve, and I don't want to do anything to her ship while she's gone. It really does feel like she's coming back, like she went on a brief mission while I hold down the fort. I'm being optimistic, and I know my expectation could bite me in the ass later. But I wouldn't be able to function if I thought she was dead. She doesn't feel dead. In my mind I still picture her out there somewhere.

It's been four days now, and I've not had a single panic attack. I've been sleeping better and haven't felt like I'm not doing enough. It's hard to admit, but I think the medication the doctor gave me is helping. I'd been expecting the usual pattern. When things don't go right, I tend to fixate, and that turns into a slow dive. I mope for days and then start to panic that I'm not doing enough, so I come up with projects to keep me busy, which helps. Within a day my mood lifts and I'm back to normal. But with whatever I'm taking, none of that happens. Four days of smooth sailing.

On the fifth day it all goes to hell.

It started off great. We got a new quantum computer hooked up to our system. It was different than our old one, but Hartley said he could make it work. And for a while it did, but then something went wrong. Hartley's still not sure what. Then systems started shutting down, including our emergency systems.

I was on the bridge when the environmental system failed. If you run backup systems with no main computer, as Hartley pointed out on several occasions, there's no warning system. And oxygen doesn't immediately dissipate when the system making it stops working. It takes hours for us to suck up all that oxygen and breathe out carbon monoxide. So while we were going about our day, we were slowly killing ourselves just by breathing.

Also, oxygen deprivation and carbon monoxide poisoning affect everyone differently. And it's not always easy to see the signs. I guess it's fortunate that Vasa tried to kill me by locking me in the filter room and sucking out all the oxygen because I know what it feels like.

I was on the bridge early this afternoon when the front porthole became blurry. When I stood up to take a look I stumbled, and that's when I noticed I wasn't the only one looking sluggish.

I staggered to one of the portable oxygen tanks we keep throughout the ship and began rounding up people to evacuate the ship. We got everyone out without any injuries. Nothing the doctor can't fix with some pain medication.

But now we're without a ship.

Hartley assures me the failures were bound to happen, that they were only a matter of time. Hartley says I'm being paranoid. It was our first night on the *Kudo*—that's what the illya call their ship. They'd just shown us to our cabins—mine is twice the size of the one on the *Persephone*—and Hartley turned to me before entering his. "You only feel this way because you're in charge." His smile was sympathetic, which is unusual for Hartley. He doesn't have a lot of empathy for people. "Don't worry. We'll get the *Persephone* back together again."

I nodded but didn't say anything, too choked up to respond. He's right though. I feel like a failure. The *Persephone* is sitting empty in their ship bay. I feel like I've abandoned my only child.

Meanwhile, Hartley is in geek heaven. Their technology is centuries ahead of ours. Stepping onto their ship is like traveling through time. I don't even recognize the materials used for the bulkheads or the covering on my cabin floor. It's so strange, but the carpet reminds me of the Tartan Track on the *Persephone*. It has a give to it, but more than that, it molds to your feet when you walk on it.

My room has a view of the planet, but I haven't wanted to look. It makes my stomach tight. I find it hard to drift off to sleep tonight. Too much is going on in my brain right now. I keep thinking about Jordan. If she were here, would we still be on the *Persephone*?

I already miss our ship. If I were there now I could go for a run on the track and clear my mind. Running is the only thing that's ever helped. I contemplate for a millisecond running around the corridors of this ship, but my thought is gone in a flash.

I lie in the soft bed and pull the covers over me, hoping the act of getting into bed will help. It never has. I usually lie awake for hours staring up at the ceiling. For some reason, tonight a strange thing happens. As soon as my head hits the silky pillow, my brain begins to mellow. My thoughts scatter, and I'm drifting off before I can wonder how I got so tired.

The next few days pass in a blur. We have so much to accomplish in such a short amount of time. The illya have been very helpful. I'm surprised by how much they know, even about our technology. It's like asking Hartley to work on the first engine ever invented.

Every morning I meet him in the mess for breakfast, and we discuss the day's projects. Hartley is still the slowest eater I've ever encountered. By the time I arrive in the morning he's already been there an hour, and I still finish before him. It's a good thing he works fast or he'd never get anything done.

I hate to admit it because it's like treason, but the food is so much better than on the *Persephone*. They have real meat. Okay, so they don't actually raise their own livestock on board, but it's grown in a lab. Hartley assures me that it's real; it just hasn't ever been alive. All the benefits of taste without the negative moral dilemmas to go with it.

This morning Hartley is sitting with Yakovich, who I haven't seen much of since our talk outside the escape pod. I had a meeting with Bragga the first day to ask if they could scan for Jordan's escape pod. So far, nothing. They said we could leave orbit and begin the search today. I find it hard to believe we haven't found a trace of them. Something should be left over from their rocket burn.

I take a seat at the table next to Hartley, and before I'm even sitting an attendant is placing a plate with several slabs of pink meat and a hunk of what they refer to as loaf, which resembles our bread. I tend to pick around the vegetables, which don't taste as good as the rest. Hartley, however, has discovered their hot sauce. He slathers it over everything, even the loaf. It's best with the greens. If I liked my food spicy, I'd consider it. I bet it helps with the bitter aftertaste.

"So what's on the agenda today?" I ask.

Hartley pauses, his fork halfway to his mouth. "The environmental systems went down because we tried for too much right off. We need to work backward, so I'm starting with the least essential systems and working my way up." He lifts the utensil to his mouth and inhales a piece of meat slathered in a bright-green sauce. "Today we're working on integrating the door-locking system."

"I don't want to be on this ship any longer than we have to. Don't spend all your time on non-essentials. We have to get the *Persephone* livable as soon as possible."

"Aye, aye, Captain." He salutes me with his fork.

"I get a promotion I haven't heard about?" When I don't smile back, his grin falls.

"No, Lieutenant."

I jump at the tap on my shoulder and turn to find Vonn bowing his head at me. The young man is still holding the translating device in front of him like a shield.

"The captain would like to have a word with you, Lieutenant Ash."

I hope this is about the search they're doing for Jordan's escape pod. I bid Yakovich and Hartley good-bye and follow Vonn out of the mess. I'm expecting Bragga, but instead I'm led to the bridge and introduced to another man, Kalve. He's the tallest man on the bridge and possibly of the crew. Still, the top of his head only reaches my nose. His uniform ripples along his arms and legs, hiding powerful muscles. I have no doubt that this man could kick my ass if he needed to.

He's introduced as the captain, which means Bragga isn't in charge of the ship, only the illya. That must get confusing. He waves me over to a console with a star chart on it. Their bridge is the largest I've ever seen—two floors, with lifts on both sides leading to a lower deck. I hear a low murmur of voices speaking below us but can't actually see anyone. The deck we're on almost looks like it's floating above the other. In front of us are the planet and expanse of stars beyond. We're currently orbiting the dark side, so no details of the planet are visible. It almost looks like a black hole where stars should be.

Kalve directs my attention to the map, zooming in on our location. "After accounting for your escape pod's thrust potential, we mapped the farthest in the system it could have traveled and searched in all directions by sending out short-distance probes. We've encountered nothing."

I feel like I've jumped into a tub of ice water. "What does that mean? You're giving up?"

"We also searched for debris and found nothing. They couldn't have gone farther than our search pattern on their own without being picked up."

The tub of ice water thaws. "So there's hope?" I try not to sound so goddamned relieved, but I can't help it.

"The only other ship in the area is your own, the main ship you mentioned before. I forget the name you said. It's possible they rescued them."

There's no way the *Posterus* picked them up. Their engine is down. Or it would be if they still had one. They're months away from being mobile. But it's possible the *Brimley* picked them up. The other Union-fleet ship headed out in the opposite direction of us. I'm skeptical, but anything to get us away from this hellish planet.

"Okay. When do we leave?"

"We will be under way within the hour."

"Good." I turn back to the giant display in front. The alien sun is cresting the edge of the planet, bathing it in light and creating a cascading haze of purple along the thermosphere. It would be beautiful if I didn't know what was lurking below.

CHAPTER EIGHT

Jordan

"I can't swim," I say. Tup has brought me to the edge of a large pool. The water stretches out a good twenty meters below us. From this height, objects beneath the surface shimmer, distorted by the waves generated from some unseen force on our end. The other end splashes up onto a platform almost two hundred meters away.

Tup's smile grows bigger, showing off his giant teeth. "Good." He slaps me on the back. "When you make it to the other side, your feat will be all the more impressive."

I look at him like he's crazy. "And if I don't make it?"

"Then you will have an incomplete. Obviously."

I frown. They're just going to let me die? Tup's not looking at me like I'm about to die. He's got that shit-eating grin on his face I associate with Sarka. "I can't breathe underwater," I say to make it clear that's what I mean by fail.

"You'll do fine." He slaps me on the back and pushes me over the edge.

I don't even have time to gulp in a lung full of air before I smash into the water. And I mean smash. All the wind whooshes out of me like I've hit a hard surface. Isn't water supposed to be yielding? I get a brief view of Tup bent over his knees laughing before I sink.

In an instant my lungs are on fire. I want to breathe out so bad I almost convince myself it wouldn't be a huge mistake. I may not have been in this situation before, but I know breathing out would increase the pressure on my lungs. Everyone in Union fleet goes through decompression training.

That need to release your breath isn't actually lack of oxygen. It's carbon monoxide buildup, which can be as dangerous as running out of oxygen.

As I sink lower I try not to panic. Instead I assess my situation. The pool isn't empty. They've designed it to look like the bottom of an ocean or a lake. Dark-green plants flowing from the bottom are scattered throughout. They undulate with the current, making it hard to see.

It reminds me a little of the pond Ash and I found on the planet, the only time I've ever been submerged in water. Growing up on Delta I didn't have an opportunity to swim. There aren't any pools, for it's a waste of water resources that are better used for crops and livestock. They come first.

Ash, having grown up on Alpha, could swim. She seemed embarrassed about the admission, so we didn't get into how she learned. But one thing she said stuck with me. She said everyone can float, that it doesn't take any skill. My arms flail at my side. Everything feels heavy and dull. It's getting darker as I sink lower.

I point myself toward the surface and kick as hard as I can. I make a little headway, but each time I do, I sink below again. I let a little air escape from my mouth and regret it immediately. It only makes the pressure worse on my lungs. I kick again, but I'm falling too fast, faster than I can kick. I search for anything I can use to haul myself up, but all I see are the plants, which would sink with my weight.

How far will they take this? Will they actually let me die? I can't see Tup anymore. In fact, I'm so deep now I can hardly see anything but a deep gray that's closing in on me. And what if I do fail this test but survive? Will they put me in the fields? I need to stick with Sarka, even if I don't want to. All these thoughts flutter through my head in a blur. I'm starting to lose focus.

Fuck, I don't want to die.

Ash will blame herself, which is stupid, because it's me who couldn't muster enough energy to kick back up to the surface. I'm not sure if it's the idea of failing or not seeing Ash again that does it, but I manage a strong kick, and then another, and another until the water begins to brighten around me. I'm getting closer. One more kick and my head breaks free and I gulp in a lung full of air before sinking again.

I kick again and use my arms, but that only splashes water into my face. I need to get onto my back, which is easier said than done. It would help if I weren't flailing about. I kick my legs and pinwheel my arms until I'm almost flat on the surface. It takes a couple of tries, but soon I find a system that works. It helps if I hold my breath, filling my lungs with air.

Now that I'm floating I take a few moments to reassess and figure out what to do next. I have to make it to the other end of the pool over two-hundred meters away. Can I even propel myself without sinking? The edge of the pool is only a few feet from me. Maybe I can use the walls to push myself along.

Even maneuvering toward the wall is difficult. After some trial and error and a few mouthfuls of water, I find I can use one hand to paddle one way and the other to paddle another. I make some headway. By the time I make it to the wall, I'm exhausted. My whole body aches. Before this whole ordeal I would've said I was in good shape, but now I'm not so sure.

As soon as my hand touches the wall, my whole body bucks as if it compresses in on itself. The shock of what happens makes me lose my concentration, and I sink, gulping water as I go under again. I thrash to the surface, sputtering. If I'd known I would need this skill, I would've gotten Ash to teach me some basics. But who would've thought I'd need to know how to swim in space? This whole exercise is cruel. I'm certain that's the point, but it doesn't make me feel any better or get me closer to the other end.

Obviously the exercise tests your endurance as well as your ability to maintain a calm head in an emergency. Are the exercises tailored to each person? And if they are, how did they know I couldn't swim? Those scans must have been more than just medical. Perhaps they can probe your mind. That's a scary thought.

Luckily the current is moving me toward the end. It's excruciatingly slow, but it gives me time to think. I can't wait for it to push me all the way. I'll die from hypothermia before that happens. I hadn't noticed when I first entered, but the water's freezing. The suit does a good job of keeping my body insulated; however, my hands are starting to cramp.

I stare at the high vaulted ceiling above me, unable to do much but float. I can't use the walls because they've added some sort of current. I doubt it's that, or the whole pool would be electrified. Nothing floating in the water to use to propel myself forward.

I'm not sure how long I drift, probably a long time, because my fingers are not only numb, but they've wrinkled up. I'm halfway when a small wave crests my body and slaps me in the face. Another one. Soon I'm surging and plunging, and the movement topples my fine balance. The water closes over my head once more. My legs ache as I thrash, kicking toward the surface. It's no use. The waves are too high now. Even if I could catch the surface, I'd never be able to stabilize myself. I have to find another way. They wouldn't just chuck someone who couldn't swim into deep water without a way to get out. Or would they? I don't know these people. Maybe this is how they get rid of people, a little entertainment beforehand.

As I sink, the pressure on my lungs becomes unbearable. I force myself to calm down, to focus on my surroundings. That's when I notice the tiny bubbles rising to the surface. They're coming from a pipe running the length of the pool.

If I can sink to the bottom and maneuver my way toward the pipe, maybe I can use the oxygen to breathe and the pipe to pull myself toward the edge.

Of course I have no idea if they're oxygen bubbles. Why would they even have a pipe carrying oxygen along the bottom of the pool? Why the hell would they have a pool on a goddamned spaceship?

I let out the air in my lungs slowly, which helps me sink lower. Funny how instinct takes over. I've never been in a situation like this, but it's like my body knows what to do.

When I reach the bottom, I lightly tap my foot to the floor to make sure it's not charged like the sides. Nothing happens, and I take that as a good sign. I propel myself along the bottom until I can hook my foot under the pipe and pull myself down to grab ahold of it. I wrap both hands around and take a moment to figure out how best to breathe in the air coming out. My lungs are screaming.

It's dark this deep. The pressure in my head is making it hard to concentrate, and my eyes have started to burn. I pull myself toward the pipe and wrap my lips around one of the openings. I try to suck in but end up inhaling water as well. A deep panic clamps me as I try not to choke when the air left in my lungs explodes out of my mouth. I wrap my lips around the opening again and this time just let the air flow into my mouth. It tastes foul. I don't care. I stay here like this, ten or so meters below the surface, hands wrapped around the pipe, lips kissing the cold surface, breathing. The oxygen takes some of the panic away. My mind calms, and I begin to focus again on the main problem— getting to the other end. It's hard to see from this angle, but as far as I can tell, it'll take me to where I need to go.

After a few more gulps of air I begin hauling myself forward one hand over the other. Every few feet I stop and draw air into my lungs from the opening in the pipe. I don't worry if the pipe will end or the holes will disappear. I just put one hand in front of the other.

I begin to relax into the motions. This is going well. I can even see a slight incline toward the edge of the pool as it raises onto a fake beach at the other end. The water is clearing up as well, and I can see more of my surroundings. The plants have even thinned out.

Then something swishes by on my right. I'm not sure at first if I've even seen it. At this depth the waves aren't as fierce, but perhaps that isn't the case as I get closer to shore. I keep my pace. The quicker I can pull myself along, the sooner I'll be out of this hellish ordeal. After a few more minutes I begin to think I imagined the flip of a tail in the dark.

As I make it closer to shore, the holes get farther apart. I quicken my pace to make up for less air. And then I see it again. This thing is real. Its skin is a deep blue, which helps it blend into its surroundings, with a long tail and arms with claws the size of my fingers. Its head is all jaws and two big eyes boring down on me. At first it appears to hover a few meters away. Then in an instant it flicks its tail and charges. Its mouth opens, and I see rows and rows of sharp pointy teeth aiming for my head. I scream, and all the air escapes my lungs as I fling myself out of the way. A sharp claw drags along my thigh as it passes. The adrenaline in my system jacks up a notch. I grab the pipe and haul myself toward the next air hole. I can't look back, not until I get air. And that's when I notice the lack of air holes. The pipe ends a meter in front of me. I swivel, searching the dark water behind me for any sign of the creature. But it's still and murky.

Now I have to decide if I backtrack to one of the holes or try to push to the surface and let the waves carry me the rest of the way. The dark plants sway in the current, hiding God knows what. No. I'd rather risk the surface. I crouch and push from the bottom, propelling myself up. It's not as deep here. I break through the surface as something latches onto my leg and pulls me under.

I flail, grabbing for something to keep me from going back under, even though I know nothing's in reach. Its hand clamps my calf, its claws digging in. I reach forward and swat at its arm, but there's too much resistance underwater.

We're traveling the far end of the pool now, water rushes over me, and I have to close my eyes for a second to still the vertigo, the panic. I treasure the lungful of air I managed to grab before it pulled me under. I can't panic now.

We circle back to the shallow end. I need to get free before I run out of air and we loop around again. Why the hell doesn't this fancy fucking suit they've given me have a weapon built into it? But I guess that's the point. Instead I opt for brute force, which is more like blind panic. I start kicking with my free leg. It doesn't matter, whatever I can hit. I hit its arm a few times, but that doesn't do anything. It takes a swipe at me. Finally I connect with its face. Bubbles rise from its mouth.

It didn't like that. I kick again. This time it lets go to readjust its hold on me, and I kick with both legs. The momentum propels me back, and I hit something hard. The beach. I claw my way out of the water as fast as I can and flop onto the makeshift shore. My chest heaves, sucking in air in great big gulps. The sand digs into my cheek, gritty and wet. There's nothing beyond the sand except a stark-white wall and the faint outline of a door. Something splashes behind me, but I don't turn. I can't face that thing again, not even from the safety of dry land.

My eyes close. Can I fall asleep here on this strange fake beach? But I don't get a chance to find out. Before my heartbeat evens out, the door snicks open and Tup marches out carrying a pack and a blade the size of my leg.

"That was brilliant." He hauls me to my feet, fits the pack over my shoulders, and hands me the blade. "I told you you'd do fine."

The blade's solid weight smashes into the sand. I can't even lift it, so how the hell am I supposed to carry it?

"It's best if you can get the dull bit over your shoulder. And better to use two hands when wielding it."

Who the fuck am I going to be wielding it against? My face asks the question before my mouth can, and his eyes light up.

"You're not done yet. You have several more exercises to get through."

Several more?

Christ.

CHAPTER NINE

Ash

My eyes snap open. It's dark, and I don't recognize where I am at first. Then the noise settles into a familiar pattern—well, familiar enough— and I remember I'm on the *Kudo*.

I'm not sure what's woken me, so I lie still until my eyes adjust to the room. The cabins on this ship are massive compared to ours. Everything on this ship is massive, even compared to the *Posterus*, which is huge. Nothing moves or breathes. It must have been a bad dream. And then I notice a faint blue light behind my head. It dims until it goes out. I press the panel next to my bed and raise the lights. Nothing on the headboard jumps out as strange. I run my hands along the panel but don't feel any seams.

"Huh." Nothing else in the room is out of the ordinary. The quiet hum of the engines filters through the walls and floor. It must feel off because we're not used to it. I'm not afraid to say this place gives me the creeps. It's not only the sound of the engines or the people who stop to watch us when we pass by; it's everything. The food tastes good. To me that's the most bizarre. For as long as I've served on Union-fleet ships, the food has never tasted good. You can't spruce up canned goods, no matter how hard you try. Everything on the *Persephone* needs to last months, sometimes years. The *Posterus* is a different story. The ship has greenhouses and living walls, but that wasn't always the case. When you set out on a mission you might not be coming back for half a year. There's nowhere to stock up, so you have to pack an entire mission's worth of food in one go. Here they have meat. Real meat.

It's not like growing up we had a lot of opportunity to eat meat, even on Alpha. Everyone thinks we have everything because we're the seat of the government. And it's true that some indulge, but my father always believed we should be an example to the other families, so we ate meat only at Christmas. He raised me to believe that meat is a privilege. Eating it at breakfast everyday feels wrong.

Today when I see Hartley I'll ask how much longer until the *Persephone* is ready. I don't want to stay on this ship any longer than we have to. But after meeting up with him, my heart sinks. We have more problems than we thought. Fitted out in our suits we trudge through the *Persephone's* decks logging all the issues we still have to fix before we can even bring the new main computer online.

"The problem is the power conversion." Hartley's voice is tinny through the suit intercoms. We're kneeling in front of the bridge's navigation console. It's a mess of polymer wires as Hartley pokes through the back, showing me where the console gets its power. "See these circuits? We need to replace them to take the type of power we'll be feeding it."

"And how many of these circuits do we have to replace?"

Hartley sits back. It's awkward in his helmet. He grabs the edge of the console to stop from toppling. "Geez, thousands."

"Jesus Christ, Hartley. Why can't we just change the power coming out of the new computer?"

He shakes his head, and the helmet bumps against the side. "I don't know their technology well enough to adapt the computer to fit our systems. It has to be the other way around."

"Even if we pull every single crew member into the task, that'll take weeks, months even."

"We don't have to do every system. Just the essentials to get us up and running. I figure it'll take us a week."

I stand and smack my hand hard into the console; the dull thud from my suit glove doesn't provide much satisfaction. Hartley stands as well, his expression grim. The light coming through the front glass is dull and gray, casting the bridge in a somber mood.

"Do we have other options?"

Hartley chews his lower lip and gazes out the front. His brain must be going a mile a minute. And then the strangest thing happens. He comes back with a one-word answer. "No."

I'm still thinking about that "no" hours later. Usually he has a suggestion, any suggestion, even if it's bat-shit crazy. I don't know if I'm overreacting. Should I worry?

Vonn finds me later, working on the bridge by myself. The sooner we get started on the power conversion, the better. His beak is even more pronounced with the glass from his helmet magnifying its round shape. He fiddles with his translation unit attached to his suit. They've fitted us all with the same unit to make it easier to communicate with each other.

According to him, my senior staff has been invited to dinner tonight. My senior staff. I still don't think of it as mine, nor is the *Persephone* mine. I'm a placeholder until Jordan gets back. I'd rather eat one of these power converters than go to a formal dinner, but since we're guests I can't very well say no. I accept as graciously as I can and return to my task.

Vonn hovers a few inches behind me. He reminds me of one of my father's aides growing up. Kurt was this meek little man who always gave the impression he was wringing his hands. Delivering bad news was cause for a panic attack. Kurt would hover behind my father and tap on his sleeve to get his attention. My father hated Kurt. He hates any sign of weakness.

I turn back to Vonn. "Was there something else?"

He doesn't wring his hands, but he does wipe them down the front of his environmental suit, even though there couldn't possibly be anything to wipe off. "It's just that…well, all this time spent breathing air from your tank. Is that healthy?" He peers around at the disarray on the bridge. Most of the consoles are in shambles, ready for their new power converters. "You've been at this for hours."

I shrug and return to my work. "Nothing's wrong with the air I'm breathing." Would they rather we sit on our assess all day? "This work needs to get done. It's going to take longer than we have." He still doesn't leave. "Would you like to help? It would go a lot faster."

He shakes his head and leaves after wishing me their version of good luck. "May your hopes be easy." What an odd little man.

It's three in the morning *Persephone* time. I've tried to keep the crew to our regular schedule, even if it doesn't line up with the illya's. And here I am again working by myself on some project that should have a whole team attending to it. A small part of me is keeping an eye on the door. I'm not worried about the air being vented; there isn't any to vent. Vasa is under guard on the *Kudo*. So why am I on edge?

The night has always been my best time to think. I like to hole up with a project that doesn't require my whole brain and sort through what's going on. The doctor would say it's unhealthy to isolate myself. It may be, but this is what works for me.

I hear a scrape behind me and almost jump out of my enviro suit. I leap to my feet and turn, clutching my chest. Yakovich is standing near the navigation console with one of the old power modules in her hand.

"Sorry. Didn't mean to scare you."

"What are you doing up at this hour?" I check the time in case I've misplaced a few hours.

"I got off watch and wanted to talk to you about Vasa. He doesn't look so good. We should let the doctor check him out."

"What's wrong with him?"

"He's sweating a lot and complaining of pains in his arms and legs."

I nod. It never occurred to me that the illya might carry diseases that our immune systems can't handle. It would make sense. It's a good idea to have the doctor take a look. I'll ask him to keep an eye on the rest of the crew as well. "Have the doctor check him out. Stay with him when he does. It could be some stupid escape plan."

"Where's he going to go?" She flings her arms out, displaying his lack of options.

"It's a precaution. Desperate people do stupid things." My mind immediately goes to Sarka and the look on Jordan's face as he pulled her out of engineering.

Before Yakovich leaves I call her back. "One more thing. They've invited us to a formal dinner this evening."

Yakovich's eyebrows shoot up her forehead. "And you're telling me because...?"

"It's for senior staff, and as head of security you're required to attend."

Yakovich's jaw drops. "Please, Lieutenant, don't make me go."

"If I have to, so do you. No one gets out of it. I don't want to risk insulting anyone." I hate formal affairs as much as the next person.

The last one I had to attend was to welcome Hartley and me aboard the *Persephone*. That was only two months ago, but it seems like forever.

Yakovich huffs but doesn't protest any further. "What do I wear? Normal uniform?"

I have a flash of what Jordan was wearing that night. It was conservative but still sexy. I, on the other hand, had opted for something a little more revealing. "Dress uniform is probably the safest." Who knows what might offend the illya?

When I was younger—especially after my mom died—my dad used to cart me to all the formal functions he had to attend. With a seat on the Commons it was a pretty regular occurrence. I hated it. He didn't force me to dress up or make small talk with stupid people who couldn't give a shit about what I had to say. Instead, he showed me off, like I was some sort of prize. "This is my daughter, Alison. She's in A levels at the academy." I'd get a limp handshake while they continued to look at my father. "Top of her class," he'd say, and they'd congratulate him as if he were taking my classes. The more revealing my dress, the less they heard. I figured the less I looked like a top student, the less he'd want to take me to these events. But my rebellion just pushed his buttons. The more we fought, the more I hated going. By the time I graduated the academy, I was spending most of the events holed up in the restroom.

I still hate attending these things. No one's here to show me off, but I still feel like I'm on display, which makes everything awkward.

I arrive first and congratulate myself on my diplomacy.

Hartley enters the giant dining hall and smacks into one of the waiters carrying a tray of food. The commotion is enough to turn everyone's head, and I un-congratulate myself. I pick Hartley off the ground, direct him to a table with napkins, and help him scrub off whatever is all over the front of his suit. It's brown and sticky, like syrup, and smells foul. My stomach tries to make a run for it.

Yakovich arrives next. Her dress uniform is like a second skin, taut where her muscles bulge. She spots Hartley and me and makes her way over.

"What happened?"

Hartley balls up his napkin, now covered in sticky residue, and shoves it behind a centerpiece. "One of the waiters attacked me."

Yakovich raises one thin brow. "Yeah?" She surveys the room. "Which one? I'll follow him into the kitchen and take him out when everyone's distracted."

"I'm kidding. Calm down." Hartley scrubs his beard with his fingertips. "Did you get my note about your help with power conversion?"

She nods. "I'm not on watch again until eight hundred hours. I can help any time before or after my rotation."

"Great." Hartley's about to give her a playful punch in the arm but shifts and reaches for his beard again.

Out of everyone in the crew, Yakovich and I are the most similar when it comes to work. If it gets results, she'll go as far as it takes. If that means overworking herself or pushing through an injury, then that's fine with her. I respect that. But that limp she walked in with has me worried. I'll ask the doctor when he gets here. I want to make sure it's healing. I'd ask her, but she'll tell me it's okay.

Five of us attend the dinner: me, Yakovich, Hartley, Dr. Prashad, and Julianna Olczyk, our helms officer. There should be seven senior staff, but the captain relieved Vasa of duty, and she of course is missing. Not for the first or last time do I wish she were here. Jordan can make everyone feel at ease in stressful situations, especially me. She has this calming effect.

Our little group is overwhelmed by the number of illya. I count at least twenty-five of them scattered around the table. They've interspersed our crew at the table so we're not all bunched together. I know why they did that, but I wish we weren't separated. I'm also sure they thought we'd have more senior officers.

Bragga is at the head of the table, no longer in uniform. Instead he's wearing a long white cloak that resembles wings in some strange way. It reminds me of the avians, and I wonder if it would be polite to ask if they're related in some way. On his right is Vonn. On the other side is Captain Kalve and then a bunch of nameless faces. They introduced everyone earlier, but the unfamiliar names and the similarity in faces makes it difficult to tell who is who.

Hartley's curiosity overrides any nervousness because, as soon as we're seated, he asks, "So how far is your home planet from here?"

Vonn closes his eyes in obvious horror, and now I wish I'd had a briefing with everyone first to go over appropriate dinner conversation. Jordan would have.

Bragga smiles indulgently—at least I think that's what that smile means. "We no longer have a home world." He spreads his hands, indicating the table and the ship beyond. "This is all that is left of our once-abundant species."

CHAPTER TEN

Jordan

"So Sarka's your father?" Tup wraps his meaty hands around his knife and hacks at something dark green on his plate. It looks like a roll of protein ground up and pressed into a log.

I hesitate. I'm uncomfortable admitting our relationship. I've hidden the fact that the leader of the Burrs is my father for so long, it comes as second nature. We're sitting at an empty table in the mess. Most of the tables are empty at this hour. It's well past dinner. My training took most of the day, and even though I'm starving, I don't have the energy to raise food to my mouth.

"Yeah, why?" I ask.

He shrugs giant shoulders. "Curious, I guess. I didn't know my father. He died before I was born, or when I was young. My mom was kind of vague about that point. It hurt her to talk about it."

"He die in the war?"

Tup nods. "Almost everyone does."

Why is conflict universal? What about intelligence also breeds contradiction? Or do our intelligence and individuality give way to friction?

The last wars on Earth were long over before I was born, but my father fought in them. They were brutal. Billions died. They put all that effort into weapons, but imagine what they could've done to save our planet instead. Those last wars were pointless. Instead of working against each other, we should have combined our efforts to find a way to save the planet. Or at least keep it habitable. In the end, everything they did was too late. Only after we'd lost our only home did we see the pointlessness of war. I wonder if the umquashi and breens will ever get there. Will they find a way to end this war peacefully or will they destroy each other before that happens? Tup doesn't look all that sad about it, though.

"I'm sorry to hear that."

"Nah, don't be." He speaks around the food in his mouth. "They're in the skylife now."

"Skylife?"

A loud thwap interrupts us. Sarka drops his tray on the table and collapses next to me. He looks as beat as I feel. "That was bullshit." He doesn't even bother with utensils. He uses his fingers to shovel the food straight into his mouth. "I'm so fucking hungry I could eat a goddamned cow."

There's another scrape, much quieter than Sarka's, and one more tray joins our table. The man who sits is well built like Tup, although not as stocky. He's all muscle. His skin is a light green, and he has a shock of bright-red hair that starts from his forehead, swoops over his head, and ends somewhere down his back. He looks kind of like a naked mole rat with a mohawk.

Tup points to the man. "This is Frage." I recognize him as umquashi, the species in charge of the *Avokaado*.

We've been on board for only a day, but already I've seen more strange species than I could ever imagine. While walking back from the training center with Tup, I saw about a dozen different aliens. It's strange to think of them as aliens, but using our human definition, that's what they are. Of course, they probably think we're the aliens.

When we stopped at one deck, the doors opened, and I thought no one had boarded the lift. But when I looked down I realized four worm beings had slithered on. Each of them had one large eye in the middle of their head but arms and hands that protruded from their middle abdomen. One was carrying a tablet of some sort and the other an engine part.

When they left I asked Tup about them, and he said they were ulods. Basically they're the grunts of the ship because they refuse to fight.

"And you're okay with that?" I thought everyone had to fight.

Tup laughed a great big belly laugh that echoed beyond the lift. "They have a point. They're so small they get stomped underfoot before they make it to the front line. They help in their own way because they can reach places most of us can't."

I'm sure this ship has even stranger things I haven't seen yet. Tup says that over a hundred species are on board, all of them working toward stopping the illya. What a pointless existence.

Sarka burps and licks his fingers. He's very much in his element right now. I'm surprised he's agreed to try to escape. Where does he expect we're going to go but back to the *Persephone*, where I'll arrest him. I would think he'd want to stay here and war. Of course, maybe after a hundred years of being at war, he's tired of it, especially since this isn't his fight. Or he doesn't like the idea of being forced to do something. He's been in charge of himself for well over a hundred years now.

I can't fathom that time span. When I was a kid I asked him one day how old he was. At eight even twenty seems old, but he told me he was a hundred and thirty-three. I thought he was lying, but then he showed me a card with a picture of him on it, and it listed his birthday. It looked official, so that was good enough for my eight-year-old self. He's had more change in his life than anyone. Does he ever get tired of just living?

I shake off the morose thoughts and return to what we were talking about. "So you were saying about the skylife?" I ask. I still haven't touched my food. My arms are resting on the table, the same position they've been in since we sat down.

"Everyone leads three lives: the waterlife, the walkinglife, and the skylife. Everyone starts out as waterlife. You," he points to me and Sarka, "me, and him." He points to Frage. "Waterlife is when you're Masha, when you're first introduced to the world. You begin as microbes, bacteria, single-celled organisms. It's simple. Lets you enter the world in a calming manner. The current of water becomes the current of life. After that comes the walkinglife. This takes many lifetimes as you work your way up to the higher intelligent beings. All of us," his hand circles the table, the ship, "we're all in the last stage of our walkinglife. But this life is weak. You are weak. You are learning what it is to be of the body. After this is skylife, which is the ultimate, the reason for life. When we die here, our journey finally begins, and we become nothing and everything all at once. We are bound by nothing—space, dimensions, time. We know all and see all. And this is why you must go through the waterlife and walkinglife before you reach this state. You take the wisdom of everything you know and use it for good."

Sarka and I exchange a look. I've never been religious myself, but this smacks too much of wishful thinking. How many fables and myths have we told over Earth's history of what happens when you die? It's always sounded like people unable to face the truth. You die and that's all. Does Sarka worry about what happens after he dies? He will die eventually. Even with all the work that Ethan Burr did on those soldiers, they could die and did. The biological pieces will run out long before any of the mechanical ones, but what happens when he runs out?

I don't want to insult Tup, so I nod.

"I'm excited to meet my father for the first time. When I begin my skylife, everyone who has come before will greet me, including my mother." Tup waves me off before I can offer my sympathies. "She lived a long life for a Varbaja. She didn't get to die in battle, but that honor isn't bestowed on everyone."

"How did she die?" Sarka sucks at his fingers. I kick him under the table, but no one else seems to think the question is rude.

"An accident on one of our incubator ships."

"Incubator ships?" I ask.

"We have several ships, much smaller than this, that can connect to ours but detach if needed. I was twelve at the time. Breen—my species—can enter battle and become a man at the age of fourteen. My mother was visiting our ship when a hull breach occurred and sucked her out into space." He puts down the meat he's eating and wipes his fingers on his pants. "I'm glad it was fast."

The way he talks, death must be very common out here. Parts of the Belt are probably like this, such as Eps, where they do most of the mining.

Frage grunts. "If you can't die in battle, it's best to die fast."

The mood at the table dips low as everyone contemplates that last sentence. I'd rather not die at all, but I don't think that's a popular opinion here, so I change the subject to something less dour.

"Do you get back to your planets often?" This whole idea of inhabited worlds has me a little giddy, if that's the right word. We as humans don't even have one planet to call home anymore, and these people can just flit from one to the next. I can't understand why they would want to spend all their time up here stuck in space.

Tup shakes his head. "I've never been to my home world. I grew up here. The illya drove us from there a long time ago."

So much for a lighter topic.

Frage puts down his utensils and stares long and hard at me. "This is why we fight." He thumbs at Tup. "He doesn't know any different, so he's happy to fight. Most breen are. None of us has a choice. A planet is a target, a place where the illya know to find us to poach our species. When they come, there are no negotiations. They rip you from your home, the younger the better." He looks down at his plate, and I think he's done until he looks back up at me with eyes so sad I lean back. "I was only five when we finally abandoned the umquashi home world. They came in the night, hundreds of ships full of troops numbering in the hundreds of thousands.

"The city where I lived was on the water, a lake so big you couldn't see the other side and so clear you could see all the way to the bottom, even at its deepest. The noise their ships make over water is deafening, so we had a little warning."

Everyone at our end of the mess stops eating to listen to Frage's story. Some I can see have heard it before, yet for others like me and Sarka, this is all new.

"They'd invaded different cities before, so we were prepared. As kids we grew up learning emergency procedures. But not everyone was lucky enough to see them coming. Their ships could evade our defense systems. The only way to detect them was to see their ships or to hear them.

"I remember waking to a roar that filled my head even when I clamped my hands to my ears. At first I couldn't believe they were here. I'd had fantasies about it. I would lead my family to safety and stop the illya once and for all. But the reality of it..." He looks over at Tup and shrugs. "I wet myself when I heard the ships coming over the water. I didn't even have to guess what the noise was. We all knew.

"My father rushed in and pulled me from my bed. He hid my mother and me and my three brothers in the attic, while he stayed in the house so he could try to fight them off, keep them from finding us." Farge's voice is low, almost a growl. "When my father fell, my oldest brother Tarro slipped out next, ready to defend our family. I watched as the illya raiders cut down one after another of my brothers. My mother tried to stop my brother Hurd, who was only two years older than me, but he slipped out of her grasp and made it out of the attic before she could stop him. His death was the hardest. I couldn't look, but we heard him cry out almost immediately.

"When my mother slipped out she made me promise to stay hidden no matter what happened. I was supposed to stay until everyone was gone and not move until morning. I watched through the slats in the vents as she too was killed and carted away. By that time I was numb. You see, they don't need you alive. They only need a small sample of your cells." He coughs and swallows hard. "So when you ask if we get to go home often, the answer is no. We won't have a home until every last illya is killed."

I clamp my lips tight. I have no words of comfort to offer, nor do I think they'd be welcome. But Sarka is oblivious to the man's pain.

"Why don't you go far away? To another system?"

Frage shakes his head. "They would find us." He picks up his fork and continues to eat. "Your home world is far, yes? Farther than any of us know, but here you are."

"We got here by accident," I say.

"You sure about that?"

CHAPTER ELEVEN

Ash

"What happened to your home world?" Hartley asks, oblivious to the looks Vonn is giving him.

Bragga again takes Hartley's curiosity in stride, but it's obvious the reactions around the table indicate this is a painful subject. "A plague. An organism infected our water, and we can never go back. Millions left our world. Thousands of ships carried our people to another planet to rebuild. But the umquashi forced us to leave. They used it as farmland, and we were unwelcome. A few months into our journey we realized that the plague on our planet had followed us. Soon we numbered a few thousand. We have managed to stop the plague, but it has left us depleted." His eyes fall to his empty plate, and we all sit in silence. I can sympathize with them. I never lived on Earth, but I'm what's left of the castoffs. It can't be easy not belonging anywhere.

"Why haven't you settled on the planet we were just at?" Hartley asks.

Kalve and Bragga exchanged worried looks. "We are afraid we would infect the planet. We still don't know very much about it."

Our crew subtly stops eating and regards each other. A plague? And they have no idea how it's transmitted?

Bragga waves away our concern. "Eat. Eat. We can't spread it to you through the food you share with us. It doesn't transmit in this manner. You are safe on the ship. I promise you. We wouldn't have offered to help you if we thought we would harm you in some way."

The doctor leans forward in his seat. "Do you know how it's

transmitted? Does it pass on…" He pauses to look for the right word. "To your children?"

Bragga pauses. "It's in our DNA. We can procreate only with medical intervention, but even then, it pervades our offspring."

"And that's its only effect? Sterility?"

Bragga shows his teeth with a gracious smile. "I'm not sure of all the details. Perhaps if I put you in touch with some of our doctors, they will be able to answer all your questions."

"I'm sorry. I don't mean to pry. Pandemics fascinate me." The doctor smiles sympathetically. However, he's stopped eating.

"It's no bother. We encourage curiosity." As Bragga says this, Kalve and another crew member exchange looks. I suspect the opposite is true. We need to be careful where we stick our noses with these people.

A man farther down the table thumps his fist on the surface. This is their way of announcing they'd like to speak. He addresses Hartley. "I've heard that it'll take over a month to refit your ship to take the power from the new main computer. Can we be of assistance?"

I raise my hand to object. No way am I letting a group of illya roam the *Persephone*, even with an escort. "That's a very nice gesture, but we can manage on our own."

As I speak, Hartley pipes up. "What did you have in mind?"

"We could assign you some of our nanobots. They could get the job done in a fraction of the time, which would free up your crew to work on other repairs instead of spending all your time on such a tedious task." As it turns out, the man is the *Kudo*'s head of engineering, Gadzir. He's tall for an illya, with elegant gestures. He strikes me more as a diplomat than an engineer. But if I had any doubts, Hartley and Gadzir break into a discussion about robots that lasts almost the entire meal.

By the end I'm so bored and exhausted from being on for the whole night, I want to vanish as soon as it's polite.

As I'm heading toward the door, Hartley stops me. "What do you think, Ash?"

"About what?" If he's asking me what I thought about the dinner, the whole thing is a blur. I remember trying everything but couldn't tell you what anything tasted like.

"About the nanobots to help with the repairs?"

"I'm not sure. I don't like the idea of strange machines coming onto our ship and mucking about. We'd have no idea what they were doing."

"Okay. Why don't we have Gadzir give us a demonstration tomorrow, and you can make up your mind after you've gotten a little more information. He's offered to show us."

I nod and agree only to end the conversation. I'm itching to get out of there. I really need a run, but they don't have a track on board the *Kudo*, and I doubt donning an enviro-suit to use our track would be a hot idea.

The next morning I meet Hartley at the entrance to engineering. I've decided it's a good idea to keep an open mind about what they can do. After all, the sooner we can get off this ship, the better. He's already been here a few times. I think he demanded a tour as soon as we were brought on board. But it doesn't stop him from bouncing around in giddy anticipation. Sometimes Hartley reminds me of a puppy. Nothing ever fazes him; he's this ball of pure enthusiastic optimism.

When the doors part I can see why he's so excited. It's ginormous. Like their bridge, the room is multiple floors, I count at least five. Up the center is—according to Hartley—their dark-matter engine. He delves into an explanation that I immediately tune out. I step close to the edge of our deck and peer down. From my untrained eye it looks like a glass tube filled with liquid light. Some sort of substance inside flows in and around itself. It's all colors and no colors and glows a comforting hue that casts the length of engineering in sunshine.

Gadzir greets us. Coming around the circular deck bathed in the drive's light, he looks happier than any person I've ever seen, especially from this species. Happy people make me nervous.

"Welcome," he shouts. "Come. I have lots to show you." He leads us down a side corridor and into another room off main engineering. The ceiling isn't very high, but the length is impressive. Down one side is a bank of computers. Inside you can see energy zipping through circuits. "Captain, take a look at this."

I think for a moment I misheard him, but when he says it again, I stop him. "I'm not the captain."

"You're in charge of your ship, yes?"

"Temporarily. Until we find our captain."

I look over at Hartley, whose eyes won't meet mine. He doesn't think we'll find her. I don't know why or how, but that one gesture destroys my confidence. I've never actually allowed myself to think we won't find her.

"What happened to your captain?"

I turn away as Hartley explains the situation and walk to one of the computer banks. Up close they don't look like computers at all. Inside, the circuits look organic, not mechanical. It's as if millions of tiny machines are zipping along roadways of their own making, the more used the brighter the line. I see a number of different colors, but the blue stands out the sharpest.

"These are our nanobots," Gadzir says.

I nearly jump out of my skin, so absorbed I hadn't noticed his approach. "Those are robots?"

He places his palm on the glass covering. He has long, elegant fingers that taper to sharp points. "Microscopic robots. The cover acts as a magnifying glass. They're actually much smaller than this."

Humans once experimented with nanotechnology. Back in the mid twenty-first century we created nanomachinery to devour plastic. But before the project was even off the ground, things started going wrong. They began eating more than the plastic. At first it was other materials in their habitats, then it was their enclosures, and soon they were eating anything they came in contact with—even each other. If they hadn't become cannibalistic, Earth would have faced a very different end.

"How do you keep them from evolving and taking over?" asks Hartley.

"That's a good question." Gadzir's face brightens, and he beckons us to another station halfway down the long hallway. "Early experiments showed that if made to reproduce themselves, they would evolve too quickly for us to maintain control." He brings up a map system on the console in front of him. It's laid out like a bees' hive, millions of brightly colored tunnels running in every direction. "So we engineered them to be like olmigas—tiny insects on our home world that organize themselves into a hive society. They have a queen who is the only female, and all reproduction is done through her. So that's what we did." Gadzir zooms in on the map to one section at the far end. "We created a queen that all reproduction and instructions go through. This way, we only have to control one nanobot, not billions."

Hartley bends down to examine the microscopic queen. Even though she's twice the size of the other nanobots, she's still so small, a comparison is unfathomable. The only way to make the comparison is to reverse it. I once had an instructor at the academy use this example: let's say if a nanoparticle is the size of a pineapple, then a virus would be the size of a chicken, and a human would be the size of planet Earth.

So imagine how impossible it would be to stop something that small from destroying the planet if it ever had a mind to. With the prevalence of AI at the time, nanotechnology was soon outlawed.

Hartley almost has his nose pressed up to the map watching as the hive goes about its day. "Are they self-aware?"

Gadzir shakes his head. "We feed them simple yes/no instructions. They're not built to learn—only to take orders from the queen."

"Then how do you propose they'll help us build new power converters if they can't problem-solve?"

"We feed them the exact specifications."

Hartley and I exchange looks. "Not all our systems are identical. Some require more power, some less. If they have the same set of instructions, then some systems will overload."

"It's not a perfect system, that's true. We'll have to tweak the output manually." He taps on the glass in front of him, as if the nanobots are animals stuck in a cage. "Otherwise, they'd overtake us in a matter of days. We lost an entire ship that way. When we went to investigate, nothing was left. No trace. The nanobots had consumed every last particle of matter on the ship and dispersed into space. I still have nightmares that we'll run into a giant mass drifting through space."

"Like driver ants," Hartley says. The look of horror on his face stops me from asking, but Gadzir doesn't hesitate.

"Driver ants?"

"On Earth—our home world—we had creatures called ants—very tiny insects that could combine themselves into structures. They could create towers and bridges to reach prey. Driver ants are carnivorous and can devour human flesh in a matter of hours. They were one of the deadliest species on our planet." Hartley holds his thumb and index finger a little less than a centimeter apart. "Tiny but deadly."

"Jesus, Hartley." As if I don't have enough nightmares to contend with now, I'm going to be worrying about flesh-eating nanobots coming for us in our sleep.

He shrugs, sheepish. "Sorry, Ash. It's not like they even exist anymore. Nothing exists on Earth anymore."

"Would you like to see a demonstration?" Gadzir asks.

Hartley and I both nod. I might be reluctant to let this technology loose on the *Persephone*, but that doesn't mean I'm not interested in what it can do.

Gadzir leads us to a simulation room at the end of the hall, and as it turns out, what it can do is better than Hartley or I could ever have dreamed of. Less than a minute after Gadzir gives the nanobots instructions, they've not only fixed a power supply to take the new energy settings, but they've also built a new power module from scratch. It looks like the thing appeared from thin air as if by magic.

"How is that even possible?"

Gadzir grins. "The same way the biological reproduces. By dividing what already exists."

"Vague. But I doubt I'd understand an in-depth explanation."

In the end I decide to allow the nanobots onto the *Persephone*. We'll still have to do a lot of the work manually, but that means we'll be able to maintain some control of the situation, which eases my mind.

Two weeks later and we're days away from finishing the repairs, almost three weeks ahead of schedule. Hartley and I are in engineering going over the last-minute repairs before we can bring the new computer online. The main bench is scattered with bits and pieces of electronics. Hartley's somewhat of a tinkerer. He likes to take things apart and rebuild them bigger and meaner than before. Most of his projects have been pushed aside for the time being. It's hard to do much with the gloves of our suits.

I'll be glad when we can stop working in our enviro-suits. They're hot and suffocating, and unbearable.

I nudge Hartley for the second time during our discussion to get his attention. "What's up with you? You've been zoning out for the past ten minutes."

"Have you noticed Yakovich acting strangely lately?"

"No. Why?"

"I was supposed to have dinner with her last night."

We both widen our eyes at the same time, Hartley's to assure me it wasn't a date and mine because I definitely think it was supposed to be a date.

"And she didn't show?"

"She came very late, then was distracted the whole time. I'm not always the greatest interacting with other people. But I know when I'm being tuned out. If I've learned anything from years of dealing with people, it's how to tell they aren't paying attention to me anymore."

I feel like I should be patting him on the shoulder at this point, but that would be more awkward than it's worth. "We're all under tremendous stress. And Yakovich is spending a lot of her time guarding Vasa. I still have a rotation going, so she's probably exhausted. Don't worry. It'll be better when we get back on the *Persephone*. We'll be able to use the brig again and won't have to keep watch on his quarters."

Hartley shakes his head. "I don't think it's that. She mentioned something he'd said that sounded very strange."

"What did he say?"

"She wouldn't tell me."

I've been avoiding Vasa, but it may be time to pay him a visit, see if I can't get something out of him. I know both Yakovich and Jordan questioned him and came up empty. Maybe he'll feel guilty and tell me.

Hartley drifts off again. This time when I nudge him, he turns to me, white as a sheet, and faints.

CHAPTER TWELVE

Jordan

Sarka's fist comes toward my face. I duck at the last second, and he misses. "I've made a couple of contacts, and I know how to get us out of here." He pivots around me, looking for an opening.

"Shhh." I bounce back a few feet to get out of range. "Someone might hear you."

We're on a mat in one of the training rooms partnered to work on our hand-to-hand combat. It's clear that Sarka is levels above me. I'm bruised and sore, and he's going easy on me.

The next time Sarka gets close he says, "We need to start a revolt."

"What?" I say it a little too loud and lower my voice. "A revolt?"

"We'll discuss it at lunch, but think about it."

I don't have to think about anything. I don't want to help start a revolt. I only want to get the hell out of here. We've been stuck here for almost three weeks now. Our daily routine consists of preparing for battle, eating, and sleeping. That's all. The breen are the most gung-ho, war-hungry people I've ever met. They eat, sleep, and breathe battle. I made the mistake of asking one of our tablemates about his armor the other day at lunch. He gave me a demonstration of all the weapons you don't leave your bunk without.

Their uniforms include a jacket, but most of the breen don't wear it because it gets in the way of their weapons. No breen should leave their quarters without at least five weapons. They include two knives, one for throwing and the other for when the thrown knife doesn't come back.

"How do you get any of them to come back?" I asked.

"Usually the person you're throwing it at is coming for you. You just pull it out when they drop at your feet." Sarka is eating this all up. I even catch him checking out the pockets in his own uniform, assessing which weapons will fit best in each pocket. That's if we're ever given any. I hope not. The second Sarka gets a weapon, we're all in trouble.

Then you gotta carry two guns: one sonic blaster for wide range and the other a water vaporizer for maximum damage. Basically it's a dehydrator. Shooting it at an enemy will dry out all the liquid in their body. I'm told it's a painful way to die, almost as bad as space exposure.

The last weapon is for emergencies only. The man pulled out a thin tube, and inside was a long dart. He said it's more for using on yourself if you're caught. It holds the saliva of a Krab beast found on his home world. He pointed to Sarka and said that one drop can kill someone Sarka's size in under a minute.

Sarka huffed. "I doubt that. I'm immune to poisons."

"Not this one, mate. The only being immune is the Krab beast. And even then, some have died from licking their own wounds."

I find Sarka later sitting at our table. It's the farthest from most of the other soldiers and gives us the most privacy. More often than not, Tup will come sit with us, ending any discussion between us. For the past week Sarka has talked of nothing else. At first he wanted to steal an escape pod. But we'd be back where we started. His next plan wasn't any better. He wanted to hijack the ship. The two of us. Unarmed.

I set my tray down and dig in. I'm starving after today's training. While I wouldn't say I love the food, it's grown on me a bit. Sarka eats like someone's going to steal his.

"So you're not actually thinking of starting a revolt on here, are you?"

He takes a bite of some loaf that reminds me of soggy bread. "Not everyone's happy with this war." He leans in. "Do you know the last time they actually engaged the illya? A decade. That's right. Ten years." He swirls his fingers around the mess. "Every single soldier sitting in this room has never seen combat before. All they do is train for it. All day, every day, and have since they got on here. They want a change. And we can give them that change." His dark-blue eyes glow with a new challenge. I imagine he must miss being at the center of conflict.

He's spent the majority of his life in one form of war or another. It must become the norm for him.

When I was very young my mom told me that he was a product of his time. Born at the worst possible moment in history, caught between before and after, he would always live on the cusp. He can remember Earth, but it was a broken Earth. By the time he was born, oil had peaked and the new technologies were struggling to keep up. Two hundred kilometers on either side of the equator were uninhabitable. Citizens fled for cooler climates where food would actually grow. People died in the hundreds of thousands from drought, famine, disease. Mass extinctions happened monthly. Every day, every new catastrophe brought the planet closer to chaos.

Sarka was thirteen when the resource wars started. When he was sixteen he paid a man to hack into the national database to change his age to eighteen and enlisted. After the wars he had nowhere to belong. The military as he knew it had no use for him as a soldier, and the colonies were afraid of the Burrs, afraid the tech would malfunction. So they were left on Zeta, a remote asteroid, to fend for themselves. Is it surprising they rose up against this injustice?

My mom never said it excused his behavior, but it went a long way to understanding it. I don't think she condoned what they did, but she couldn't side with the Union on the matter either. The Burrs should've been reintegrated into the early colonies with programs. But everyone was struggling to build the first settlements and establish a rule of law. There was no room for them, so they were abandoned and forgotten until Sarka led a revolt to free them from Zeta. He united the Burrs in a common cause, the destruction of the Union. And now he's trying to do it again.

"And how does this help us escape?"

"One of the men I've been talking to said he'd take us back to the *Persephone*. For a price." He waves this detail off. "But nothing we couldn't afford."

"And you'd be willing to go back to the *Persephone*?"

"I'd be willing to swing by the *Persephone* and drop you off. My pilot and I would carry on."

"Ah, so this is really a way for you to escape. I'm lucky you'll let me tag along." Plus, he gets the bonus of leaving this place in chaos.

"I could very easily leave you here to deal with the crazies."
And he'd do it too. I grab my tray and stand to leave. "Go to hell."
"If you're out of the planning, you're out of the rescue effort."
"Fine by me. There's no way—" I smack my tray back down.
"You're reckless. You never think of anyone but yourself. Go ahead. It'll never work. You'll never get enough people to bring this place down, let alone escape from it."

"Ye of little faith." He grins and shoves a piece of meat into his mouth. To him this is a game. He doesn't give a shit if people die because of his actions.

I storm off like a five-year-old and jam my full tray in the composter. My stomach rumbles as the lid slams shut. That's the last food I'll see until tomorrow at the midmorning meal. Usually I wouldn't mind missing a meal, but here you need every bit of energy you can get.

There's still a few hours before lights out, so I wander the corridors. I don't know what it is about my father, but he can goad me like no one else. Maybe Ash. She gets under my skin, but in a different way.

I find a lift and exit on the walkway. The stars fill the glass expanse. I rest my forehead against the clear surface and stare out at the millions of stars on the horizon. I wish I could know for sure that I'd see her again, that this would all work out. It's the not knowing that's the worst. I keep replaying that moment on the *Persephone*. Why didn't she come for me? The Ash I know wouldn't let anything stop her. Forget safety or what's best, she would've done what she wanted. That's the irrational side talking, because I know she would've saved me if she could. I can only assume she's doing everything she can to find us. In the meantime, I need to find a way off this ship. Sarka's crazy if he thinks his big showy revolt will get results. But he has the right idea about finding someone to pilot us out of here. Maybe we can bribe one of the pilots? We don't need a revolt for that.

I stroll to the other side of the walkway. Halfway there I feel a buzzing throughout my body. By the time I get to the other side I'm ready to explode. I drop to my knees and grab my head. The pain is unbearable. Someone grabs my arm and drags me back down the hall. The farther we move from the door, the less my head hurts. By the time we reach the other side I can open my eyes.

The person dragging me is Veera, the woman from our briefing a few weeks ago. For someone who stands only thirty centimeters she's sure as hell strong. She bares her pointed teeth at me.

"Didn't they warn you?" She points to my arm. "That thing in your arm isn't only a tracker. It stops you from going into off-limits areas of the ship."

I rub the spot on my arm where there's still a crescent-moon scar. It's faint now, only a shy reminder of what lurks beneath the skin. I wonder if it will disappear altogether one day, in hopes that I'll forget it's there. It doesn't help to have your prisoners feel like prisoners. "No, they didn't." She steps to the side as I stand. But once I'm standing I realize it's harder to see her. She only reaches to my knees.

"Well, the training area is off-limits after hours. People used to go down there and try to rig the tests, thinking no one would notice. Now we just keep people out. Saves us all the headache."

I laugh. Not everyone.

She blinks up at me. Her face is all eyes, big black eyes. I'm reminded of the Cheshire Cat from *Alice in Wonderland*, minus the whiskers. "I remember you. You came in with that big gentleman, the one with the strange face."

"That's right. Do you guys get a lot of new recruits?"

"Used to. But not a lot to choose from these days. Those who know about us stay away, and everyone else has already been recruited to the cause."

"How long have you been here?"

Veera gestures toward the lift. I follow, slowing my pace to match hers. "Twenty years or so. I know what you're going to ask next. And the answer is no, I don't miss home. Don't miss my family. Don't have either, so this is both my home and family now." When we reach the lift, she does an impressive jump to reach the controls. The doors open, and I wait for her to enter so I don't accidentally step on her.

She watches me with shrewd eyes as the lift moves through the ship. She's pressed the deck that will take me back to my bunk.

"Can I give you some advice?" she asks. "Watch your step. You may not want to be here, but there are worse places to be in this galaxy. The Varbaja take care of their own. The second they think you're not one of them, they'll kill you."

"So fight and maybe die or don't and definitely die."

"The last combat mission we had was many years ago. Mostly we take care of each other."

Over the last few weeks I've seen how they take care of each other, and I'd rather be back on the *Persephone*. If there isn't a fight in the games room, then there's one in the mess. People who spend their whole lives beating the shit out of each other for practice know how to relate to each other only with violence after hours. This is not my idea of a family.

Veera places a hand on my calf. "It gets better. Trust me, but you don't want to get into trouble here."

The way she's going on I worry she might know something. Sarka's not exactly subtle, and I'll be condemned by association.

The doors to the lift open on my deck. Before I exit she says, "Is it worth it?"

I don't pretend to misunderstand her. In that one knowing look she's said everything. Is what I want to return to worth giving all this up, worth my life? I think of Ash. Her stubbornness, her laugh, that look she gets in her eyes when she's persuading me to do something I know is against my better judgment. I think of the *Persephone* and my crew and the thrill of being in command, being out in space on one adventure after another. There is no question. No doubt.

"Yes."

She nods and the doors close.

As I lie down in my cramped bunk, I know I have to get off this ship. I have to return to Ash and the *Persephone*. I also know I've set something in motion that won't be stopped now. I have no idea what Veera will do now that she is aware I want to leave, which means time is running out.

CHAPTER THIRTEEN

Ash

"He's stable. That's about all I can tell you," Dr. Prashad says.

I'm pacing in front of the doctor as he runs scans over Hartley. Dan Foer and all his massive girth is pacing opposite. We had to bring Hartley to the medical center on the *Kudo*. We still won't have access to the *Persephone* until we get the main computer fully connected.

"What's wrong with him? Does he have what they have?" I lower my voice so the *Kudo*'s medical staff doesn't hear me.

Dr. Prashad spreads his hands. "I have no idea until I run more tests. I've sent Chloe to the *Persephone* to get a few instruments that will help me. Their technology is impressive, but I'm still not comfortable with some of their devices. I'd rather have my own."

I don't want to push, but seeing Hartley pale and quiet causes my anxiety to peak. "How long until you know more?"

The doctor shrugs. "Ash, you know I can't give you absolutes."

"Would it help if we could get you back on the *Persephone*? If we get it up and running, would that help?" I turn to Foer. "How long until we can turn on the main computer?"

"I'm sorry, Lieutenant, but that's not going to happen. Not without Hartley it's not."

"What do you mean? You can't do the final initialization?" Does Hartley do everything in that department?

Foer licks his lips and ducks his head. "Turning on the computer isn't the problem. It's the access codes." He takes a moment, and I'm not going to like whatever he's going to say. "The access codes were never restored. And you never took charge of the *Persephone* officially. So…" He's talking about when Jordan had Hartley set up backdoor codes, which means the only people who know these codes are Jordan and Hartley.

"So without Hartley, we have no way of programming the new computer to take our commands."

"Exactly."

I turn away from the group and survey the medical center with my hands on my hips. It's pristine. White and sterile. It says reliability and professionalism with every piece of equipment and red-coated medical officer hustling through the large room. We're tucked to the side, away from the rest of their personnel. There are more doctors than patients. We haven't nailed down the number of illya on board, but six doctors is too many.

Dr. Prashad places a hand on my arm. "Why do we need to get back to the *Persephone* so badly? We're not in any danger here. The illya have been nothing but hospitable."

"And their ship is much much faster than ours. Like thousands of times faster," Foer says.

"We're heading toward the *Posterus*, and they're searching for Captain Kellow as we go, so why don't we take one thing at a time? Let's focus on finding out what's wrong with Hartley. The *Persephone* can wait," Dr. Prashad says.

I grip Hartley's hand. If I don't have something to focus on, I'll obsess. The work on the *Persephone* is the only thing keeping me from worrying about Jordan. But they're right. It would take years to search for Jordan with the *Persephone*, and by that point she would be dead. If she isn't already. I haven't let myself go there yet. But the possibility is hovering in the background all the time. Keeping busy is the only thing that stops it from crowding my thoughts. They say you can feel if someone you love is alive or dead, but I don't believe that. I don't feel anything. In fact, I feel numb.

"Okay, Doctor, keep me posted. Foer, you're with me. I want to talk to Gadzir about hacking back into our system without the access codes." Just in case. I can't bring myself to say it out loud, but if Hartley doesn't ever wake up again, we're going to need a backup plan to establish control of the ship.

I take one last look at Hartley before leaving. The first time I met him he was brash and arrogant. He's still brash and arrogant, but behind that is an insecure, kind-hearted person who has surprised me with his bravery on more than one occasion. I don't want to do this without him.

The one good piece of news I learn is that our access codes are ridiculously easy to hack. That's not how Gadzir phrased it, but his expression told me as much. Thanks to Foer, I receive a crash course in encryption technology. The *Persephone* uses UES, the Universal Encryption Standard, to encrypt all our data and ship functions. That means we use a secure hash algorithm first designed in the late twentieth century and improved over the centuries. It's based on a symmetric block cipher that, according to Gadzir, is an antiquated way to encrypt data. They've been using DNA cryptography for centuries. As Foer explained, it's easier for them since they use molecular biology hardware instead of silicon-based hardware.

"Actually, we're going to have to find something that will integrate with the *Persephone*. We have to dumb down their technology to fit."

I raise my eyebrows. I've never heard of the *Persephone* referred to as antiquated. She may be old, but her engines and computer system were first-rate when we set out on this mission. "Are you saying the *Persephone* isn't good enough?"

"No. I'm saying it would be like trying to repair a Model T with our current technology. It can be done, but we'll have to improvise."

"Model T?"

"One of the first cars ever invented." He grins. "I have a thing for ancient engines. I once recreated a two-stroke kerosene engine when I was a kid. Of course I couldn't test it because we don't have kerosene. But it was pretty cool anyway." No wonder Hartley and he get along so well. They both speak geek.

"What's the timeline on this?"

Foer turns to Gadzir, who shrugs. "I haven't seen your engine room, so I can't make an assumption."

"But it's your computer that we'll be interfacing with."

He shakes his head. "Hartley supplied the specifications for us. We've never used quantum-computing technology. We may have built the computer using our components, but its use is unknown to me. Foer will have to show me how it works before I can estimate how long it will take to access the command functions on your ship."

"Foer, can you show him what he needs on the *Persephone*?"

He nods and Gadzir smiles. "This should be fascinating. I'm always interested in learning primitive modes of transportation."

"Excellent," I say. His grin grows wider, my sarcasm lost on him. With nothing to do myself, I go in search of Captain Kalve. I want to see how the search for Jordan is going. If they'd found anything I would be the first person to know, but I need to do something. I find him on the bridge. Their ship is starting the morning shift. Over the last few weeks I've converted to their time, despite my best intentions. They have a thirty-eight-hour day as opposed to our twenty-four-hour day. I guess up here it doesn't matter, because we based our original day on Earth's sun rotation. But we got used to it, so why change now?

He invites me into his office, which is on the lower deck of the bridge. There's not much to it: a desk, a huge window, and a small cot in case he wants to sleep but still be close by. On the *Persephone* Jordan's office and cabin are one and the same. Her room is located next to the bridge, so she's never far from her command post. Another reason being in command sucks. That need to constantly be on is stressful. And even though my position is almost always a precursor to command, we have very different tasks. I maintain the crew and assignments while she handles ship operations. All decisions, including mine, go through her before they're approved. That's a lot of forms to sign.

Kalve presses a small button on his desk, and a clear thermos with dark-reddish liquid rises from some unknown recess. "Would you care for some juua?"

"What is it?"

"Originally it comes from the stones of a barb. I'm not sure if that's the right word. Their bodies naturally produce pellets that taste sweet. When boiled it creates a pleasing drink." He pours the liquid into a small cup and offers it to me. "We of course don't have barbs on board, so this is synthesized to taste the same."

I take the cup and look into dark, swirling fluid. It coats the sides and slides back. Steam rises from the surface. I take a whiff. He's right, it does smell sweet. I don't know if I should be happy that it's synthesized. After all, if it wasn't fake, it would be animal poop. I also wish he hadn't told me what it was. I could probably have enjoyed it in ignorance. Now that I'm holding the cup in my hand I can't refuse. That would be rude.

Kalve's eyes close as he sips his. A murmur of satisfaction escapes from him. I stare into my cup, trying not to gag. Our eyes meet across the table, and his lips curl into an understanding smile. "It's okay if you don't want to try it. The idea must be foreign to you. You won't offend me."

No way am I going to back down from that challenge. I hold my breath and take a small sip and swallow fast. It's synthetic, it's synthetic, I tell myself. After a moment, when I don't die, I take another larger sip. It reminds me of watered-down maple syrup. I don't even want to know what was in this animal's diet to make it so.

Kalve laughs, a boisterous sound that slams into me. It's warm and accepting. Instead of being embarrassed, I'm delighted. I laugh too. There's something comfortable about this encounter, and for the first time since Jordan left, I don't feel lost. In fact, something's so familiar about this.

I peer around the room again and notice a lot more of the details, especially a picture on the wall next to his desk. "Is this your family?" A short woman has her arm around Kalve, a younger boy standing in front of him. He has one hand on the boy's shoulder. Instead of looking at the camera, the boy is gazing up at Kalve with such an adoring expression I can feel the connection, like they were actually tied to each other.

His expression softens. "Yes. My wife and son."

"I can tell. He has your..." I motion around his small beak area, not sure what they call it, so I settle for "Nose."

"We were lucky about that, yes. But the men in our species don't contribute to the genetic gene pool. Not since the plague."

"Oh." A million questions pop into my head, but it would be rude to ask any of them. "Are they on board with you?"

"They died over ten years ago."

"Oh." Jesus, I'm really killing this. "I'm so sorry. I didn't mean to bring up bad memories."

He holds up a hand. "I have no bad memories when it comes to my family. Even now they are my joy in this life. Sometimes I think it's better that they died. The life we lead is a hard one. We're never able to stay in the same place, constantly on the move and no place to call home." He drains his juua and places the cup on the table. "Bragga plays the diplomat a little too well. He would have you believe that our life on the *Kudo* is all any of us want, that this ship is enough. It's not. Most of us are tired of being hunted into extinction."

"Hunted? Who's hunting you?"

"The Varbaja. Ever since we settled on their farming world, they've had a need to destroy every last one of us. Their army is massive, numbering in the hundreds of thousands, and we're a couple of thousand. That's not enough to defend ourselves, let alone win, so we run." He waves a hand at me. "I'm sorry. I know you have your own problems and probably don't want to hear ours."

"My father used to say, 'the best way to distract yourself from your own problems is to hear someone else's.' I don't mind, honest. Our species grew up isolated in our galaxy. Until a few weeks ago we didn't even know for sure if other species existed. I mean, we hoped, assumed? I'm not sure, but all this is science fiction come to life. It's exciting."

"Life on a ship is never dull." He nods toward my cup, but I shake my head. It's too sweet for me. "I've captained the *Kudo* for over ten years now and even without skirmishes we have our hands full keeping her together."

I laugh again. "We've been interstellar travelers for a few weeks now and have almost destroyed two ships." I've almost destroyed two ships. That thought hits hard. I can keep telling myself that I made the right choice, but what happens if I'm wrong?

"The *Posterus*, the one we are taking you to, this is the other ship that's adrift?"

I nod. "We're not exactly sure how we got here. But we had to eject the engine or it could've exploded and taken all three ships with it." It's strange how comfortable I feel talking to this person. But something about him makes me want to trust him. Maybe it's the way he doesn't seem to offer judgment, only acceptance. It's almost as if I've known him longer than three weeks. It's happened very few times in my life. Jordan and, to an extent, Hartley are the only people who come to mind, but sometimes I just connect with people.

"What is it you need? I know you didn't come to try juua."

"As tasty as it was, no. I came to see if you'd found any sign of Captain Kellow's escape pod."

He places one of his fingers into a small groove in the table. Nothing happens. But after a few moments I realize he's no longer looking at me. His attention is focused on some unknown spot a few feet in front of him. His eyes skim back and forth until he removes his finger and returns his attention to me. "No. We haven't found anything yet. We entered the base elements that construct your escape pods in case there may have been an explosion. We haven't found any significant amounts in any of our search patterns. But we won't give up."

Where is she? I can't let myself think the worst. "Could another vessel have picked them up?" Are there that many space-traveling species in this galaxy? And if there are, what are the chances they're friendly?

The intercom interrupts Kalve.

"Captain, we've reached the other ship."

"The *Posterus*?" I ask.

Kalve nods and stands. "Excellent. I'll be out in a few minutes."

"You should know, sir, they're not alone. The *Avokaado* is here as well."

CHAPTER FOURTEEN

Jordan

I'm sprinting down an unknown corridor blind. Smoke envelops me. It's hot and sickly sweet. Something's on fire, and whatever it is terrifies me. The sound of boots pounding on the metal floor behind me drowns out the faint shouts farther ahead. Sarka catches up to me and has the gall to grin as he does.

"Told you it'd work. You gotta learn to trust me."

I don't have to do any such thing. I almost trip on a body lying on the floor in front of me. I vault and stumble until a thick hand wraps around my arm and yanks me up. It's Sarka. He's still got that grin on his face, along with a large gash over his left eye.

"We need to get to the flight deck. They're waiting for us." As he tugs me along, I wonder how the hell I got myself mixed up in all this.

After my conversation with Veera I knew Sarka was on to something. There's more unrest on this ship than even Sarka knows. In the last two days I've only scratched the surface of the real issues. That's no surprise. After all, what were they expecting, filling up a warship with restless thugs? They've got nothing to do but harbor resentments toward each other. I've been here only a few weeks, and I already resent half the people on this ship.

This is what happens in overpopulated situations. It happened on Earth in the late twenty-first century when the population soared over ten billion. Kindness and understanding are not able to flourish in close quarters. They need wide-open fields and vistas as far as the eye can see.

I don't know about the species on this ship, but I don't think any of us were meant to live permanently in space. If I ever make it back to the *Posterus* and the *Persephone*, I'll probably spend the rest of my life doing just that, but it's for a greater cause. It's so my decendants don't have to.

Sarka yanks me down a side corridor, and we reach a small chute like we have on the *Persephone*. I'd almost forgotten how spoiled I'd become in the last few weeks using lifts to get everywhere.

"Where are we going?" I cough. Smoke is filling the corridors. It's not as bad here, but I can see it creeping around the corner.

"Flight deck. That's forty decks away."

I balk. "And we're going to climb there? What's wrong with the lifts?"

"The ship's burning. The lifts automatically shut down when there's a fire."

How does he know this? Because he already tried to use the lifts or because he's been reading up on the specs? I'm not sure, and I don't care right now.

"Up or down?"

He slaps me on the back. "You didn't think I'd make this easy, did you? Stop being a baby. Let's go." He beckons for me to go first.

Fuck. I grab the ladder and hoist myself up. Even with weeks of training and being in good shape to begin with, I find the climb excruciating. I stop trying to count the decks. It's not distracting enough. All it does is focus my attention on the heaviness in my arms.

None of this would've happened if I'd listened to my gut. After spending most of the night coming up with a plan, I realized the simplest was the best, and Sarka had already laid it out for me. I just had to find a pilot I could bribe and have them fly me off the ship. The problem with confined spaces is that information has a way of taking on a life of its own.

The first few days I'd kept my head down and listened to the chatter. I sat in a different place in the mess, not only because I still wasn't talking to Sarka, but I wanted to get a feel for the people. We'd kept ourselves isolated, and because of that, I had no idea what the people on board were like. For all I knew, interspecies mingling could be considered dangerous or ill advised. I didn't want to push my way in where I wasn't invited. But the more I listened, the more I understood what Sarka had been talking about. They were restless and angry. A dangerous combination.

After the second day I got up the nerve to talk to one of the pilots I'd heard complaining about the guy who bunks above him. Turns out he tosses and turns in his sleep. And apparently he's a heavy guy. That day at midmorning meal I took a seat opposite him. He was a species I wasn't familiar with. His skin was pockmarked and rough, leathery brown. His nose was nonexistent, two small holes above his mouth that flapped when he laughed. He was also hairless, including his head.

I only ever learned his nickname, Tink. He got that name because his nails make a strange tinkling sound when he throws the stones in one of the chance games they play in the lounge after hours. I never learned what species he belonged to, but I'll steer clear of them from now on.

As I sat, Tink gave me the once-over but didn't comment. I was trying to find a subject to start a conversation when another of his species sat down next to him.

He cocked his head toward me. "Who's this?"

Tink shrugged. "Never seen her before."

Tink's companion smiled, showing two neat rows of razor-sharp teeth. "What's your story, honey?" I'm sure the word wasn't honey, but I got the gist.

"Why do I have to have a story?" I spooned something that looked an awful lot like porridge but tasted like soap into my mouth, beginning to see my mistake.

"This is Tink." He pointed to Tink. "And I'm—"

"Why you gotta be such a big mouth all the time?" Tink hit him with his utensil. His porridge flew onto the cheek of another man across the table who stood up.

Tink's friend didn't notice. Instead he plowed on. "What?" he asked. "Why don't you want people knowing your name?"

"It's not my name. I hate when people call me that. You know that. I tell you that every time."

The man who got hit with porridge made his way around the table and lifted Tink's friend up by the collar of his uniform. That's when I stood and slid my tray off the table. My back was turned and I was three chairs down when I heard the telltale sound of a fist hitting cheekbone.

This is probably why I didn't have many friends when I was a kid.

I preferred being on my own anyway. A good book and the tall safety of the cornstalks were much better companions than people. Especially ones my own age.

Halfway up the ladder I'm forced to stop because someone's closed off the rest of the chute. It could be due to the fire, but either way, without the access codes we won't be able to get through.

Sarka smacks my leg. "No time for breaks. We need to keep moving."

"We'll have to find another way to the flight deck. Look." I point above me.

Sarka strains his neck to see. "Son of a bitch."

"Let's climb down to the last deck and see if there's another chute somewhere that leads up."

"Won't work. If this one's shut, they're all shut. We need to find another way," he says.

"We won't know until we try."

"And while we're trying every chute on that deck, they'll be gaining on us. No. We need to find the service hatches. Those won't be blocked. The emergency crews will need access to the decks. We need to find them." The last bit is muffled as he's already started climbing down. Below, something bright flashes. A few seconds later I hear the boom, and a wave of heat slams into us.

"Hang on." I wrap my arms around the rungs of the ladder.

Sarka doesn't grab on in time. The blast catches him, and he pinwheels backward before latching his leg into one of the gaps. I hear the snap even above the echo of the explosion. But Sarka doesn't make a sound. He hooks his other leg in to take the weight off and hoists himself up with his abs. He does have the decency to grunt as he disentangles the broken leg from the ladder. I swear you'd have to cut off a limb to get an actual scream from the man. He descends using only his arms. I follow, keeping a close eye on him.

I examine the injury. It's good and truly broken. He's lucky it's not a compound fracture, but I'll attribute that to the fact that a Burr's bones are harder to break than a regular human's.

"Well, you're useless to me now, old man."

His eyebrows crawl up. "Old man?"

"You're almost three times my age. You going to debate me on that fact?"

The corridor we're in is empty. For now. I have no idea where we actually are. I was counting on Sarka to guide us. Now I'll have to leave him here and get help. I relay this to him and get up to leave.

He catches my arm, holding it in a tight vise, and pulls me back down. "You're not fucking leaving me behind."

It's my turn to raise my eyebrows. "And you're going to stop me? I got this far no thanks to you." Of course that was his plan the whole time. Make me do all the work.

After that disastrous first try with Tink, I decided the mess wasn't the place to approach people. If their reaction to our training was similar to mine, they were starving and grouchy by the time they got some chow. Not many people want to be disturbed while they're shoveling food into their mouths. No, the best place to reach people would be the lounge after hours when they're fed and relaxed. Plus, I quickly realized I had an easy in to talk to people.

After the evening meal I waited until the lounge filled up but wasn't crowded. It was my first time inside since we'd come aboard. Along the far wall stretched a long bar staffed by grumbling barmaids who looked exhausted even though their shifts had only started. They offered only one thing to drink—a gelatinous red goo that dribbled out of the bottle, easing itself into the glass after a day of hard labor. I decided my life was more important to me than trying it. But I didn't want to look out of place, so I ordered a drink and vowed to never actually take a sip.

A group of breens in the back was playing a game of chance that involved three stones. The stones were roughly the same size but were all different colors. After watching for a few minutes, I thought it seemed simple enough but figured the best way to get to know people was to ask how to play.

I watched a few more rounds before stepping forward and asking to participate. I'd never cruised bars in my life, not even the few on campus at the academy. I don't recall going once. It occurred to me only after I stepped forward that my actions could be misinterpreted. I was greeted with four huge grins, which told me everything I needed to know. If any of these breen thought I was going back to one of their bunks, they had another think coming. To be fair, if anything identifying as female had approached them, they would've shown interest.

I surprisingly managed to dodge any awkward moments by being up front with them. In fact, telling them I mated only with females— their words—endeared me to them more. They pulled me into the fold as one of the guys and, with that, all their grumbles. They bitched about everything: the food, the bunks, their training, the scarcity of battles. They lamented the lack of opportunities to mate, although the word they used was something even the universal translator couldn't convey, so I assume it was obscure slang. They left with the impression that we all bonded over the fact that females are crazy. I've never understood how telling a group of guys you're a lesbian means they forget you're still female.

The night was a success. I learned how to play hea mang and made some important contacts. It also gave me the first crack in the wall. It would take only a few more days to find out if any of them were interested in escaping and how best to do that. That had been the plan anyway.

I try to pull away, but Sarka's grip is so tight it hurts. "Let me grab help," I say.

He shakes his head and pulls me closer, close enough that I can feel his breath on my face. "We don't leave people behind." He's almost desperate as he says the next part. "You're not leaving me here." I look down at his leg, any damage hidden by his uniform pants. He's going to be some serious dead weight. I'm strong, but I'm not sure I'm up to this task. When I look back into his eyes, I spot a hard edge to go with the pathetic pleading. I don't doubt he'd crawl after me if I tried to leave him behind.

"Okay. But you're a huge pain in my ass. Next time try not to get hurt."

"Great advice. You should write motivational speeches for a living."

"Shut up." I grunt as I heave him up on his one good leg. He drapes his right arm over my shoulder, and we begin our hobble down the hall. I have no idea how we're going to make it through the service hatches now. They'll be even more cramped than the chutes we were in. I hear shouting up ahead. Well, fuck.

CHAPTER FIFTEEN

Ash

We enter a bridge in chaos. Crew run back and forth, checking instruments, yelling reports at each other from the other side of the bridge, and in a few cases, I hear muffled responses from the deck below. Kalve rushes into the middle of everything. I melt into the background to stay out of everyone's way, but also so I don't get asked to leave. I'd like to be here for the action.

Jordan would never let her bridge get this crazy. First she'd calm everyone down before proceeding with a well-thought-out plan. I'm trying to think how I would handle it if I were captain, when Kalve beckons me to his side.

"Your ship, the *Posterus*, what kind of defenses does it have?"

"Why?" A thread of alarm snaps taut in my belly. Have I misjudged these people?

He points to a giant ship off the bow of the *Posterus*. It's immense and looks hostile. "That's the *Avokaado*. It's very unlikely they're here to make friends." The ship is ten times the size of the *Posterus*, the largest ship the human species ever built. It's a city drifting over us. The observation screen zooms in on the top decks of the ship. Five rows of cannons lift their protective shields, ready to aim and fire on our ships.

"They're going to attack us? What for?"

"They're known as the Varbaja. They recruit people against their will for war. Specifically, war against us. They probably approached the *Posterus* to add to their army. They'll board the ship and capture anyone they think will be good fighters."

"My people will fight back." I don't even have to question that

• 125 •

assertion. The majority of people on the *Posterus* are scientists, civilians, people who will help create a balanced society. The *Persephone* and the *Brimley* were the only military personnel on the mission, and it doesn't look like the *Brimley*'s returned from its mission. But humans are resilient. Every person on the *Posterus* will immediately defend it. We've spent twenty years preparing for this mission. We won't let it fall to pieces the second we leave the gate.

"They'll lose," Kalve says.

"Maybe." But it would be poor strategy to take too many of the *Posterus* crew. Over forty thousand humans are on that ship. That's a large number to take all at once, not to mention the aftermath. That many members of the same species working together from the inside to escape would cause chaos. "Do you know if they've boarded yet?"

Kalve turns to one of his men, who shakes his head. "No. They haven't. Which is strange."

"Can you disable their ship? Or destroy it? Isn't that something this ship is designed for? To defeat these people?" All we've done since we landed in this galaxy is get ourselves stuck in the middle of one conflict or another.

He turns kind eyes on me. "If it were only that simple. Do you know how many people are on that ship? How many of them don't want to be there? Even if we could destroy it, should we?"

"Can we talk to the captain on the *Posterus*?"

He nods. "Raise the *Posterus* on the comm."

After a few moments of figuring out how to bridge the technology gap, Captain Wells appears on screen. I've never met her, but I've heard horror stories. She may appear diminutive with her short stature and kind features—in another environment you might expect her to pull an apple pie out of the oven—but she's anything but the kind grandmother she appears to be. Behind that exterior lies a cunning and brilliant woman who won't hesitate to strip you down.

At first she looks confused until she spots me. Her eyes widen.

I step forward. "Captain Wells, I'm Lieutenant Alison Ash, the *Persephone*'s first officer. We—"

"Where's Captain Kellow?"

I flinch. Of course she'd ask about Jordan, but I hadn't prepared what to say ahead of time. "She's missing. We're searching for her."

"Missing?" She has the ability to make that one word a

recrimination with so many facets. It's an accusation against me, my inability to keep my captain safe, my crew, our ship.

"Davis Sarka took her hostage and escaped using one of our pods." Before leaving on our mission Jordan had argued against keeping Sarka on the *Persephone*. Wells overruled her, stating the *Persephone* was better equipped to handle a Burr. Even if they didn't have a brig, they could've converted an empty cabin. They also have more security personnel than we do. We have four members of our crew for security, whereas they have over a hundred. I know it's petty to dwell on this subject, but I partially blame Wells for what happened on the *Persephone*. We were in no way prepared to take care of Sarka and embark on our mission. Not to mention, Jordan shouldn't have had to deal with her own father. Not that Wells or anyone else at the time knew Sarka was Jordan's father.

"The *Persephone* was unable to capture an escape pod with limited propulsion?"

"We were dead in space at the time, and they disappeared behind a barrier." Kalve grabs my arm and shakes his head very subtly at me. I get the idea. He doesn't want me to tell others about our experience on the planet. For the time being it's in our best interest to follow his wishes. "It's a very long story, one we don't have time for right now. The ship off your bow is very dangerous. Have they been in contact with you?"

"What are you doing on that ship? Where is the *Persephone*?" I hate people who respond to questions with questions.

"It doesn't matter right now. That ship off your bow—"

"Is a warship." Kalve interrupts me. "They will destroy you if given the chance. You must prepare for an invasion force as soon as possible."

"And who are you?"

Kalve and I share a look. This woman is infuriating. Is it some power-trip thing, a need to control what's going on even though in reality she doesn't have any real power over me or the *Persephone*. She's not Union. None of us are now.

"I'm the captain of this ship, and I know what that ship is capable of. If you want to survive, you will listen to us and follow our advice."

Her face pinches together, evaluating both of us. "What other ship are you referring to? What invasion force?"

I turn to Kalve with surprise. "Why can't they see the ship?"

"It's possible their sensors aren't calibrated properly."

"Is there any way to fix that?" I ask.

Kalve beckons to one of his officers and whispers something low. The officer scurries off, and Kalve turns to me. "We have something that might help, but we'll have to transport it to their ship."

"What is it?"

"*Avokaado* has technology to mask their signature. We have the ability to counteract that ability. It's a small sensor that would enable them to detect the ship."

I whisper, "She's going to want to know more about what's going on. It's best if we speak to her on the *Posterus*. Is there a way to do that safely?"

He nods and beckons one of his men over. "We'll send a stealth ship. They operate on minimal energy output, which makes it difficult for the *Avokaado* to detect them, especially with other ships around. You can take the sensor with you."

After arranging the ship to the *Posterus*, I decide to take Yakovich with me. If we're attacked in flight it'll be handy to have a security officer with us, plus safety in numbers.

The ship isn't very big, with two seats up front for the pilot and copilot and two in back for passengers, plus a small hold for cargo. I sit up with the pilot and Yakovich is in back. From my vantage point in front I have a better view of the *Kudo* as we leave. The *Posterus* looks dwarfed among giants. The *Avokaado* looms over both like the predator it is. The first time I saw the *Posterus* I thought it was impressive. But seeing these two ships next to one another, I have no concept of how anyone would build something so massive. It took twenty years to build the *Posterus* and thousands of workers. Imagine what it took to build the *Avokaado*.

As we round the aft of the *Posterus* I can see some of the damage the explosion caused. They've patched the holes, but the scorch marks are still visible. The patch job is raw and ugly. I still don't understand why Sarka tried to stop us, but why should he care? He said it was a perversion of our species to separate us from where we evolved, that we would lose who we were if we left. But I don't buy that. Only a fraction of the species left, while the majority stayed behind. It sounds like the rantings of a deranged man. And Sarka may be a lot of things, but he isn't crazy. It makes me worry for Jordan all the more for being stuck out there with him.

We come up to one of the cargo holds. It was a little tricky figuring out how to gain access to the *Posterus*, as our docking is meant for large ships, specifically the *Brimley* and the *Persephone*. The only other option was to land inside one of the cargo holds. Once we land we'll re-pressurize the hold. As we pull into the ship, I glimpse the *Avokaado* alongside the *Posterus*. It's so huge it almost blocks out the rest of space behind it.

Captain Wells and her head of security Kurt Gladwell meet us as we land. I have met him. He interviewed me after the explosion on the *Posterus* while I was still in their med center recovering. If ever there was a distinction between the *Posterus* crew and the Union fleet, he's it. The guy makes me want to sleep with the lights on.

Before Captain Wells has a chance to step forward, he holds her back with an arm thrown out in front. He's not a very large man but he's imposing by the creep factor alone. His face is all angles, almost as if he were built with sharp edges. His eyes are black, and his tendency to squint makes them appear smaller than they are. But I swear, I always end up looking at the cleft in his chin. Everything on his face converges on that point.

"Captain, we should scan them before you go near. We don't know if this is a trap." He stares at me as he speaks. He still thinks I was somehow in on the plot to blow up the *Posterus*, like I volunteered to have a bomb planted in me. He recommended that Jordan relieve me of duty. Luckily he has no authority on the *Persephone*.

I raise my arms. "Scan away. We're here to solve problems, not create them." It's too bad we can't say the same for him. Wells stays far back. She doesn't look as intimidating up close. In fact, if I had to guess I'd say she looks scared. Gladwell's probably filled her head with all sorts of worst-case scenarios.

"Is anyone else in the ship?" he asks.

"Sergeant Yakovich and their pilot."

"One of them is in there?" Gladwell asks.

"One of who?"

"The aliens."

I beckon for Yakovich to come out, along with the pilot. This might become stupid real fast. "We have no idea how to pilot their ships. They were kind enough to provide this service in the first place." They could've left us here to deal with a warship on our own.

The pilot steps out from the ship next to Yakovich, who is a foot and a half taller than him. Gladwell's men, who had entered to do their scan, stop. Everyone stares. I wonder if I looked that dumb the first time I saw one of the avians on the planet. I hope not. I lean in toward the pilot and whisper, "Introduce yourself."

He raises his hand. "I'm Pana." Still no one moves. I nudge him again, but his eyes grow round, and he shrugs at me.

"Now that everyone's had a good look, let's move this along," I say.

Gladwell nods at his men, who spread out to scan every centimeter of us.

"Who are these people?" He steps closer to me, squinting and eyeing Pana as he asks the question. "How did you end up on their ship?"

Yakovich hands over a small disc. "This will help you detect the other ship."

Gladwell eyes it but doesn't take it. "I'm not going to allow the installation of unknown equipment on this ship before properly inspecting it."

Yakovich shrugs. "Go ahead."

Wells steps forward and holds out her hand for the disc. "How long have you been on their ship?"

"A few weeks." I pause, because in truth I don't trust the illya. Not entirely. And the whole time we've been on board I've been trying to get my crew off the ship. So I have no idea if this disc actually does what it says it does. "I don't blame you for not trusting them. But I do know one thing for sure because I've seen it with my own eyes. There is a giant, and I mean massive, ship off the bow of the *Posterus*. Now, even if they're not here to invade you, the fact that they haven't made themselves known is a bad sign."

"I want to see this ship," says Wells. She hands the disc to one of her crew. "Have a look at that, see if it contains any viruses if possible." She turns back to me. "Can you take me there?"

"Take you where?"

She sighs and places her hands on her hips. "The ship," she motions outward, "that you just came from. I want to see it for myself."

"I don't know. They weren't expecting company." I look back at Pana and Yakovich. Pana shrugs. I'm sure he doesn't care who he's flying. Yakovich's jaw is flexed. She's not keen on the idea.

"They don't need to roll out a welcome mat. This is a lot to take in." Wells runs her hand through her short white hair.

I shift my gaze to my boots and then back up to the hard stare of Wells. The woman doesn't budge. She's made up her mind that she's coming, even if she has to strap herself to the back of Pana's ship. "All right. Let's go."

Gladwell steps forward to join us, and I hold up my hand. "Only room for four. Sorry." I try to look sorry, I really do.

He points at Yakovich, giving her the once-over. "She can stay here until we return."

"Yakovich is my head of security. She'll make sure we're all safe. She's also fully briefed on the situation and the illya. There'll be fewer questions and guesswork this way." Wow. Diplomacy. If ever there was a "suck it, bitch" moment, this would be it. Jordan would be proud that I stayed civil.

Wells holds up a hand. "I'll be fine, Gladwell. I want you to take charge of looking over that disc, but don't do anything until I get back." She steps forward, and we have a moment like we both know why I brought Yakovich. Like I said, safety in numbers.

Back on the *Kudo* I take a moment to pull Yakovich aside. Wells is busy being in awe of the massive size of their cargo hold compared to the *Posterus*'s. "I probably don't have to say this, but Gladwell—"

"Keep an eye out for him? Yeah. I got that impression," Yakovich says.

"Good. I don't trust that man."

"You shouldn't. I've seen him before. He's not Union fleet, but he went through the academy. He was a year ahead of me. I don't think he's here only to act as head of security for the *Posterus*."

I pull Yakovich farther away from the group. "What do you mean?"

"He's special operations. No way would they appoint someone like that to head up security unless they were worried about some other problem."

"Like Sarka?" We fall in behind the others as we make our way to the bridge.

She nods. "Yeah, like they knew the Burrs would try to sabotage us."

"His head must be exploding right now."

Yakovich laughs and slaps me on the back. "I would give anything to hear what he said as soon as we took off. I'll remember the look on his face when you told him no forever."

As we enter the bridge I have this strange feeling, like I'm watching the scene from the outside. Yakovich and I walking side by side, sharing a joke as colleagues. A few weeks ago I wouldn't have thought that possible. In the past few weeks, with Jordan and Sarka gone and Vasa confined to quarters, it's almost as if I could forget the crew's earlier animosity toward me. And as I have this thought I look up. The *Kudo*'s commscreen is live, and standing in the background, behind several very tiny people, is Jordan. Our eyes meet, and my laugh dies instantly. She's alive.

CHAPTER SIXTEEN

Jordan

"Down here." I guide Sarka into an offshoot passage, away from the voices. We stumble through an open door and into a dark room. I tuck us into a far corner, and we wait for the voices to fade. There isn't much light from the corridor, but I can see it's one of the classrooms where Sarka and I were first brought. There are three rows of desks and chairs. At the very front is a large screen that stands blank.

"How did you even break your leg? I thought you had reinforced bones."

Sarka groans as he shifts. "Despite what everyone thinks, we aren't gods."

"No one thinks you're gods."

"You know what I mean. We can and do die."

"Spare me the 'we're just like you' speech."

"Shhh."

Instead of moving farther away, the voices get closer. We are, of course, unarmed. Not having passed basic training yet, we haven't been entrusted with our own armory like the rest of the crew.

Sarka nudges my arm. "See if you can get one of the chair legs loose and use it as a weapon."

I crawl to the nearest set and yank the chair up. It doesn't budge. "They're bolted to the floor."

"Of course they are. Kick it free. Use your brain."

I circle the room looking for the chair closest to the wall so I can use it for leverage. I position my back against the wall and kick one of the legs as hard as I can. It doesn't even vibrate. I kick a couple more times and still nothing happens.

"Put some force behind it."

"What do you think I'm doing? Playing footsies?"

"Stop fucking around, Jordan, and get it done."

That does it. My blood boils. I stomp my foot against the base of the chair leg as hard as I can again and again and again. All the rage and helplessness I've felt in the past few weeks comes out in a burst of fiery temper. Sarka taking me hostage, the Varbaja recruiting me into a war I don't want to fight, Ash letting Sarka escape, all of it. A shooting pain starts at the tip of my heel and radiates up my leg, and still I stomp my foot against the chair. I'm panting and sweating, but I couldn't stop if I wanted.

The only thing that stops me is Sarka. He pulls me away from the chair, which hasn't even budged. "That's enough," he says. "It's dead."

I pull free and stalk to the other side of the room still panting, still seething. This is Sarka's fault. I should leave him here and escape to the flight deck myself. Why am I even bothering? I grab the back of a chair and grip until my knuckles turn white. Why? I don't need him to survive, not anymore. He deserves to be left behind. This is all his fault.

"It's my contact," he says.

I have a hard time figuring out what he means. "What?"

"You're debating whether to leave me behind. Well, it's my contact on the flight deck. I'm the one who's going to get us out of here." He hobbles closer.

"I have my own contacts."

"Those idiots who started this whole mess? Not that I'm not grateful, but they're probably dead."

"Please don't act like you haven't been behind this whole thing. I know when I'm being manipulated."

He spreads his arms wide and grins. "And yet."

"Fuck you."

"Here we are. Exactly as I planned it."

I storm toward the door. The voices in the hall have stopped. I hold my hand up for Sarka to stop talking, then peer around the door and find the frame blocked by three giant bodies.

I wish Sarka wasn't right about how this all started, but there's no other explanation. The three soldiers I met in the lounge that night turned out to be easily persuaded. I set the idea in their head about escaping, and the rest snowballed from there.

We were playing hea mang when Karm, the tough guy of the group, asked if I'd ever been in combat. Now, my life hasn't been anything like most of the soldiers on this ship. Many grew up here and have never known anything except fighting, but my life hasn't been cushy. After escaping the Burrs I grew up on a farm where we worked every day. And I'd like to think I held my own against the avians. While I've never been at war, I've been in life-or-death situations. Even simple everyday decisions as captain force me to put people's lives in danger.

"Why?" I asked.

"I was thinking about what you said the other day, about how we're stuck fighting an unwinnable war." He turned to the other two. "Right? How can we win when we can't find the enemy?" They all nodded. One of them, Bruto, slammed the three rocks from our hea mang game on the table. "All we do every day is get ready for battle that's never going to happen. Most of us have never even seen the illya in person. It's time we take back our lives." He gulped the rest of his drink and slammed it on the table. "Who's with me?"

And that's all it took. I didn't mean for it to happen. I wanted to find someone to fly me out of here, but instead I helped start a revolt.

The bodies blocking the door move aside for a small figure who pushes through their legs. It's Veera. She spots us in the small corner and waves the men off. "Go check the other rooms."

"Well, you've been busy," she says to me.

I'm not going to pretend I don't know what she's talking about. But I can't take credit for all of this. "Not really." I mean, all I did was mention that I wanted to get out of here, and the right person happened to hear me. Besides, Sarka set the whole thing up. He put the idea into my head about a revolt, knowing I would try to be more subtle than that.

"What happened to him?" She walks over and begins poking around his leg. He tries to swat her away, but she persists. "Broken. That needs medical attention. Can you manage with him?"

I'm at a loss. Do we follow her? Is she part of the revolt or the establishment? Judging by her comment the other day, I'd guess she's for the revolt.

"Depends on how far we have to go," I say.

"There's a medical bay at the other end of this deck. I know one of the doctors who'll help him. No point struggling with a broken leg if you don't have to."

Sarka pulls away from me. "We're better off on our own."

Veera bares her teeth. I think she was going for a grin but it didn't work out. "If you're on your own, I give you half an hour before you're found and killed. The Varbaja are sweeping the ship looking for any dissidents. With that leg you won't get far." She stalks to the door and turns. "Your choice. You'll last longer with me, though."

I pull Sarka's arm over my shoulder. "We're done doing it your way." He grunts as he adjusts his weight to hobble on his good foot.

"Your way would've failed," he says. We follow Veera down the hall. "We need the revolt to cover our tracks. While they're busy getting things under control, they won't notice one ship taking off. If you'd done it as a lone getaway, you would've been caught in an instant."

"Thought the whole thing through, did you?"

He smirks. "Always."

"Well, did you think about the authorized takeoffs? Twice a week they have two crews go out to mine nearby asteroids for resources. We could've bought our way onto one of those."

"Okay, smart-ass, then what? When they discover we're gone, they'll immediately call in those mining ships."

"I hadn't worked that part of the plan out yet. The point is, there are other ways of doing things."

"Neither plan would've worked." Veera pipes up from up ahead. "You think you're the first people who wanted to escape? They search all vessels leaving, which means a security officer goes through the entire ship before it departs. Then it's scanned as it's leaving. If you had found a way to avoid the officer, the device we implanted when you arrived would've sent an electromagnetic pulse to your brain as soon as you passed that scan point, killing you instantly." That point shuts us both up. Both our plans were obviously flawed.

Veera stops in front of a door with their medical symbol painted on the front. She enters a code, and the doors slide open. "This is the top-ranked Varbaja medical bay. It should be empty now. In a few hours that might change."

The place is large and white, with minimal equipment. I don't see any medical staff, but most would've evacuated after that first blast.

The first assault came an hour before everyone's alarm. The

perfect time to cause the most confusion. Someone rigged an oven in one of the mess kitchens to explode. It was right below the crew bunks. Everyone heard it. I'm sure many thought it was an attack, something long awaited by many, especially the breen. But it became clear soon that the assault came from inside.

My first thought was that Ash had come with the *Persephone*—irrational, I know. Then the shouts started up. Soldiers banging on the doors of our bunks ordering us up and out to fight for the new regime. In that moment it hit home that she wasn't coming for me. Ever. I hadn't even realized I'd been holding on to the hope that she would rescue me. The second my boots hit the ground, Sarka grabbed my arm and steered me in the opposite direction.

We find a lone doctor hidden in one of the far labs. He must be Veera's contact because he doesn't balk at helping Sarka. I'm awed by their facilities. As much as humans have progressed in the medical field in the last couple of centuries, we haven't come as far as some might have thought. When you break a limb it's still excruciating, it still takes weeks to heal, and the best you can do is set it right and stay off it as much as possible. The illya have better medical knowledge than we do.

He instructs Sarka to sit on one of the medical beds and lie down. He squints up at the ceiling. Everything is so white it's hard to stare at anything without shielding your eyes.

"How did you know?" I ask Veera.

She hops up onto one of the beds adjacent to Sarka and sits. "Know what?"

"The other day, you asked me if it was worth it."

She taps her head. "I'm an aju. We know things."

I jump up on the bed and sit beside her. "Know things?" This sounds far-fetched. I read in books about people claiming to read another's mind, but I don't think that's possible. Our thoughts are a mess of electrical pulses transmitted via neurons.

She tilts her head toward the ceiling. "We know things about people. Sometimes they don't even know it about themselves. Take you, for instance." She studies me with her dark-purple eyes. "Most of you isn't here. You live for another. And you will do everything you can to get back to this person."

"But how did you know all this would happen?"

She laughs. "We can't predict the future. But I saw an opportunity."

She spreads her arms. "The aju are very good at seizing moments. We listen to the signs. The unrest on this ship has been building for years, and then you come along with your need to escape and your ignorance of the Varbaja. No one escapes the *Avokaado*, but you didn't know that, and that element led to this moment." She slaps my knee. "You and this man were the only ones who could've started this revolution, only because you didn't know it couldn't be done."

Sarka grunts from the table. "That's stupid. You just have to decide to do something, then do it."

"But don't you see? The Varbaja don't think like that. That thought would be chaos to them."

"All done," the doctor says. We all stare at Sarka's leg. It looks exactly the same as it was before. I didn't even see what the doctor did.

Sarka lifts his leg a little and bends his knee. He grips his thigh with his hands and squeezes. "What did you do?"

The doctor frowns. He's umquashi like Farge, Tup's friend. His skin is dark and he has long white hair. "I treated you. That's what you wanted, wasn't it?"

"Already?" I ask.

Sarka sits up and tests his leg, putting a little weight on it, then more, until he's hopping up and down on it. "Well, holy shit. It's fixed."

The doctor grabs Sarka's arm. "Go easy. I've repaired the bone, but the bonds will be weak for a few days. Try not to overdo it."

I roll my eyes. Good luck with that.

"How did you do it?" Sarka asks.

Again the doctor looks confused. "How did I do what?"

"Fix it so it wasn't broken anymore."

In that second I discover an expression universal to all species—disdain. The doctor glances from Sarka to me. "If I have to explain it, you won't understand it."

Veera slips off the table. "Thank you, Doctor." She asks Sarka, "Would you like to stay here to rest for a bit? The doctor can find you a bed."

"Why would I want to rest? My leg's better."

"Our forces have taken the bridge. I need to be there to oversee the end result." She beckons us to follow. For better or worse, we're in it now. Veera has claimed us. I have no idea if this development is good or bad.

CHAPTER SEVENTEEN

Ash

Jordan is alive. It's the only thought I can make sense of at this moment. Everything else is white noise. She's dressed in a strange uniform, and even from this distance, the pain and anger in her eyes are unmistakable. It takes Yakovich nudging me to break my stupor.

"How did she get on that ship?" she asks.

I have no idea, but her presence fills me with dread. Everything Kalve has said about the Varbaja is a nightmare. She may be alive, but that doesn't mean she'll be alive for very long. Sarka steps into view. He's wearing the same uniform as Jordan. Did they get recruited? Kalve mentioned something about the *Avokaado* recruiting people. Do they brainwash them too? Why would she be on the bridge standing there like she's part of the crew?

I step toward Wells. Kalve is speaking to the tiny representative on the other ship, but I'm too absorbed in Jordan to understand what's going on. If Jordan's on that ship, we need to rescue her. I tap Wells's arm as she turns toward me.

"What is Kellow doing there?" she whispers.

"I don't know." I keep my voice low as well. "They must have picked up the escape pod. We need to get her back."

"I don't think now is the time to worry about that." She bites her lip and looks up at Kalve, clearly sorry for ever coming aboard. I don't blame her. She's been thrust into the middle of someone else's problem. We all have.

The commscreen goes dead. I turn to Kalve, whose face is stone. "What's going on?"

His jaw tightens. "They want to talk peace."

"But you don't believe them."

He shakes his head. "No. This isn't the first time they've spoken of ending our conflict. Every few decades there's a revolt. They talk of peace, but it's only a trap. I'm not falling for it this time. When they come we will be ready."

And while they're fighting it out, we'll be stuck in the middle. Yakovich and I share a look. She's thinking the same thing. We need to get the *Persephone* ready to depart as soon as possible.

"What's going on? Who were those people, and why was Captain Kellow on board?" Wells asks.

"Captain Kellow?" Kalve asks.

"Our missing captain. She was on their bridge," I say.

He shrugs. "It's unlucky then. You will find it very hard to get her back."

I stop him with a hand on his arm. "No. We need to get her back."

With compassion in his eyes he says, "It can't be done. No one leaves that ship unless they're already dead. You're better off helping us so that she dies quickly." He walks off, leaving me stunned.

Since Jordan vanished in that escape pod, I've never thought she was dead. Some part of me always knew I'd see her again, that we'd get her back somehow. The way he casually drops her death on me, like it would be the better option, paralyzes me. I cannot leave it at that. We need to rescue her. And the only way to do that is to get Hartley well again.

Almost as an afterthought, I remember Captain Wells, who is still standing in the middle of the bridge looking shocked. I tug her arm, motioning for her to join Yakovich and me as we leave the bridge.

In the lift Wells is still enthralled by the ship. She peers up at the ceiling, which is transparent, allowing us to see where we've come from. "So how exactly did you find yourselves aligned with these people?" The way she says "these people" makes them sound despicable.

I don't want to recount how, under my command, I managed to strand the *Persephone*. As Hartley pointed out earlier, we're lucky we got rescued. I don't find it lucky. The fact that we had to be rescued in the first place is the issue. Given the circumstances, Jordan wouldn't have had the same outcome. I also have to remember that, technically, Wells isn't my commanding officer. In one sense, as a captain, she outranks me, but she isn't Union fleet, which means she has no real authority over me.

"It's a long story."

"I have the time to hear it."

The lift stops on the medical deck. "We need to get Jordan off that ship before these people blow each other up and us along with them." I'm already halfway through the medical center before I realize I've called her by her first name. My face flames red. I bite off my next sentence before I dig a bigger hole for myself.

I find Dr. Prashad in one of the labs perusing Hartley's blood work.

"If we need to get Captain Kellow off that ship, why are we in the medical center?" Wells asks.

"Because the man who can help us do that is here. This is our doctor. Dr. Prashad, this is Captain Wells from the *Posterus*." I realize as I introduce the two I have no idea what her first name is. You'd think I should. After all, during most of our travels we'd be attached to the *Posterus*. Only in extreme cases were we ever to disconnect from the main ship. Maybe her name is something else I've forgotten.

"This is the man who will help us rescue your captain? A doctor?" She examines Dr. Prashad with the same scrutiny she seems to give everything.

"You've found the captain?" he asks.

I nod, trying not to grin. Jordan's alive, and even though she's in the worst possible place, I can't help but find pure joy in the fact that she's living.

"And no," he says to Wells. "I'm not the person to be rescuing anyone."

"How is he?" I ask.

"As far as I can tell he should be fine. Nothing indicates illness in any way." He motions for us to follow him through the other side of the lab into a dimmer area of the med center. Hartley is lying prone on a bed in the far corner. Empty beds line the walls and fill several examination stations in the middle of the room. We have the place to ourselves.

"He looks dead." Yakovich takes a spot at the head of his bed and pokes him. "Feels dead too." She frowns. "He's not, right?" He does look dead. His skin is gray, and he's so still he doesn't even look like he's breathing.

"I've examined everything, done every test I can think of, but I can't find anything wrong with him. Besides the fact that he won't wake up."

Wells circles to the other side of the bed.

"What about a diagnostic cube?"

"I don't see what that would tell us that a test wouldn't. I don't suspect any internal injuries, and he certainly doesn't have a mind knot."

"A mind knot?" Well's eyes widen. "Why would you think he has a mind knot?"

I shake my head at Dr. Prashad. I don't want everyone knowing I have this intruder inside me. Even if the doc says it's dormant, people will still be prejudiced. The only people who have mind knots now are the Burrs, and I certainly don't want to be associated with them.

"It was just a thought. Because of Sarka." He looks at me, assessing, then sighs. "Well, I guess we could use a diagnostic cube. I've run out of all other options. It will take me a while to get Chloe over to the *Persephone* to get the necessary supplies."

"Actually, I'd like you to do the procedure over there. I'd like to be present as well," I say.

"But there's no life support. We'd have to suit up and ventilate Hartley. That's a lot of work."

"I know." I don't expand because I don't know Wells enough yet to trust her like I do the doctor and Yakovich. Something about this ship still bothers me. I've been trying to get off it since we boarded, and sometimes I feel like I'm the only one. But at times even I feel this pull to stay. The longer we stay, the stronger it gets.

The doctor gives me the benefit of the doubt and nods. "I'll ask Chloe to join us. She won't be happy about having to do this procedure in an enviro-suit."

"She'll deal." She always does. Chloe, the doctor's nurse, complains a lot, but she always gets things done in the end. I had to drag her into the jungle when we went to rescue the captain, but she handled herself fine.

I turn to Yakovich. "Can you find Foer? I want him to give me a progress report." Maybe they've been able to crack the encryption and gain access and we won't have to wait for Hartley to get better. But as I stare down at his prone form, a deeper worry creeps up. I'll feel better when he improves. Something's very scary about the way he's just lying there. His usually brilliant grin is slack, and those bright, playful eyes are hidden. It's not right. The *Persephone* needs her head engineer. It takes a couple of hours to set everything up. With Chloe complaining it feels longer. I had Yakovich take Wells with her. With a battle pending, the illya don't have the spare resources to return her to the *Posterus*. It's just as well. I'd rather have her here instead of at the mercy of Gladwell's bad advice.

We're in our med center. In fact, I think this is the exact exam table the doctor did my procedure on. I'm happy to be on the other end of it this time. Chloe's stripped Hartley to his boxers and attached a ventilator to his mouth and nose to make sure he gets air during the procedure.

The doctor picks up a scalpel to cut into Hartley's hip. "Confirming patient is unconscious." His eyes flick to mine for a brief second as if to say, "See, this is how it's supposed to be done." As painful as it was, I don't regret being awake for the procedure. I trust the doctor, very much, but something about giving up total control devastates me. At the time I was terrified he and Jordan would keep me in the dark for my own good. More than anything, I needed to know what was wrong with me.

"Confirmed," Chloe says.

As Dr. Prashad cuts into Hartley, I wonder what Jordan must have thought watching me. She was my only source of comfort during that whole experience, but she must have thought I was bat-shit crazy to refuse pain medication. Watching the doctor slice Hartley open and insert the diagnostic cube into his hip, even I can concede I was bat-shit crazy to let him do it without anesthesia. I feel like I should be holding Hartley's hand, even though he can't experience pain. I'm not really the hand-holding type, though.

His face is still slack under the ventilator. He hasn't moved since the procedure started. He's fine. I can't understand why I'm so nervous for him. But when the doctor pulls the suture out to stitch him up, I take an involuntary step back. Something deep in my gut just wedged itself in my throat. I can't believe I was awake for this procedure.

After the doctor finishes stitching him up, Chloe turns on the monitor to view the data the diagnostic cube is sending back. The doctor squints up at the screen, where a red sensor is beeping in the left corner.

"Well, that's interesting."

"What?" I circle the table to get a closer look. Not that I'll understand what I'm seeing.

The doctor shifts the screen and enlarges a section that shows a list of numbers running up the side. He brings up another slide with more numbers and mounts the two beside each other.

"What do those numbers mean?"

"The diagnostic cube passes blood through its sensors as it makes its way through the body. We can program it to look for certain things, but it does this automatically. So far we've found nothing wrong with Hartley. Everything we've tested for has come up negative. But this sensor," he taps the screen, "is indicating an anomalous reading. I pulled up an early medical record, and he definitely has something in his blood that shouldn't be there."

"Could that be causing the issue?"

"I won't know for certain until we do more tests, but it's definitely possible."

I know the doctor well enough to realize I won't get anything more out of him. "Keep me posted. I'll check back in later." I next stop to check in on Yakovich and Foer to see if they've made any progress. We need to get the *Persephone* back up and running now. I don't want to wait. Whatever happens with the illya and the Varbaja, I don't want the *Persephone* stuck in this ship. I'm sure their cause is worthy and the Varbaja deserve what they get, but we need to get our crew off or we'll get caught in the middle. We didn't come thousands of light-years from home to get blown to pieces.

Walking the empty, dark ship in my enviro-suit is creepy. With the engines silent and no one on board, it's like being on a ghost ship. On one of my first assignments, we responded to an emergency call from a mining ship. They'd been struck by an asteroid that had torn apart a good section of the hull. By the time we got there, the airlocks had failed and left nothing but an empty ship. The entire crew had been blown out the hole—all except the helmsmen, who we found wedged between his seat and the console. He'd had the good sense to get into an enviro-suit but had long since run out of air. I remember thinking what a horrible way to die. At least if he'd been sucked out the hull he would've died with the rest of the crew. Quickly. Instead, he had time to sit there at the helm thinking about how he would eventually run out of air and suffocate to death. That's an excruciating way to die.

As I'm about to enter the chute down to engineering, the ship lights blink on. I'm blinded for a moment as I orient myself. Then they begin to pulse red, and an alarm blares through the corridors.

CHAPTER EIGHTEEN

Jordan

When the view screen goes blank, I can still see the imprint of Ash. I'm stunned. What are she and Yakovich doing on the illya's ship? I've been busting my ass to get back to the *Persephone*, back to Ash, and now she's sided with the very enemy we're up against? I can't concentrate on any of the surrounding conversations. Only one thought absorbs me. What the fuck did Ash do with my ship?

Sarka nudges me, pulling me back from the brink of explosion. When I turn to him I'm seething, and for the first time my rage isn't directed toward him. I've been mad at Ash before. With some of the shit she's pulled, how could I not be? But I've always been able to see it from her point of view, realize she was trying to do what she felt was best for everyone. Even selflessly trying to commit suicide was, in her mind, the best for everyone. Sacrifice the one for the many. But I have no context. I have no information whatsoever, and that's gnawing at me.

"What?" I growl.

He points to the view screen. "Well, you don't have to worry about those bombs I set. Alison made it through just fine. All the pieces are there." As he says this, a dangerous thought enters my mind.

"Some of the crew may have made it out, but I don't see my fucking ship anywhere, do you?"

He pauses, and I can see him going through the thought process. "That's a good point. Huh. I really thought she'd figure them out. They were dead simple to disarm."

Before I can redirect all my anger at Sarka, where it belongs, Veera steps forward and pokes my leg to get my attention. "We're going to send over a delegation to their ship—"

"I want to be part of that," I say. I need to see Ash, and not just through a screen. I want to talk to her face-to-face and find out what happened.

"No, you don't." Veera's voice is flat and hard.

"Yes, I do."

"The soldiers we'll be sending over there will be on a suicide mission."

"What?"

"They'll be strapped with explosives. If we time our attack right, we'll destroy their command structure and take out their main cannons."

"Won't work." Sarka shakes his head. "You don't think they'll be ready? You've been at war for centuries. More than likely they're planning a similar strategy. Why else would they have agreed so easily?"

Veera turns all her attention to Sarka, gauging if he's worthy of her time. Before this she'd almost dismissed him as another thug, but now it seems she's sensed something more useful from him.

"I would listen to him." I hate to side with him, but if we're caught in the middle of this situation, I'd rather have the time to get my people out of the line of fire before they blow each other up. "He's been at war probably as long as you guys have been, and he's still alive."

Veera jumps up onto one of the consoles to even out the height difference. "What do you suggest?"

"We have people on their ship." He turns and points to me. "Captain Kellow's crew is over there. At least her first officer and head of security are. It's likely they've found themselves in a situation similar to ours. If we can get a message to them, we can have them sabotage the ship from the inside."

"How do you know they're not on the illya's side?"

"The captain here just needs to give the order, and her crew will follow. They'd follow her anywhere."

Veera paces back and forth along the console mumbling to herself. "It's an idea. It's definitely an idea. How do you propose we get in touch with them?"

Sarka taps his head. "I have a piece of technology in my head that can communicate with Captain Kellow's first officer. It's rudimentary, but we can get a simple message through that I believe she'll understand."

My vision actually goes white from blind rage. It's a visceral response to the concept that Sarka's connected like that to Ash. I'm jealous of that connection, as he knew I would be. He's taunting me with the idea that he'll be more intimate with Ash than I could ever be. He glances at me sideways, and that's all the proof I need. He's been waiting for this opportunity, biding his time until he could thrust his knife in.

And the worst part? I have no choice but to agree, to submit Ash to that invasion, because if we don't, the outcome is so much worse.

"Okay. This is a good plan. But we need to devise a message that will convey our sabotage strategy. The illya's ship will not be easy to undermine," Veera says.

"Get your engineer guy to help, Jordan. I'm sure he can destroy anything," Sarka says.

I say, "We don't even know if he's on their ship. We have proof that Ash and Yakovich are there, but what if they're being held prisoner?"

He places a hand on my arm, and I jerk away. "Do you really think Ash would leave the crew behind? If she's there, the rest of the crew are there."

"But once they do sabotage the ship, how do we get them off?"

"We'll have to leave that to them," says Veera, who's still up on the console conferring with one of the other aju. "We don't have the resources to help in that matter. Now, come with me." She jumps to the floor and beckons for us to follow her. Something about the tiny woman scares the shit out of me. But if she thinks I'm going to sit back and hope my crew has a way off that ship before all hell breaks loose, she's nuts.

Veera shuts Sarka and me in one of their classrooms with one of their engineers to brainstorm. We need to figure out how to configure Sarka's mind knot to talk to Ash—it's not as easy as he made it sound—but also what message to send.

The message has to be simple because we don't want to overload the mind knot on the first go. But it's hard to figure out how to send a simple message with a complex meaning. We want to give them the instructions for how to disable the ship, something Veera's engineer hasn't figured out how to do yet.

It's best to ignore Sarka. It's been a day since I saw Ash on the bridge of the illya's ship, and it's killing me not to know how she's doing or how she got on that ship.

"Isn't there some self-destruction timer you can get them to hit?" Sarka's squished into one of the chairs with his boots resting on top of the desk. "That would be an easy message to send. HIT. DESTRUCTION. BUTTON."

The engineer, Troer, ignores him, as he's ignored most of what Sarka says. So that makes two people now. And the more we ignore him, the more he talks. Troer is an umquashi with one long patch of flowing red hair right down the middle of his head. He must be a lot younger than the others I've seen, most of whom have very white hair. His eyes are black specks sitting in the middle of his face. His lips are also black, which makes his face look like a round white plate with three black beans sitting on it. He's had his head buried in a tablet since we arrived.

"What if we tell them to blast a hole in the side of the hull? That would decompress the ship, and in the chaos you guys could charge in and blow them up." When this suggestion is also met with silence, Sarka drops his boots onto the floor with a loud thunk. "What about taking another smaller ship and ramming it into the bridge of the ship? Or an engine?" He drums his fingers on the table. "What if—"

"Enough." I slam my palm on the table. "Leave if you're not going to be helpful."

"Me? I'm coming up with all the ideas. You guys are just sitting there like lumps of shit." He points to Troer. "And this guy, you're the one that's supposed to know the most about their ship, and you haven't said shit. What are you doing over there? Reading a novel? We're running out of time."

For the first time Troer lifts his head from his tablet. "I'm studying our historical database on the illya to find any mentions of their ship configurations. I've never seen an illya ship before, so forgive me if I'd like to enter this assignment with knowledge instead of guessing, like you're inclined to do."

"We need to find a solution that won't make the illya aware of our intentions." I turn to Sarka. "If it were up to you, we'd go in guns blazing. I have crew on there I don't want killed. We also need to find a solution that's a slow burn. Something that gives them time to escape."

"You can't have both, Jordan."

I ignore his comment. I can't worry about all the worst-case scenarios. For my own sanity I have to focus on what we can accomplish and trust that my crew can do the rest. Outside the classroom I hear a stampede of boots rush by. Things have calmed down for the most part. The revolt is over and there's a new regime. For the first time the aju are in charge—people who lead with their brains instead of their fists. Perhaps that will make a difference. Not that they'll stop fighting. We've already seen that the goal is the same, to destroy the illya.

"Have you come up with any ideas of how my crew can sabotage the illya's ship?" I ask Troer.

"Yes, but all require too much instruction. The trick is coming up with something simple that can be compressed enough to be sent through your friend's device."

I also ignore the friend comment. "How much space do we have to work with?"

"About a hundred gigs."

"That's it?"

"What did you expect? It's centuries-old technology. We're lucky we have it to use," Sarka says.

I leap to my feet and tower over him. "Lucky? Is that what I should be feeling?"

He stands, taking the challenge. "Don't start."

He's a foot taller, but I don't back down. "And don't pretend like you didn't have this planned in the back of your mind from the start." I jam a finger into his chest. The anger that's been building since he came aboard my ship escapes its cage, and its power makes me feel strong and, most importantly, right. "You love the fact that you can shove this situation in my face. You know, she won't even tell me what you did to her, because it's so bad she doesn't want to relive it. You treat people like they're objects. You use the ones who are useful until nothing's left and discard those who have no value." Sarka takes a step back, obviously unsure where this is all coming from. To be honest, I'm a little surprised myself. I rarely lose control like this. But now that I've started, I can't stop.

"I've seen you do it my whole life. You think you're this great leader, but people don't follow you. They're afraid of you. Mom hated you so much she chose death over staying with you." God, I want to hurt him. I want to hurt him like he hurt Ash, like he did Mom. But nothing I say will ever accomplish that. "You're nothing but a fucking bully and screw-up. God. This whole mess"—I slam my fist on the desk—"is your fault. We're stuck on this fucking ship because you had the bright idea to jettison an escape pod into fucking nowhere." I push him, but he doesn't budge. "Even worse, we're lost in this fucking solar system because of you. Because of your grand, stupid, fucking ideas. If you hadn't meddled. If you hadn't gotten involved—where you didn't belong, I might add—then none of this would be happening." I punctuate each of those last words with a slap to his torso. His face has turned to stone. I can't read him at all. "Get out of here. You're no use to us. We'll solve this without you."

"Jordan—"

"Out. You're not wanted."

He doesn't say anything as he turns to leave.

I'm still panting several minutes after he's gone. I'm on the verge of tears, but I'll be damned if I'm going to cry in front of Troer.

To Troer's credit, he hasn't reacted in the slightest. In fact, when I turn to look at him, he has his head down, engrossed in whatever he's reading on his tablet. For a split second I wonder if Sarka's right, and he is reading some novel instead of coming up with ideas for how we can sabotage the illya's ship.

I drop into the seat Sarka vacated to calm myself before getting back to work. I'm exhausted. I've expended more emotion in the last minute than I have in my entire life. At least it feels that way. Silence fills the room.

Then Troer lifts his head and says, "Do you think your crew could build a small bomb?" He points to something on his tablet, and when I stand I see it's a schematic of the illya's ship. "If they can place it here in this section, they'll be able to disrupt life support. If they take out the emergency life-support systems at the same time, the ship will descend into chaos."

"Yes. I have no doubt they can build a bomb." I'm sure Hartley could build a bomb out of air if you gave him enough time.

CHAPTER NINETEEN

Ash

I've almost reached engineering when I run straight into Yakovich. Our helmets clash, and the force knocks me down. Yakovich is all muscle. She pulls me up by my arm.

"Sorry, Lieutenant."

"What's wrong with the ship?"

"Foer and Gadzir were able to bypass the encryption, except something went wrong." I motion for her to continue as I steer us toward engineering. "Foer thinks it's a fail-safe Hartley installed in case Sarka was able to get into the system when you and the captain were on the planet."

"What exactly are the alarms signaling, and can they shut them down?"

"I didn't stick around long enough to find out. You'll have to ask Foer."

When we reach the doors to engineering, I stop her. "I need you to take charge of evacuating the ship. There aren't many people aboard. The doctor, Chloe, and Hartley are still in the med center, but beyond that I'm not sure. But double-check there aren't any others."

"What should I do about Wells?" she asks.

For a moment, I'd forgotten about her. "Where'd you leave her?"

"She's in engineering with Foer and Gadzir."

"Okay. Leave her with me. Go take care of the evacuation."

She nods and heads in the opposite direction. If this is a booby trap set up by Hartley, we're in serious trouble. Jordan was very adamant about not letting Sarka grab control of the *Persephone*. She gave

Hartley a sweeping mandate, and knowing Hartley, he would've taken that to the next level. He's most likely got this thing rigged to blow, which is overkill. I'd rather let Sarka take over the ship and stay alive than kill us all.

Foer and Gadzir have their heads bent together over a screen of code. Foer towers a few feet over the diminutive illya. Wells is on the other side of Gadzir, peering at a screen blinking red. She looks up when she sees me.

"What's going on?" I ask.

"Lieutenant, thank God." Foer seems relieved to see me. I don't know why. I'm one of the more useless people who could show up. "We tripped something, and I'm not sure what."

"How much time do we have, and what's going to happen when that time runs out?" I round the station to take a look at their screen. It's all in code that I can't read.

Foer shrugs. His hair is plastered to his head, even though his enviro-suit keeps the temperature in there a perfect twenty-one degrees. "He's rigged the computer to shut down, at the very least. But this is Hartley, so there's more to it than that. I doubt we're about to explode. But it's a very good thing we're all in enviro-suits just in case."

Wells takes a step back from the console like she's about to bolt.

I wrap my hand around her arm just in case. "Do we have a time frame?"

Again Foer shrugs. "No clue, Lieutenant."

"These alarms are from your own personnel? What kind of ship are you running here?"

I pull Wells to the side. "Captain, we don't have much time. Explaining will take longer than we have. I need you to either shut up or be helpful."

I'm not sure if she's about to protest or storm out or smack me. Her face goes through several shades of red before she nods and takes a step back, folding her hands in front of her.

I turn back to Foer. "Didn't Hartley share any of this with you?" Foer looks confused, like we're talking about someone else. I hold up a hand. "You're right. This is Hartley. What can we do? Can we at least shut off the alarms?"

Foer is beginning to look very uncomfortable with the amount of noes he's given me in the last few minutes. He looks behind him and back at me with an expression that, if possible, is even more apologetic. "Well, there is one thing we can try, but it's dangerous."

If it gets the ship up and running and shuts off these fucking alarms, I'll try anything. "What is it?"

"We can bypass the main system and run everything through the emergency circuits. It would only be temporary until we figured out what the real access codes are, and then we could reroute it back."

"That sounds like a good plan. Do that."

"There's no way you can do that with the system on lockdown. It won't take any of your commands," Gadzir says.

Foer gives me a look I know well. Tekada uses it every time he needs me to fix the filter lid in the storcell. "He's right. It can't be done from here. It has to be bypassed manually from in there." He points to the system core. "You have to reroute the circuits from the main board to the emergency system, and that should circumvent the lockdown."

The system core is a solid wall from floor to ceiling, making it fifteen meters high. I have no idea what's behind it and can only guess it's not easy to access or Foer wouldn't be this nervous. "And I assume you need me to do it."

"The access tunnel is meant for engine bots. It'll barely fit you, and that's without your suit."

I look at Gadzir, the smallest of all three. While he's definitely shorter than both me and Foer, his shoulders are much wider than mine. And to be honest, I don't trust anyone but my crew crawling around in one of the most important parts of the *Persephone*. "Wait. Without my suit? How am I going to breathe?"

"Life support is back up and running. That's not actually the problem. The temperature in there is going to get hot. We have vents, but they're probably shut, and I won't be able to cool the tunnel without access to the system."

"How hot?"

"But if we move quickly it might not be so bad."

"Foer?"

"We should have the doctor on standby, though."

I put my hands on my hips and give him my best hard-ass stare.

"Fifty? Fifty-five?" he says. "And it'll get hotter the longer you're in there." He turns away as he says the last bit.

I unhook my helmet and remove it. "Tell me what I have to do."

When I take that first breath the air is stale but breathable. I strip the rest of my suit off as Foer explains my assignment. I only half listen, the rest of my mind focusing on getting my suit off as fast as I can. Speed is going to be my savior. The longer I sit around and debate whether this is a good idea, the hotter that tunnel is growing.

"I think you should wait for the doctor, Lieutenant."

"We don't have time. He's still busy with Hartley. Inform him, but I'm going in now."

We don't have any comms working, so we're just going to have to do it the old-fashioned way, yelling back and forth. Foer unhooks the hatch and sets it aside. He sticks his arm in, testing the air. The opening is tiny, leaving a few centimeters on either side of my shoulders if I'm lucky. I'm not claustrophobic, but I have no idea how the heat will affect me. It's not like we have a choice. We need the computer back online before whatever Hartley has planned happens.

"Wish me luck," I say.

Wells steps forward. "You're not going in there, are you? What happens when you don't come out? Who will be left in command?"

When I don't come out? Nice confidence booster. "If I don't go in there right now, it won't matter who's in command because we'll all be dead." I grab the sides of the tunnel. It's awkward getting in because I don't have much room to squeeze my upper body into the opening. For a few scary moments my arms get pinned at my sides and I'm worried I'm already stuck. I wiggle my shoulders from side to side until my arms come free. By the time I make it all the way into the tunnel, the heat is clogging my throat, making it hard to breathe. I'm blasted by the hot breath of the core. It's worse than being on the planet under the hot sun. There's no breeze or humidity, only the constant heat.

It's a slog to get through. I haven't made it very far, maybe a meter, and sweat is pouring down my face, pooling under my arms and between my breasts. Foer shouts something at me. It's muffled, but I don't need to hear him to know he's telling me to move my ass. It takes a few more moments to perfect my technique. Using my arms to pull and my feet to push gets me going a little faster.

After a few meters the tunnel is completely dark. My body blocks any light from behind, and there's no light up ahead. Shit. How am I going to see what I'm doing without any light? Panic grips me, and I have to stop and take a few deep breaths and refocus. I can't do anything about the lack of light in the middle of the tunnel, and the sooner I make it through, the easier it will be to think. It's so dark in here it doesn't make any difference if I close my eyes or not.

It's getting harder to breathe too. The heat seeps from the tunnel, through my uniform, cocooning my body. The walls of the tunnel are made to withstand this heat, but I'm not. It's not burning my skin. Yet.

I feel like I've been crawling for an hour and start to freak out. What if there's no end to this tunnel and I keep crawling until I boil to death? Instead of letting the panic in, I concentrate on pulling myself forward inch by agonizing inch. How do I get myself into these situations? By agreeing to do crazy things.

As I'm having this profound realization, my hand hits open air. I've made it. I still can't see anything because the entire space is dark. You would think there would be indicator lights, even if they were faint. It's like I've crawled into the belly of a giant beast, like Jonah and the whale. It's a silly story when you stop to think about it. But as a child I believed you could live inside a whale for months. In all my dreams I never pictured it this dark or humid. My uniform is molded to me with my own sweat, my hair is plastered to my head, and I feel a hundred pounds heavier.

I search for a handhold to hoist myself out of the tunnel. In the dark it's impossible. We didn't think this through. This space is meant for engine bots equipped with their own lights. I manage to scramble down into the hold. As soon as my feet touch the floor, the whole place lights up in an ambient blue.

"Yes." I pump my fist. "I'm through," I call down the tunnel. My voice echoes in the chamber.

From this end I can barely make out a far-off light. I hope they can hear me because I don't remember Foer's instructions. I'm supposed to replace the main system cables with the emergency system's cables. I see literally thousands of cables, and none of them are labeled.

"Which cables do I switch?" I yell as loud as I can.

After a moment or two I hear, "Two panels to the right of where you entered is the main-system configuration." A few seconds pass and then, "Switch those with the cables to the right of them. They're color coordinated. Make sure you switch color with color. And hurry."

He doesn't need to tell me that. I've already been in long enough that my head is starting to spin. Ten more minutes of this and I'll faint.

I turn to the panel with the main system cables and begin swapping. A new wave of heat smacks into me, and my vision blurs. I drop one of the cables, and it takes me a moment to grab hold and trace it back. My coordination isn't what it should be. I give myself one more minute before I have to leave whether I'm done or not.

That thought derails me. I look over at what I've done and forget which one is the main system and which is the backup. My brain won't focus. I lean into the tunnel and yell, "Which one's the main system panel?"

A few seconds later I hear, "Two panels to the right."

Two panels to the right. I repeat the words to myself as I slog back to where I was working and count two panels. That would mean three panels over is the backup system. Right?

Breathing is an effort. Every breath feels like I'm sucking in a furnace. I rest my head against the panel and take a moment to regroup, pushing the rising panic down deep. I need to do this. The *Persephone* needs this if we're going to get out of here and rescue Jordan.

My eyes snap open and I pick up where I left off. The last three cables are the hardest. I keep missing the opening for the cable. But I get it done. As soon as the last cable goes in, the alarms stop. They'd become background noise. Now, without them, the silence is ominous.

It's been a little over a minute, and I don't waste any time climbing into the tunnel again. "I'm on my way back," I shout. My voice isn't very loud. I don't have the energy for loud.

It's worse going back. My stamina is zapped, and it has to be hotter than fifty degrees. I feel like I'm trapped in hell. My world becomes the actions I need to perform to get out of this place. Pull forward with my arms, push with my feet.

The second I make out the light from engineering up ahead, the alarms begin again, and this time the ship lists, rolling to the right. I don't even bother trying to hold on because there's nothing to hold on to. But my stomach roils and I almost vomit on myself. And now I really start to panic. I do not want to end up dying in my own sick stuck in this tiny tunnel. I pull and push with everything I have.

In the end, I'm not sure how I get out of the tunnel. It's all a blur. But by the time I'm pulled out by Foer, the alarms have stopped and the ship has righted itself. When my vision clears I'm staring into the deep-brown eyes of Dr. Prashad. He wrinkles his brow in concern. And then Hartley's head pops into view.

"Ash, you look like shit. It's like the ship crapped you out of its asshole."

Foer groans and grimaces. "That's a mental picture I never wanted."

"Hartley, you're okay." My voice is raspy.

"And it's a good thing too. I don't know what you guys were trying to do, but you almost messed the ship up beyond repair."

"Nothing's beyond repair."

Hartley smacks Foer in the arm. "You didn't think I'd booby-trap the backup system as well?"

"We had to try something. Next time, share."

"He's right." I try to sit up, but Dr. Prashad pushes me down, still examining me. I let him. I feel like ass.

Later, after I'm checked out by the doctor and have given Hartley instructions to get only the essentials back up and running, I collapse on my bed. I'm drenched, but I don't want to move to take off my clothes. I doubt the showers are working yet. It's going to take engineering a while to test all the systems with the new computer. I have faith that it'll get done, but showers are low on the priority list.

My cabin is a mess. When the ship listed it scattered everything off my desk and shelves. From the comfort of my bed, I pick up a few tablets and place them on the desk. One I don't recognize is jammed in the back. I pick it up and turn it on. It's the last communique from my father. I haven't watched it yet. I didn't want to hear another lecture about how my choices reflect badly on the family, et cetera. As soon as the tablet turns on, the video autoplays. My father's head replaces the black screen. He looks angry and agitated. I'm about to turn it off when his first sentence stops me dead.

"Alison, you have to turn the *Persephone* around. You can't let the *Posterus* leave for its mission." I drop onto my bed. "The mission isn't what you think. The *Posterus* was never meant to be a generational ship but instead a payment. A species known as the illya have been poaching us for centuries. It's only since we've been on the Belt that the disappearances started to get noticed. Twenty years ago, the Commons took a vote and decided we would offer the illya a small selection of

· 159 ·

our species. They could take them and set up a colony somewhere. In return, they would leave and never return." He sighs and scratches his head. When he looks back at the camera, I see tears in his eyes. "I never meant for you to volunteer. If you don't turn the ship around, you'll die."

CHAPTER TWENTY

Jordan

I have to get off this ship. It's the first thought that enters my head as I wake in the morning. My head hits the ceiling of my coffin bunk, and I forget where I am for a second. The purple glow gets brighter every few moments until it's blinding. You have no choice but to escape and start your day.

We sleep in our uniforms, which at first I thought was disgusting, but the material is designed to clean you in your sleep. It's why I don't smell like armpit most days, even though I haven't showered since I arrived. I shrug my boots on and open my cubby hole. Everyone is streaming out of their bunks. There are a lot less people now. Some died in the revolt, although way less than you'd think. They don't want to waste bodies because that's not good for the war effort. Not that there is much of a war effort. This is the first time most of the soldiers—at least in my unit—have ever seen an illya ship.

"And what are we doing?" one of them asked at the mid-morning meal yesterday. "We're sitting around talking about it. Isn't this what we've been training for since we came on board?" I see a lot of nods but am glad we're not rushing into anything, and not because Ash and my crew are over there, but because rushing into conflict without strategizing first is asinine. I keep my mouth shut during mealtimes. By the sound of it, my opinions would not be welcome. Most of my unit is breen, and their only interests include fighting and arguing about fighting. It doesn't matter who they're fighting or arguing with.

Besides, Veera has a solid plan. I can't say I exactly agree with it because it puts my crew at risk, but at least we're not charging in with weapons loaded, asking questions later. I've washed my hands of it all. After my outburst with Sarka, I left Troer and Sarka to work out the details. My goal, and it grows stronger every second I'm on board, is to get the fuck off this ship. My only problem is how to do it.

This whole thing is going to play out one of three ways. The most optimistic is if Veera and Sarka's plan works and they cripple the illya's ship and the attack from our end is successful. The most probable is that my crew isn't able to sabotage the ship and the *Avokaado* attacks anyway and we suffer huge loses. And the third—which I really hope doesn't happen—is that everything goes tits up and we all get blown into space.

As I climb down the ladder to join the queues at breakfast, I've never been so sure of anything. I need to get off this ship. I can't wait for other people to decide what happens to me. I'll find a pilot to fly myself off this ship, find Ash, find my crew, and get us away from all this. We may have lost the *Persephone*, but we still have the *Posterus*. I'm not looking forward to losing face with Harrios. I'll never live down the fact that I lost the *Persephone*. He's not my boss, in fact we have the same rank, but he is our representative from Union fleet, and he'll judge. He's the type.

I pull a tray off the counter and begin slopping stuff onto a plate. I'm not paying attention to what I'm grabbing. I'm looking for Karm, one of the hea mang players. I know he can fly their scout ships. We'll still have to find a way to bypass the sensors, but I'm sure there's a way. They say no one escapes this ship, but I'm pissed off enough to prove them wrong. I spot Karm in the back. He's not with any of his friends, and for the first time he doesn't have that big grin on his face.

I sit down across from him. "Hey."

He brightens when he sees me. "Hi, Jordan. I see you came through the revolt on the right side."

I try to smile. Is there a right side to a revolt? It's all how you choose to look at it, I guess. Every side thinks they're right, and whether they are or not it doesn't matter. In the end the victor chooses how it's remembered. I'm not sure who said it, but history is written by the winners. The aju won this revolt, and now they'll choose how it's remembered until the next rebellion happens a decade from now. This is not my war. That's how I choose to look at it.

I look down at my plate, not recognizing a thing I've chosen, and

I've had enough bad experiences with the food here to just plow in. I pick through a few of the choices and settle on something that looks like bread. When I bite into it, the satisfying sponge feel on my tongue confirms I've chosen wisely.

I look around to make sure no one's listening in on our conversation. It's not much of an issue on this ship. By the time people make it to the mess they're too hungry to care. "I have a proposition for you."

Karm leans forward with an eager expression and catches his sleeve in something bright orange and slimy. "Will it bring me glory?"

"It might. No one's ever done it before. At least that's what they say."

He leans away and scans the nearby tables. When he speaks his voice is no longer friendly. "You're not still planning that, are you?"

"Of course I am. More than ever now. My crew is on the illya's ship. I have to rescue them, and I'll need a good pilot to help me."

He shakes his head and wipes the orange mess off his sleeve. "You'll have to find someone else for that kind of glory. I can't risk it."

I can't understand this sudden change. "A few days ago you were all in." In fact, after a few drinks from the bar, they were ready to take on the entire crew of the *Avokaado*.

"A few days ago I was low ranking and had nothing to lose. Now, I'm in charge of my squad, I've moved four bunks lower, and I have everything to lose." Of course he's right. I hadn't even thought about the other side to winning a revolt. New leaders arise, high on their need to prove they can do better than the last regime. Previous leaders are either killed or jailed or made an example of. I'm curious where our previous leaders are now.

"Congratulations," I say.

He huffs. "I'm not saying this to brag. I'm one of the lucky ones." He points to the empty spots on either side of him. "Bo and Meek didn't make it, which I guess works in my favor because Meek outranked me. My point is, things are different now. But that doesn't mean I'm not with you in here." He points to his head. I guess it's the same as saying you're with someone in spirit, which helps me not one fucking bit. "And I'll even point you in the right direction to prove it. If you're serious about leaving, really serious, the people you should be seeking are locked up on deck three. In the prisons."

Even if I didn't have a very good reason for getting the fuck off this ship, I'd be hard pressed to find a soldier that ranked lower than me. My bunk is several meters up. In fact, I'm at the top, which ranks me pretty fucking low. "I'm dead serious about leaving. But how do I get into the prison? They're not going to let just anyone in."

"True, but now's the best time to do it. Everything's chaos. No one's really sure who's in charge and who isn't. Go in with a lot of bravado, and I mean a lot, and tell the guards you're there looking for information about something. Tell them Veera sent you. But you gotta believe it, or else they'll throw you in there with the prisoners. Trust me, you don't want to end up in the prisons."

Later that day as I'm heading down to the prisons, I realize I didn't ask him how to get the prisoner out once I find someone dumb enough to pilot me off this ship. I'm still not allowed weapons. That's how low my rank is. And getting a weapon is out of the question. Each soldier gets their own weapons, which are programmed to be operated only by their owner. If I try to pick up someone else's, it'll zap me with a charge strong enough to kill. It's an effective deterrent. The only other place where you can find a weapon on this ship is in the armory, and that's guarded.

I wish Ash were here. She'd know what to do in this situation. In fact, I'm sure she'd have a weapon already. Of course there are other weapons to be had, and I don't mean makeshift ones. I know from Tup that the two knives all breen carry don't have a fail-safe to stop someone from picking up one that isn't theirs. I have no skills when it comes to picking pockets, but that doesn't mean I can't figure out a way to get one out of someone's bunk. They lock us in at night, but locks can be picked.

It takes me a few days to get everything in place, but I luck out in such an extreme way I don't mind the delay. The second day, as I'm coming down the ladder, one of the bunks I pass has its door open. Karm is sitting on his bunk. He puts a hand on my arm to stop me.

"If you're serious about your plan, you're going to need this." He looks around to make sure no one's paying us any mind. When he's confident we're unobserved, he gives me a mean-looking knife.

Without thinking, I stuff it into one of my cargo pockets. I nod a thanks and keep going. I don't even stop once I hit the floor. If you want to get away with something, the cockier you are, the better. I'm not sure where this pearl of wisdom came from. It's not like I've lived a life of crime or even mischief. The most you can say I'm guilty of is ambition. But I've never stepped over someone to get where I am today. I may have used information to my advantage. My position and success can be attributed to never giving up, even when I should have. Call it tenacity, enterprise, stubbornness—whatever it is, it's gotten me my own command at thirty-four. Not many captains can say that. Now I just have to take that drive and put it to a new use: getting the fuck off this ship.

The next part of the plan isn't going to be so easy. I've been observing the security guarding the prisoners. I haven't encountered their species yet. They're covered in a thick black hair that makes them look like they're walking around in stuffed uniforms. I can't see their eyes or much of their face because they too are covered by this black fur. And what they lack in height, they more than make up for in girth. They remind me of a picture of a gorilla I had in a book as a kid. "Harry the gorilla is enjoying his jungle lunch. When he's finished his banana he'll have another bunch." I know gorillas were actually dangerous. Not violent on their own, but if threatened they could kill a human in a heartbeat. Somehow the gorilla seemed happier and more approachable in my book, and nothing like these guys.

I'm running out of time. I need to make a decision and go for it. But I still haven't figured out how to get past the sensors. Karm assured me they're armed, now more than ever because there's more unrest after a revolt. That makes sense. Who knows how the new leaders will run things. For a ship that houses dozens of different species, they do well to work together, but prejudices still exist. The breen and the aju have never gotten along. Most of the soldiers in the prison right now are breen. That's a big hit on their armies, because I've heard most of the best fighters were breen. Of course, it was a breen who told me this, so I'm not sure if I can take their word for it.

The longer I'm on this ship, the more I'm learning about the intricate natures of the species. Some of them even evolved on the same planet together. I read once that if there had been an intelligent species—besides humans, and even that's debatable—to evolve on Earth they wouldn't resemble humans. I try to imagine what future travelers will make of Earth when they land. By now the cities will have begun to disintegrate. Without human involvement nature will begin to reclaim its territory. As more and more asteroids rich in minerals and water pummel Earth, the oceans will refill. The current desert-like conditions will recede, and more diverse and rich vegetation will take over. In a thousand years, what will be left to say we were there? In ten thousand?

For those species that evolved on the same planet, the same conditions have produced vastly different results. Take the guy who bunks below me, Calp. He's blue with large orange dots over most of his body. He says it's to help regulate heat from the sun. His species are from the same planet as the hairy gorillas guarding the prison. Apparently the hair pulls heat from the skin and also allows them to camouflage easily, because their hair resembles the grass on several continents.

Whereas humans may look very different from one another, we haven't melted into the pot quite yet, although, in the years we've been on the Belt, things have definitely homogenized. And I suspect it'll happen even more on the *Posterus*. There are only so many breeding options. And as those kids partner with each other and breed, humans will forget different skin colors once existed. If we had evolved to look similar, would we be here now: cast out from our planet because our violent nature couldn't bring us together long enough to save ourselves? Or would we have found something else to fight about?

When I wake up the next morning, I realize I've run out of time.

CHAPTER TWENTY-ONE

Ash

I've watched my father's communique a dozen times now. It doesn't get any better the more I watch it. And every time I do, the tighter my insides get until I'm wound together like a coolant coil. I've been pacing my cabin for over an hour now. The sweat on my uniform has long since dried and is stiff and uncomfortable, but I can't seem to do anything except pace. And while I pace, one thought keeps going through my mind.

There was no planet.

They never intended the *Posterus* to reach Kepler F980 because it never existed. The whole thing was some sort of payment.

I keep pacing because I can't not pace. This is huge. It took twenty years to build the *Posterus*. This mission has cost the Belt most of its resources, and everyone agreed it was worth all the effort because in the end it meant colonizing a new planet and saving the human species. But it was never about that. It was all a scam. The Commons knew the entire time that the 45,000 people on board would never reach any planet.

This explains why my father was so angry when he found out I'd been accepted on the mission. He knew then. He knew I had just signed up for a death mission. It's not like any of us thought we would reach the planet, but we knew our descendants would. It's an entirely different thing to know you get to live a full life, even if it is on a spaceship, than to know you're not going to live to see the next month.

My pacing has become erratic. It's not using up enough of my anger. I'm so furious I want to destroy things. My father had the gall to call my life choices into question when he betrayed his entire species.

Everyone back on the Belt is under the false impression that their loved ones on this mission will live long, happy lives and that their descendants will help colonize a new world and further our species in another system. These are lies the Commons told them. They betrayed everyone on the Belt, every single person who worked on the *Posterus*, who gave their lives for this project. For what? So we could all die? What sort of payment is 45,000 lives?

How many people beyond the Commons knew? My father didn't go into detail about how complicit the government was, but this would've come from the very top. From the leaders of the Union. They certainly wouldn't approve of a project with this magnitude without knowing the real mission. Or would they? Without knowing why they sent us, it's hard to speculate.

Did Sarka know? He was trying to blow up the *Posterus*'s engine. But not just the engine. He wanted the *Posterus* to explode as well. Why else make sure it made it on board? Was it to teach the Commons a lesson? Or is he really as insane as he sounds when he said leaving would destroy our species?

I can still picture the look in my father's eyes when I told him I was going. He stood there and lied to my face. If he was so angry with me, why did he choose to send me this communique when we still had time to turn around? Did he find his conscience?

I look at the tablet in my hand. Jordan gave it to me weeks ago, but I was too stubborn to watch it. I was sure I knew what it said. I could've prevented all this: all those deaths that have already occurred, not to mention the tens of thousands of deaths that will now likely happen.

It's all my fault.

I throw the tablet against the wall. A dull thud is followed by a cushioned fall onto the carpet. I search my shelves frantically for something that will break, something to ease the rage inside. I find the photo of my aunt and me at my graduation and send it flying toward the window. It gives a satisfying crack as it smacks into the thick glass and lands on the ledge. I grab more things, more of my treasures, and fling them against the window until I'm panting so hard I'm almost hyperventilating.

When I'm out of things to throw, I sink to the floor next to my bed. I lean my head back on the soft mattress and stare up at the ceiling.

I have so many questions I need answers to and have no idea who to ask. If Jordan were here she'd know what to do. If anything, though, I need someone to talk to. The people on board I trust the most are Hartley and Yakovich. Three brains should be able to come up with a solution.

As I exit my cabin, I run into the doctor. "Ash, why are you in such a hurry?" He puts a hand on my arm. I must look crazed. That's how I feel.

"I have some urgent matters to take care of."

"You'd be served well by changing into a clean uniform and showering first." Never one to sugarcoat things, he says, "You stink."

"Thanks. Did you come here just to let me know that, or can I help you with something else?"

"I wanted to make sure you were okay."

"You already asked me that." The doc wanted to pull me to the med center for further tests. I'm feeling decent, considering my world just imploded.

He steps into my quarters and pulls me with him. "It's best if we talk in private."

He leans against my desk and crosses his ankles, and I'm at ease immediately. If something was wrong, he wouldn't look so relaxed. "I wanted to check in on you and see how you're handling the medication."

"You mean you're checking to see if I'm still taking it."

He smiles and shakes his head. "We've already seen an improvement, so there's no doubt you've been taking it."

He's right. Before the medication, something as devastating as losing Jordan would've put me into a downward spiral. I would've moped for days, stayed in bed as long as I could without anyone noticing. But that hasn't happened. I feel lost without her, and I miss her like crazy, but it's not a demoralizing defeat. And I haven't had as many urges to work through the night on projects. "I've been getting regular sleep, which isn't normal, so something must be better."

"Good. Good. We're in the early stages of treating you. And I know it must be difficult with everything being as unstable as it is. Eventually we'll look at diet, and I want you to keep up with your exercise regime. Have you noticed any side effects? Nausea, dizziness, headaches?"

"I've been getting really bad headaches. Usually late at night right before bed."

"Okay. We'll look into that. It'll be easier once the *Persephone* is functioning like her old self again." He pats me on the arm again. "Ash, for the sake of everyone you pass in the hall, have a shower."

"I told Hartley to work on getting the essential systems up first."

"Showers are essential, trust me. I heard him tell Foer to get the communal showers working. So you'll have to go down to the track in order to clean up. But everyone will thank you for it."

I grab a clean uniform from my drawers, snag a towel, and head to the track. I haven't been able to enter the locker room since I was last here with Jordan. As I walk past the threshold and hang my towel on a hook, I swear I catch a faint hint of her perfume. Even though I know it's all in my imagination, the sweet scent of apricots floats by. I turn on the shower and let the hot water sluice down my back. I have a longing so fierce I feel it as an actual pain in my stomach. What I wouldn't give to go back to that moment in the showers. I'd have a chance to make it all different. I could've turned us around and stopped all this. We wouldn't be lost in this galaxy. Those sixteen crew members would still be alive.

The water heats my skin. I turn my face to the spray. Would I change everything, or would I leave some things the same? I can still see the heat in Jordan's eyes, feel her bruising lips on mine, her hands digging into my skin, claiming me. No. I'd never have the willpower to walk away from that. From her. And as much as it's caused us problems, I don't regret it. I'm not sure what will happen if we make it out of this situation—once we make it out. But we're out here now with no way back. Fuck the rules. The Union no longer controls us. We're on our own.

As I exit the showers, still drying my hair with a towel, I notice a shadowed figure standing by the window looking out into the expanse of the ship bay. It's Wells. She's leaning against the rail. When I approach I see she has the same look of awe I had on my face when I saw the illya's ship for the first time.

"It's strange, isn't it?" Her voice is soft, contemplative. "To think we'd built this grand ship, only to find it dwarfed by the first species we encounter." She turns around and smiles, but it's a sad smile. "I never believed we were special. I knew there must be life out here somewhere. But I guess I thought our achievements would set us apart. Silly to think that, isn't it?"

"I don't know. I'm sure every species is biased when it comes to their own accomplishments." And if what my father said is true, the illya have been spaceworthy for centuries. They've had time to perfect their technology. "It's almost like stepping into the future. I'm sure our ancestors would find the *Posterus* spectacular."

"Your father is Colonel Shreves, correct?"

I inwardly cringe. Not many people know I'm related to him, which suits me just fine. I don't want people thinking he had any influence over my career.

Before I have a chance to answer, she waves off my hesitation. "I'm only asking because I'm curious if you spoke to him before you left."

I shake my head. "He wasn't too happy with my choice to volunteer."

She nods but doesn't say anything, turning to look out at the ship bay again. After a few moments she asks, "Do you trust your crew, Lieutenant?"

The question puts me on alert. Her hands grip the rail, and I notice now that she's agitated about something. "I've not been on board long enough to get to know them all, but I have full confidence in them."

"Let's cut through the bullshit, shall we?" Her tone is steel. "Do you trust your crew?" She scans the track, making sure we're alone.

"Most of them, why?" I have a feeling she didn't just come on board to see the illya's ship. She knows something.

"But not all of them?"

"No. We had a series of incidents."

She nods again, pursing her lips. "A series of incidents. Sounds familiar. A few weeks ago we had an accident never fully explained to my satisfaction. While making repairs to the engine core, an explosion occurred. We lost three crew, including Amit, my head of engineering. I've been told the engine is unsalvageable."

My mouth falls open, not just because I can't believe it can't be repaired, but that with it gone, we truly are stuck in this solar system.

She holds up her hand. "When we have time we'll mourn our

loss. But how did the engine explode in the first place? I put Gladwell in charge of the investigation, but his report was severely lacking. So sparse on data I started my own investigation, and what I found was not what I expected."

I have a feeling I know what she's going to say next, and now I have to decide if I trust her. Standing next to Wells, watching the lights play across the ship bay, I realize I've been approaching this whole thing wrong. I took command so reluctantly that I forgot to trust myself, to trust my instincts. I've been so wrapped up in what Jordan would do, I forgot to ask what I would do. It must have taken a lot of guts for Wells to come on board not knowing if we could be trusted. For all she knows she could've been walking into the arms of the enemy, and all I've done the past couple of weeks is whine about how I never wanted to be in charge.

In that moment I decide to trust Wells. "Let me guess. You found out it wasn't an accident that we ended up in this galaxy."

She gazes up at me with shrewd eyes. "How much do you know?"

"I know the *Posterus* was never a generational ship. Our lives bought the Belt's freedom." If she was checking up on Gladwell, she must have discovered communications or files. Which means, "Gladwell was in on it."

She nods. "Yes. But he's not the only one. Someone on your ship was communicating with him for several weeks. I'm not sure who. The messages were encrypted. But they were given several mandates, one of which was to make sure nothing impeded our delivery to this galaxy. They were working as an agent for the Commons."

My blood runs cold. She might not know who, but I have a good idea.

Later, I'm outside Vasa's cabin, calming myself before I go in. He's had no interaction with any of the crew except Yakovich, who brings him his meals three times a day. I can't be sure he's the agent, but no one else is working against us the way Vasa has. Not to mention, he was the one who found the planet we landed on. It would be coincidental for him to accidentally find this planet that the illya have gone to a lot of trouble to hide. At the time he made it seem so reasonable—anomalous readings coming back from his probes. But what if he already had the coordinates and took us there? He was also the one who found the asteroids that pointed us in that direction. It's entirely possible that he orchestrated this whole thing.

I enter Vasa's cabin without knocking. Even if he isn't the agent, he still tried to kill me. He doesn't deserve my consideration. He's lying on his bed with his hands behind his head and his ankles crossed. He looks relaxed, at peace.

When I enter he sits up, clearly surprised to see me. I guess he would be. I haven't seen him since before I found out he was behind most of the harsher attacks. He's tried to kill me more than once. If our situations were reversed, I'd be surprised to see me too. Actually, I'd be a little afraid. But Vasa doesn't look frightened, only curious. And now I wonder if Gladwell gave him the order to kill me.

I take a seat from his desk and straddle it so I can cross my arms on the backrest. Vasa sits there watching me, his big brown eyes blinking expectantly. He's had a shower recently, but it still hasn't done anything about his pungent smell. It permeates the room. Hell, most of the time you can tell whether Vasa's been in a room twenty minutes after he's left.

"As I'm sure you've been informed, the Captain is MIA, which puts me in charge." He still doesn't look frightened. I have a feeling he will be by the time this is over. "I'm giving you two options. The first, you can cooperate and answer all our questions, and you'll be able to accompany us back to our own galaxy after we finish repairs to the *Persephone*." He doesn't blink. "Or option two. We leave you here with the illya before heading back." I watch him, watch his face as he weighs what I've said. I know the exact moment he hears what I've really said.

"Head back? You guys are trying to get back to the Milky Way? How? You don't even know where it is."

Gotcha. "Hartley found the wormhole. He thinks he can get us back to where we started. In fact, he's not convinced it's naturally occurring. I'm confident we'll be there within weeks." I place my chin on my folded arms and stare Vasa down. "So which is it going to be? Option one or option two?"

"You can't head back."

I shrug, enjoying myself. "Why not?"

"Because it's a suicide mission."

"Hartley doesn't think so. He thinks we'll—"

"Hartley's an idiot." Vasa jumps off the bed, but I'm up and out of my chair with a sonic blaster pointed at his chest before he can take a step closer.

"You don't have to decide right away. I can come back." I take a step toward the door.

"Wait." He holds his hands out for me to stop. "Wait. Not here."

"What?"

He points to the ceiling and then points to his ear, meaning they might be listening in on our conversation. That's a good point. We don't want to tip them off before we're ready to make our grand escape. I point for him to lead the way out. This is the perfect opportunity to relocate him to our brig on the *Persephone*. Hartley has a lot of our systems up and running. I told him to use all the crew he needs, even non-engineering personnel. I don't want him taxing himself. After all, we still don't know why he got sick. For that reason, I've asked him to share access codes with Foer and to set up my command codes so we never get locked out again.

Vasa tromps toward the door. I step back several feet to keep him from reaching around to grab my gun. It takes us a few minutes before we even make it to the *Persephone*, both of us silent. We're a few meters in the door before something loud and painful reverberates around in my brain. I drop to my knees and grip my head with both hands. My vision goes white before swamping me in darkness. I blink a few times, trying to get it back to normal. That's when I feel, or rather smell, Vasa slink up close. Instead of asking if I'm okay, he grabs the gun and takes off down the hall. The last thing I hear before I pass out is Sarka's voice.

CHAPTER TWENTY-TWO

Jordan

I'm standing in an alcove a few meters from the guard station on the prison deck. The same gorillas are standing guard. However, as horrible as it sounds, I couldn't tell you if they were the same gorillas or just the same species. Same dark fur, same dark scowl.

This morning Veera informed me that Sarka was able to contact Ash through her mind knot. That was all she said. They won't know if the message was successful until they detect an explosion on the illya's ship. But they're gearing up to enter into combat. I have no doubt Ash and Hartley will come through for us, so it's just a matter of time before my window to leave is gone. I certainly don't want to get caught on a pilot ship in the middle of a battle.

So I've sucked up my nerve, and I'm standing here finding the last of it to go up and demand the guards give me entry. I'm not even sure who I'm supposed to tell them I want to speak to. Karm didn't go into details about that, so it's up to me. More than ever I wish Ash were here. She's good at coming up with crazy-ass plans.

I've timed it so that it's fifteen minutes from shift change. I figure they'll be tired and ready to leave so will give me less hassle. Of course I'm basing this assumption on human nature, not theirs. Who knows? Maybe they prefer being on duty.

I suck it up and walk forward. No point in second-guessing myself now. What's the worst that could happen? They lock me up too? I put on my game face because being in these prisons would be pretty bad.

They notice me the second I walk around the corner. If possible, they loom harder. I stand up straighter, not that it'll do much. By the time I'm standing in front of them, they're no taller than my shoulders, but I'm still intimidated.

"I'm here to talk with Tup." It's the first name that comes to mind. I'm not even sure he's being held here. I haven't seen him in the mess since the revolt. For all I know, he could be dead.

"What for?" one of them asks. The question is low in his throat, creating a deep resonating sound that vibrates around the room.

"Veera wants to know if he has any information about a counter-revolt." They share a glance, a look that speaks volumes. I'm not aware of what's in those volumes so I wait, ready to take off if things don't go my way. One of them nods. The other one shuffles to the controls and unlocks the main doors.

I sag in relief. Thank fuck. I'm not sure if my nerves could handle a chase through this ship. Before I walk through the door, one grabs me and holds me back.

"Wait." He points to the keypad. "You need to sign in."

I smile as if I've done this a hundred times. "Of course." But when I walk over I have no idea what I'm supposed to do. I stand there like an idiot for several seconds before one of them grabs my wrist and waves the arm with the device they implanted over the pad. It flashes purple. I hope that's a good sign.

Inside, the doors shut, and the darkness of the corridor surrounds me. I hear shuffling and grumbles from the cells on either side. It doesn't look like there's any barrier, only a cell and open space. For a terrifying moment I wonder if I've walked into a trap. Is this how I die? It would take less than a second for any one of these people to kill me. They could even use their imaginations. Most species we've encountered on this ship outweigh humans by more than double, some triple. They have muscle strength we could only dream of. In fact, even in our early primate stages we probably didn't have that kind of strength. It's the kind where they could literally break you in two like you were a cornstalk.

The corridor must run the length of the ship. That's a lot of cells. We have one brig cell. The *Brimley* is a little bigger; they have two. And the *Posterus* has none, which makes a total of three jail cells for the entire human population in this galaxy. That doesn't seem like much, when you consider human nature. But every single person on this mission was handpicked. Their personalities were tested to make sure they'd fit in and get along with everyone.

Here they've built an army with people who, for the most part, are here against their will. That will obviously lead to conflict. Add a revolt in here or there, and I can see how they'd need this many cells to house prisoners, although I guess it depends on your definition of prisoner.

As I continue to walk down the corridor, I notice a shimmer across the doorways. There must be some sort of field like on the planet, blocking them from exiting their cells. I breathe a little easier, but not much. It's not complicated. They could hit one button and drop all these doors. Then what? Would these guys be on my side? I doubt it.

Now that I'm in here, I'm not sure what I'm looking for. Or rather, who. And when I do find someone who's willing to fly me out of here, how the fuck am I supposed to get them out of their cell and past the two gorillas?

The cells are spaced a meter apart and are only five by five inside. There's a cot and a place to do your business, but that's all. When you consider the size of my bunk, it might not be so bad to get locked up here. Less claustrophobic. Of course, you can't do anything but pace back and forth. In fact, that's what most of the inmates are doing. Only now, as I walk past, they stop to watch me—some with suspicion, some curiosity, and a few others with hostility. I haven't encountered a familiar face since I entered, and it occurs to me that if Tup is alive, maybe he'd help me. It beats dying in this place or waiting a decade for things to sway back to your side. I'd hate to be locked up for even a second.

"Who you looking for?" an older gentleman asks. He's sitting on his bed, stooped over. He's one of the only prisoners who hasn't come to the doorway to get a look at me.

"I'm looking for Tup." I step as close as I dare. Red light illuminates the cells from a single source above their beds. It doesn't give off much light, not enough to do anything like read, but enough to see your way around your cell.

"Breen." The man grunts. "They're being held much farther down."

I thank him and pick up my pace.

"What do you want him for?" another prisoner asks. This one is much younger. He's leaning against the wall looking out his door, his thick arms crossed over his massive chest.

If there weren't a shield blocking us, I wouldn't have the guts to say, "None of your business." I'm glad the protection is there. I don't want people thinking I'm getting Tup to snitch, and I definitely don't want them thinking I'm springing him. The large man in the cell grunts and turns away.

After a minute or two I near the end of the hall. "Has anyone seen Tup? I'm looking for Tup." I start peering into all the cells, hoping I'll be able to spot him in this dim light. Every few meters I ask the question again. I keep my voice low to match the near silence in this place.

Finally someone says, "End of the row."

I walk faster until I reach the last cell. Tup is curled up on his bed either sleeping or pretending to sleep because he's heard someone's looking for him.

"Tup, it's Jordan."

I guess he was faking because he sits up right away. "Jordan? What're you doing here? Thought you were someone working with Veera to get information out of me."

How would he know what I told the guards? It's too good a guess for me to believe he didn't know. I don't speak as he grunts and stands, stretching various limbs to get the kinks out. I hear a few pops.

He walks up to the door and whispers, "You're not working for Veera, are you?"

"Were you expecting me?"

"They're friends of mine. Told me to expect a visitor."

"If they're friends of yours, why are you locked up here?"

"I'm here till something better comes up, and since you're here, looks to me like something better showed up. So, human. What can I do for you?"

I grin because my luck just turned. "You know how to fly, right? I need you to help me steal a pilot ship and get out of here. We can give you asylum and drop you where you need after."

He thinks about my proposition for a moment, chewing something I can't see. "And if I want to keep the pilot ship and take off on my own?"

"It's yours."

"Then you got yourself a pilot for hire. Let's get out of here."

My exit from the prison was much easier than my entry. A lot less stressful. Tup hadn't been lying when he said he could leave anytime he wanted. He messaged the gorillas from an intercom system in his cell, and they released him immediately. It took a few moments for my brain to overcome the paranoia that this might be a trick. After a few seconds, my train of thought switches back to how the hell we can get past the shield without getting our asses fried. I ask Tup about it as we walk the last of the dark prison hall.

"She's lying. That's how they control people here. But it's not true."

"What if it is?" I ask.

"I grew up on this ship. I'd know if they had that sort of control over us." We reach the gorillas, and Tup waves to them. They, in turn, salute. I look back when we've walked a few meters. They're not even watching us. That was much easier than I thought it would be. I was expecting to be running for my life at this point in the process. I even stretched beforehand just in case. It's a little too easy, which has me worried again. Cameras are everywhere. Any second an alarm's going to sound.

"Stop your worrying. Everything's under control," Tup says.

That sentence is probably the worst sentence in the history of sentences. It makes me even more convinced Veera wasn't lying about the shield. "Couldn't they program something to interact with our implants?"

"Implants?" Tup stops us. The lifts are only a few feet away. One short ride and we're on the flight deck. "What implants?"

I show him my arm where they injected mine, right above the wrist on my left arm. "When I arrived, they put it in." You can't see it or feel it anymore. But I know it's there. I watched them put it in. I'm sure if I have one, everyone does.

He waves me off. "You may, but I sure don't."

"How do you know they didn't put it in when you were born?"

"My mom would've told me."

"What if she didn't know."

He taps my head. "You got some serious trust issues." He steps forward and motions me toward the lift. "You'll have to recall it. If I do, all sorts of alarms'll go off."

I fold my arms. "And why's that?" He has brawn, I'll give him that, but he seriously lacks brains.

Yet he looks at me like I'm the stupid one. "When I wave my hand over the pad to recall the lift, it'll alert the system I've escaped prison. I got all the access codes, but I can't use my palm to open anything."

"And what do you think it is about your hand the system reads?"

He waves his palm in front of my face. "My print."

"Really? This magical pad can, without a camera, recognize your palm among all the others?" He studies his palm. "What's more likely? That when you quickly wave your hand in front of this sensor it reads your very detailed print or that you have a device in your wrist that it reads when you're close?" He actually has to think about this for a second. I wave my hand, facing backward in front of the sensor. The door to the lift opens. I huff and drag him in. I hope he's a better pilot than a thinker.

We reach the flight deck, and a ball of dread settles in my stomach. We need a solution before we get onto one of the ships, or we're never going to make it out alive.

The deck stretches out before us, three stories high. Neat rows of pilot ships decorated in red and white and silver line either side. They look sleek and fast, and I can feel my escape slipping.

Tup walks to a console and begins pulling up documents. The place is empty, which surprises me. Shouldn't there be mechanics working on broken ships? Yet they haven't been to war in a decade, so the only things these ships are used for is small trading and mining missions.

"Over here. This one looks good. I checked its record. Wasn't serviced too long ago." Tup walks toward a ship halfway down the line.

I follow as quietly as possible. "Where is everyone?"

"Everyone who? The flight deck is automated. Robots do all the work."

"Isn't it monitored?"

He stops. "You're starting to sound like you don't want to go."

"Of course I want to go, but I also want to survive leaving." I wave my hand around the empty bay. "This is all too convenient for me."

"You don't like convenient? Trust me, as soon as we're out those doors," he points to two large doors at the end of the hall, "we'll have plenty of inconvenience. The *Avokaado* has at least five hundred cannons and twenty-seven missile launchers. We're going to have to dodge every one of those, not to mention the scrambled manned ships after about," he looks up at the ceiling, calculating, "three minutes, give or take a few seconds."

Christ. What did I just get myself in to?

"You still want to leave?"

"Of course she does. We both do."

I turn toward the booming voice. Sarka is strolling through the concourse, cocky as all get-out.

CHAPTER TWENTY-THREE

Ash

I wake up in a deserted corridor on the *Persephone*, my brain feeling like it's filled with water sloshing from side to side. I try not to move. The blaster is gone, along with Vasa. Shit.

Without wasting another moment on self-pity, I pull myself up the wall and scramble toward the airlock. He'll be heading back to the *Kudo* as fast as he can. The bastard's probably going to ask for asylum.

I get to a commstation and message Hartley to seal the airlocks. It won't stop Vasa for long, but at least it'll slow him down, hopefully with enough time to grab him. My next call is to Yakovich, who I hope is on board. When I reach her, I ask her to bring an extra blaster. Two against one is fairly good odds, although, with Yakovich, I'd be happy with just her on my side. She doesn't even need to be armed. I once saw her take out a corporal in a bar on Alpha with only her hands. He was a big guy too, and she just dropped him.

I have one stop to make before I meet up with Yakovich. I find the doctor in his office hidden behind several monitors full of data. He looks up when I enter and smiles.

"It's good to see you took my advice."

I look down at my clean, pressed uniform. "It beats running around looking like I don't bathe. Listen, I need to know if the trackers you implanted in the crew would still be transmitting."

He purses his lips. "Yes. It would be faint at this point, but you could still get an accurate reading."

"Good. Can you pull up the location for Vasa?"

He digs through the pile of tablets in front of him and zeroes in on the one he wants. "I thought he was locked up in a cabin on the illya's ship."

"He was, but I decided to move him to the *Persephone*."

"Alone?"

I look away. I don't need him getting on my case too. I was stupid, and Yakovich is going to have a fit over this. I was so focused on getting that information from Vasa that I let my guard down. He wouldn't have gotten away if I hadn't collapsed, which is another thing we're going to have to address once we find Vasa. What the hell was that? I heard Sarka, but after my brain short-circuited, I heard nothing. Yet now I have all this extra information in my brain, and I have no idea where it came from. This isn't the time to bring it up. First, I have to get Vasa back before he gets off the *Persephone*.

The doctor pulls up a schematic of the ship and hands me the tablet. "He's the violet dot." It's moving fast along a corridor on the deck above the airlock. I check the legend to see which color Yakovich is. Her orange dot is standing stationary in front of the airlock. Did I tell her Vasa's armed? Shit. I can't remember.

I throw a thank you at the doctor as I rush out of the med center. If I cut through the forward service passage, I might be able to get to Yakovich before Vasa does. He must have taken a roundabout way to reach the airlock.

I scramble down the corridor clutching the tablet and stop at the service hatch. It's cramped and painful to climb through, but the passage cuts through half the ship. I tuck the tablet into one of my cargo pockets and duck inside, then crawl as fast as I can. Every few meters I hit my head or catch my knee on the rough grate. When I come to the other side it's with a few scraps and bruises, but quicker than expected. I open the hatch and slip out. I'm two decks above Yakovich. Now I just have to hurry down the chute and hope I get there before Vasa gets the jump on her.

When I make it to the chute, somebody's already climbing down. It's Vasa. The blaster isn't in his hand, but I can see it stuffed in his uniform cargo pocket. I hesitate for only a second before grabbing the sides of the ladder and sliding down. The bars whiz by, and when I slam into Vasa, he flies backward and we crash to the floor with a loud thud. All the air flies out of my lungs, and I lie there stunned for several seconds.

Yakovich hobbles around the corner. She's wearing a small brace on her knee joint. "Holy shit, Ash. Where the hell did you come from?"

I point up.

She hauls me off Vasa, who's out cold.

"A bit much, don't you think? It's only Vasa."

"He's armed." I poke around until I find the pocket with the blaster in it.

Yakovich grabs it from me. "How'd he get this?"

"It's a long story."

"He got this from you, didn't he?"

I grab one of Vasa's arm. "Help me drag him to the brig. You can lecture me about moving a prisoner on my own along the way."

"It is against regulations." She grabs his other arm. "You see why, right? What if he'd killed you?"

"I only had a sonic blaster. The best he could do is put me out."

"And while you're incapacitated he could stab you with a knife or shoot you with a gun. That would kill you. This is someone who's already admitted to trying to kill you at least twice before."

I knew this was coming. I can tell myself all this, but for some reason when someone else points out your shortcomings they sound so much worse. The way she's going on, you'd think I was a first-year aviator, not the first officer and acting captain.

"Okay. I get it. I screwed up. I wasn't expecting to pass out, which is how he got the gun from me," I say.

Yakovich looks over at me with concern. "Why'd you pass out?"

"I'm not sure. I needed to deal with this first. After the doctor checks Vasa over to make sure I haven't broken anything important, I'll have him look at me."

Yakovich stops. "That's a good point. Maybe we shouldn't be moving him anywhere. What if you broke his neck and we're making it worse?"

"Then he's shit out of luck. We don't stop until he's in the brig." That's all the convincing Yakovich needs. I think she took it personally that he slipped by her notice. She has a lot of pride that way.

We continue to drag Vasa down the hall. His body makes a strange swooshing sound as it glides over the metal floor. After a few moments of silence, Yakovich asks, "Where do you think he was heading? Back to the *Kudo*? Why?"

I have a choice now. I can fill Yakovich in. I'll eventually have to tell people what I discovered. Or I can hold on to it a bit longer until I finish questioning Vasa. At this point, Yakovich is already involved. I decide it's best to tell her.

"I think I know why he was heading to the *Kudo*. My father sent me a communique with some…" I slow a little. This is the part that won't be easy for people to take: the fact that I had this knowledge in my hands when it would've mattered and I did nothing because of my own stubbornness. "Some information about our mission."

We stop at the chute.

"How are we going to get him down?" she asks. "There's no way I'm carrying him."

"We'll have to put him in an empty cabin until he wakes up and can get himself to the brig." Shit. I want Vasa locked up. The idea of him free for even a few minutes makes me uneasy. What if he gets the jump on us again and escapes before we find out if he's an agent for the Commons?

I point to a door a couple of meters farther. We dump him on the bed, and I call the doctor to the empty quarters.

"You were saying about getting a message from your father?"

I sigh. "Yes. I set it aside and forgot about it." Not an actual lie. I'm only omitting the fact that I'd already decided not to watch it. "According to him, the *Posterus* was never meant to be a generational ship. We were all some sort of payment to save the rest of the Belt. Captain Wells discovered the same thing. Not only that, there's a possible agent on board this ship who's been communicating through encrypted messages with Gladwell."

Yakovich looks down at Vasa with horror in her eyes. She doesn't need to ask the question. I nod. "I'm not one hundred percent sure. That's why I wanted to question him. And not on the *Kudo*, in case they were listening. They might have something to do with why we're in this galaxy. I don't think it was an accident. Nor was it an accident that we found that planet. Vasa set this all up."

"Why? What possible incentive could he have for screwing us over?"

I shrug. This is why I want to talk to Vasa. I need to know for myself how he could do this to us. I don't know him that well. I mean, none of us knows anyone that well when you think about it.

The doctor enters carrying a med kit. "What happened?" He doesn't spare a glance toward Yakovich and me. Vasa looks fine, lying on the bed like he's passed out from too much fun.

"I slammed into him on the chute ladder."

Dr. Prashad stops what he's doing and spares me a hard look. "And that was necessary?"

"Yes," Yakovich and I say in unison.

He leaves it at that and continues to check his pulse and feel along his limbs for broken bones. "You're lucky. It doesn't appear that he's seriously injured."

"Can you wake him up?" I ask. "I want to move him to the brig."

"You can't wait until he revives on his own?"

"There's a bed in the brig. It's mildly comfortable." I should know. I spent a day there a few weeks after I signed on. Part of my adventure with mind knots and memory loss. I still can't remember anything from that missing time span, and that's the scariest thing I've ever had to deal with.

"I don't recommend waking him up, but I can."

"We're short on time. We need to ask him some questions."

"I can't promise he'll be coherent." The doctor takes a syringe out of his med kit and rolls up Vasa's sleeve. "It'll take a few minutes for it to take effect." He sticks the needle in his arm, and I look away. I wouldn't call myself a squeamish person, but I hate watching that stuff. "I'll stay until he wakes. I want to do more thorough tests later to make sure he doesn't have brain damage or swelling."

With all of us standing around Vasa's prone figure, I feel like I'm at a wake. Only I'm not about to say something nice over the body. Part of me thinks he deserves death. I read that they used to kill people as punishment. They'd hang people by their necks and drop the floor out from under them. If you were the person swinging on the noose, you hoped your neck broke. It definitely wasn't the most gruesome method they used for capital punishment, but I always thought how frightening it must be to have to wait for someone to pull a lever with the only thing going through your mind the hope your neck would break.

Vasa groans. Yakovich draws her gun.

"Is that necessary?" the doctor asks.

"Yes," Yakovich and I say at the same time, again.

Dr. Prashad shakes his head and packs his supplies. When he's gone Yakovich asks, "Do you want to ask him questions here or wait until we've made it to the brig?"

I want him in the brig as soon as possible, but I also don't want to risk missing out hearing what he has to say. What if something else goes wrong? "We'll ask him as soon as he wakes up. Then we'll move him to the brig."

Vasa groans again and opens his eyes. He touches his head. He has a goose egg forming above his eye.

"Hey." Yakovich waves her blaster to get his attention. "You awake?"

"What the hell happened? My head feels like it's twice its normal size."

"You had an accident on the chute. Now, before we were interrupted, you were going to tell me what the hell we're doing here in this galaxy and what your part was in it," I say.

He looks at Yakovich, her gun, and then over at me. He tries to sit up, evidently thinks better of it, then lies down again. "You won't leave me behind?"

I try to make eyes at Yakovich to play along. I forgot to fill her in on that point. She picks up the thread perfectly. "Depends on what you tell us."

I purse my lips to keep from smiling. "Why don't you start from the beginning. What was your mission?"

Vasa licks his lips and stares up at the ceiling. He digs his thumb nail into his palm. "When they approached me, they said it was a special mission and that the future of our species depended on me. But as they explained it to me, I realized—I said no at first. I did. I swear."

Yakovich waves her gun at him. "She didn't ask for your justifications and excuses. Give us the facts."

He pushes himself into a seated position to get a better look at us. "This wasn't how it was supposed to go. There wasn't supposed to be an explosion. They said it was going to be—"

"The facts." Yakovich kicks the bed. "What was the mission?"

"The 45,000 chosen for this mission were tribute to the illya. To stop them from taking any more from the Belt."

CHAPTER TWENTY-FOUR

Jordan

"You are not coming with us," I say. Sarka laughs, which only infuriates me more. "If you come back with us, you'll be tried and imprisoned. Why would you want that?"

"I don't plan to stay around for all that. Tup here has a ship. I'll go with him."

"I doubt Tup wants you with him."

We're squared off against each other. He towers over me, but I hold my ground, hands on hips, jaw thrust out.

Tup waves an arm between us. "As fun as your petty squabbles are, we have to get off this ship before we're discovered. I said the place was automated, but it's not unpopulated. We need to go."

I turn to Tup and point to Sarka. "Tell him he can't come."

"I can get us through the shield."

Tup nods and heads off toward our ship. "He's coming."

Fuck.

He stops in front of a silver ship with white stripes along each side. It's not much bigger than one of the *Persephone*'s escape pods. Tup opens a rear hatch and fiddles around with the controls until the side door snaps and hisses open. If it looks tiny on the outside, it's even more cramped on the inside. There are four seats, two up front and four in the rear—no room for cargo or anything else.

Tup climbs into the ship with no problem. It's obvious these were built for someone with his stature. We'll be lucky if we can all fit in here. Before Sarka can enter, I grab his arm, stopping him. "Tell us how to get past the shield first."

"Let's take our seats and order drinks first, huh?"

I swear he tries to be difficult on purpose. "I don't think you actually know how."

"If that's the case, then we're all going to die, so wouldn't you rather I come? That way you can be sure I'll die a painful death."

"Cut the shit."

"Get in, if you're coming," Tup calls. "We gotta go. Any minute now they're going to discover we're here, and that's when things get a whole lot harder."

Sarka smirks at me as he pushes past. He squeezes into a seat in back and buckles in. He tilts his head to the side, unable to clear the ceiling of the ship. I buckle in next to Tup and turn around in my seat. "So how do we get out of the shield without dying?"

He points to his wrist. "We cut out our trackers. That's how they're able to send a pulse through our system that kills us."

"You're shitting me." I look down at my wrist and wonder why I didn't think of that.

He smiles and shakes his head. I have no idea why he's enjoying this.

Tup finishes his preflight checks and says, "We'll be clear of the flight deck in less than two minutes, and we'll reach the shield barrier in under five. So if we're doing this, let's get it done."

I groan and pull out the knife Karm gave me. Sarka reaches for it. "Hell, no." I pull it out of his reach. "There's no way I'm giving you a knife. I'll do everyone's."

"Who's going to cut yours out?" he asks.

"I'll do it myself."

"As much as I'm impressed with this bad-ass attitude of yours, it's a whole different ball game when you actually have to cut into yourself."

"I'll manage." I turn to Tup. "Do you have a medical kit on board? We'll need to disinfect the knife and wrap the wounds after." He motions between my legs under the copilot seat. "Great. I'll do you first." I pull out the med kit, which isn't exactly stocked. There's two bandage wraps and a rubbery stick. I pull out my knife, which is bigger than I remember. A battle knife—long, serrated on one side, and sharp. I have no illusions that it might be sterile. In fact, if I were going to pick something to cut into everyone's skin with, this would be dead last. "Hold out your arm."

Tup rolls up his sleeve and hands it over to me. I'm impressed with his cavalier nature, as if this is some inspection he has to pass before being able to leave. I gaze over at Sarka, who's trying to look like he isn't paying us any attention.

"How do we know it's in the same place for everyone? Especially since he doesn't remember getting his."

Sarka shrugs. "If you don't find it in that arm, then open up the other one."

"Great solution. We only have two bandages." And then I remember our earlier conversation. "Hey, Tup, what arm do you use to unlock doors?"

Tup places his bulky right hand in my palm. "This one."

I heft the knife and position it where I think they've placed his tracker. He watches intently as I slice into the inside of his arm.

His blood comes out dark purple, thick and opaque, mingling with his hair. He doesn't even flinch. "Doesn't that hurt?"

"Nah. I had my pain receptors dulled. Cost me two years' wages, but it was worth it. Kept hitting my head getting out of my bunk every morning. After I had the procedure it doesn't hurt anymore."

Great. So I'm the only one who's going to feel this. I dig into his wrist with both fingers until I find a crescent-shaped object. Then I take one of the bandages and wrap his wrist as tight as I can. "We don't have anything to close the cut. We'll have to wait until we get back to the *Posterus*."

Tup nods and readies the ship for takeoff. "Everyone strapped in?" He doesn't wait for us to answer. The ship lifts off and blasts toward the flight deck exit. "You have five minutes until we reach the shield."

I wipe Tup's blood on my pants, turn, and motion for Sarka to give me his right arm.

He places it on the back of my seat. "So much for sterilization."

"Don't move." The lighting is dimmer in back. Compared to Tup's wrist, Sarka's is hairless, with faint scars along one side in even strips. I try not to think about how he got them. I take my best guess and cut in about halfway, the same area as Tup. For some reason this is worse. Maybe because we're the same species. Maybe it's because his blood looks like mine, or maybe it's just one of those things you can't explain. I'm the one who flinches when I reach in and locate the tracker. His is a much brighter purple than Tup's. I hand it to him, rip the bandage in half, and wrap his wrist as best I can.

I wipe the knife on my now-filthy pants and stare at my own arm. This is fucking crazy.

"Two minutes left." We race along the flight deck past all the other dormant ships.

I grab the rubber stick from the med kit and place it between my teeth, then take a deep breath and brace myself.

Sarka reaches for the knife just as I'm about to cut. "Don't play the hero. Let me do it."

I yank the knife out of reach and turn to face front.

"Jordan, you're being ridiculous. I'm not going to hurt you."

I take the rubber stick out of my mouth. "I don't care. The last thing I'm going to do is trust you." I wedge my leg against the console and place my arm on my thigh.

"And you don't think this is trust? Stabbing yourself with a knife? You don't even know if removing it will save your life when we cross the shield."

I stop. "Are you screwing with me?"

"No. I'm trying to prove a point."

"One minute left." We clear the ship and enter space. The difference in light is stark. I feel the cold dead of space surround us.

"Who told you we had to remove them?" I ask.

"It doesn't matter. I'm telling the truth. What do you have to lose? You've seen removing them has no side effects—"

"That we know of. What if you both drop dead in another minute?"

"Thirty seconds."

"Cut it out of your arm," Sarka yells.

Goddamn it. If he's lying I don't have time to find out. I jam the knife into my arm and cut a thin line. Christ.

I take a moment to readjust to the pain. My breath comes out in pants, and then I feel two large fingers dig into my arm and root around. I lean forward, afraid I might vomit when I hear, "We're clear." I don't feel much after that. My brain has shut down the part that hurts like hell.

There's a soft slap and I jerk awake. My arm is bandaged. There's blood everywhere—my arm, my pants, the floor, the console. I turn in my seat. Sarka is staring at me. He holds up the crescent object between his thumb and index finger. "You're welcome," he says.

I face the front. Now what? This was as far as my plan got. Hell, I didn't even have a plan for getting past the shield. Everything about this is a hope and a prayer. "How will we get onto the other ship?"

"That's up to Alison now," he says. I ignore it. He's goading me, and I have to stop letting him. "I know she got the message I sent her because the system sends an automated response back when it makes the connection."

I grit my teeth.

Tup banks to the right and heads toward the other ship, his face pure bliss. I've never seen him this happy. "It's better than I imagined. Most of our information is out of date." He leans forward to get a good look. The ship is massive. It looks like they could fit the Belt's entire population on board. I watch Tup as he studies the ship. Is this what we'll become? A species that can't even remember our home? Or, worse, our ships will become our home. That's what I signed up for. I didn't want to live the rest of my life on a ship. But it was a sacrifice I was willing to make. I doubt the illya or the Varbaja chose to live like this. But what happens when it stops? When the war is over? Will they be able to go back to the lives their ancestors lived? Lives they have no connection to?

When I signed on for the *Posterus* mission, I didn't really grasp what it would be like to live the rest of your life on a ship. Granted, it's like no other ship I've ever seen. It's more like living on Alpha. I just knew I needed to get away. But what happens to the people who reach our final destination? Will they also have problems adjusting to a life that isn't in constant motion?

"What exactly did you tell Ash she had to do?" I ask.

Sarka stretches his legs out in front of him, trying to get as comfortable as he can in this tiny ship. "To find a way to plant a bomb in their main computer to disable them."

Tup shakes his head. "That won't work."

Sarka shrugs. "It's the plan that tiny woman had me relay."

"Why won't it work?" I ask.

"Because a ship that size wouldn't have one main computer, It would have many. They would need redundancy since it's likely many systems go down on a regular basis. Veera is stupid if she thinks that will work. Even the *Avokaado* has two main computers: one for operations and the other for defenses."

We're now equal distance between the *Avokaado* and the illya's ship. So far nothing is following us, and Tup's spirits are high. I take that as a good sign.

"Alison's a smart cookie. She'll figure it out."

I glare back at Sarka. "We still need a way in." I hate to ask, but we don't have any other option. "Can you communicate with her from here?"

"There's no need. She's expecting us." He smirks, probably at my dumbfounded expression. "I had faith you'd find a way to get us off that ship. Love is a great motivator, isn't it?" When he wiggles his eyebrows, I nearly explode with rage. "And like I said before, the rest is up to Alison."

"Stop saying her name. You have no right," I shout. It's that smug smile on his lips that does it. I lose whatever self-control I've been holding onto and sink the knife I'm still holding deep into his thigh. The silence that follows is excruciating.

Sarka's eyes go wide, not from pain, but from surprise. I know he didn't expect that. Hell, I didn't know I was going to do it until I did. My hand is still wrapped around the handle. The knife is buried in the meatiest part of his thigh muscle. I can't yank it out or he'll bleed all over the place. There's a moment where I'm more pissed that I gave him a knife than the fact that he finally got me to lose my temper good and proper.

It's what I should have done in his cabin that first week. I should've just stabbed him then and been done with it. I'd have a lot less headache, and we wouldn't be in this goddamned mess. I'd be on the *Persephone* with Ash heading back to the *Posterus*. And as I think this, I realize I'd most likely be dead, killed by those avians who surprised us in the pyramid.

Christ. I could throttle him just for the confusion I'm feeling right now.

He cups his hand over mine and looks at me in a way I haven't seen since I was a child. "Steady wins the race," he says in a low, calm voice.

I nod and try to choke back tears. I wrench my hand free and swipe at my eyes. Fuck. The last thing I want to do is cry in front of him. I face forward in my seat.

Tup looks over at me, but instead of fear or a sudden wariness he shows the same excitement from before. "We're approaching the *Kudo*. What do you want me to do? Once we get too close, their proximity sensors will sound, and they'll know we're coming." As he says that it hits me. Ash knows we're coming. She'd make it so we could get in somehow.

"If you were going to sabotage a ship, one you weren't familiar with, and get us access, how would you do it?" Ash has Hartley. And Hartley is a fucking genius. He'd find a way to get us in. Unfortunately, I don't think I'm working with the same caliber of brain power here.

"I'd sabotage the toilets," Sarka says.

I turn back. He's got his hand on the knife and has ripped off part of the bandage around his wrist and secured the knife to his leg. The sight adds a layer of guilt to all the other emotions battling for prominence. "What?"

"It's the only essential system that won't have a lot of security around it. And as an added bonus, many ships will have a fail-safe that vents all gray water in an emergency." Before I can wonder if Hartley would think of that, Sarka continues. "Plus, it'll be on their minds. I placed a bomb there on the *Persephone*."

CHAPTER TWENTY-FIVE

Ash

"What does that mean? Tribute?" Yakovich says.

Vasa licks his lips and stares up at us. He looks terrified, and he should be. Yakovich's stance is intimidating, arms crossed, chin raised, pissed-off expression.

"I don't know much, only what they told me. I was approached a few months after they announced the assignments for the *Posterus*. They said they had a special mission, but that I had to agree before I heard what it was." He rubs his palms on his legs. "After I heard the mission, it made sense. There's no going back once you know. I wanted to refuse after I heard, but they promised me my parents would be moved to Alpha, where they wouldn't have to work for the rest of their lives.

"The illya have been abducting humans for centuries and using us to help them procreate. For hundreds of years humans had no idea. Because there were so many people, it didn't make any difference that a few went missing every few months. But by the twentieth century, when we started to make headway into space, things changed. They captured one of our ships. As compensation, an agreement was reached. We would supply the illya with humans in exchange for technology."

"What kind of technology?" I ask.

Vasa shrugs. "They didn't say, but I think it's pretty obvious. The technology boom of the twentieth-first century? Probably wasn't human ingenuity." He lets that thought sink in. And it does. We suddenly had technology we weren't ready for, and look where it got us. He nods when he sees my face. "Exactly. And when we had to migrate to the Belt, things got worse. The illya still wanted humans, but it was harder to hide those disappearances with so few of us left. So a deal was struck. We would give them 45,000 humans to begin their own colony on a planet in their system, and they would leave the rest of the Belters alone."

Yakovich looks like she's going to puke. "And what was your role in all this?"

Vasa hesitates before his face crumples. "It was my job to discover the planet." Great big sobs overtake his whole body. He sags in on himself.

Yakovich and I exchange a look. I'm not sure if she's thinking exactly what I am, but it's clear we agree that we have to get as far away from the illya as possible. We need to warn the *Posterus*. If I were Vasa, I'd be drowning in guilt. If what he says is true, he was willing to sacrifice 45,000 of his own people so his parents wouldn't have to work for the next ten years. Except that still doesn't explain why he's been trying to kill me for the past month.

"And why was I a threat to all this?"

Vasa continues to sob.

Yakovich kicks the bed again. "Why were you trying to kill Ash? Did you think what's one more, when I'm already guilty of mass murder?"

I place a hand on Yakovich's arm. We don't want to antagonize him. In this case it'll be better to play nice rather than be aggressive. I kneel in front of him and place a hand on his knee. "Vasa, I know you were only doing what you thought you needed to, but for my peace of mind, I need to know."

Vasa raises watery eyes. A tear escapes and runs the length of his cheek, dropping from his chin onto his leg. "The Commons have another operative aboard the *Posterus*—"

"Gladwell."

He nods. "He said I should make it look like an accident."

"But why?" asks Yakovich.

"He was worried you'd been compromised by the Burrs because you'd been on the station when they attacked."

"Why didn't they just pull me from the mission?"

"I heard Colonel Shreves tried, but they had no evidence you'd been compromised. All your medical tests checked out. And they weren't aware that the Burrs had been on the station for two weeks. They still think it was only a few hours. But Gladwell didn't want to take any chances." New tears spill over. "I'm sorry. I'm so sorry, Ash."

I pull Yakovich over to the window so Vasa won't hear us. "Now what?" she asks.

I'm asking myself the same thing. "The best thing to do is put him in the brig until we come up with a better option."

"Lieutenant," Vasa calls. "You can't take us back to the Milky Way. The illya will keep coming for us. They'll keep abducting people until there aren't any left."

"You told him we were going home?" Yakovich asks.

"I had to tell him something to get him to talk."

"So if we were chosen for this mission as sacrifices, what does that say about their selection process?"

I snort. "Guess we're the rejects."

After dropping Vasa in the brig, I call a staff meeting. Everyone is back on board working on getting the *Persephone* up and running again. The race is on now, not only because we have to get away from the illya before they make us their never-ending supply of baby makers, but because an invasion force is heading our way.

Yakovich holds up her hand. "So let me get this straight. The leader of the Burrs, the guy who left you for dead—"

"And planted bombs on the ship," says Hartley.

Yakovich nods at Hartley. "And planted bombs on the ship, sent you a message telling you to blow up the ship we're on?"

We're seated around two tables in the officers' mess. The six of us—Hartley, Mani, Foer, Yakovich, me, and the doctor—are discussing the data dump I received from my mind knot a few hours ago. It's hard to explain what it felt like to just suddenly know things I don't remember accumulating the normal way. I have to assume it's from Sarka, because how else would they have transmitted it except through his mind knot? Plus, the information is a memory of him telling me all these things I don't remember hearing before.

"Yeah," I say.

"Why would we listen to a Burr?" asks Yakovich.

I sigh. I knew this would be a hard sell. "He's stuck in this galaxy as much as we are." I haven't filled the crew in on what we learned from Vasa. "He doesn't gain much by lying to us. Plus, he's with the captain. And I don't believe she'd be on board with a plan that would harm us."

Foer leans back and folds his arms across his chest. "If that's even true. What if he's lying and the captain is dead?"

"She was alive a few days ago. I saw her on the other ship's bridge." And I have to believe she's still alive. My world doesn't make sense if she's not.

Yakovich and I share a look. We'd decided—I decided—that we wouldn't tell the crew what we knew, but this looks like it's going to be a harder sell than I thought. Trusting a Burr just isn't in people's natures. I make a choice. They need to know, to be fully informed about why it's so urgent we get away from the illya.

"There's something else," I say. "Something Yakovich and I discovered about the illya and it's not—"

"The Commons stabbed us in the back," Yakovich says.

I glare at Yakovich. I'm trying to explain this situation in the least inflammatory way. "It appears our entire mission was a cover. We were actually payment to keep the illya out of the Milky Way." This doesn't sound any less inflammatory, and the room erupts. It takes the better part of an hour to calm everyone and explain what we know.

Hartley stands up and sneaks behind the mess counter. He grabs a container of wasabi peas—the only snack we have left on board—and places them on the table in front of us. Mani and Foer scoop a handful each. The room fills with loud crunches as they munch and think. Hartley takes a pile and places them in front of himself, eating one at a time.

"So what was the plan?" Foer asks around a mouthful of peas.

I take a moment. If the last bit wasn't digested well, I can't imagine this will go over any better. "They want us to blow up the main computer. But also, we have to find a way to get them on the ship."

Hartley shakes his head and pops another pea into his mouth. "Three computers comprise the main one. All are located on different parts of the ship, and all are heavily guarded. I'm not saying it can't be done, but we don't have the time."

"Well, what do we have time for?" I ask.

"Plant a bomb in the waste-management system," he says and grins.

I hear other groans. We all remember how effective it was at crippling the *Persephone*.

"It makes sense. It's a major system we have access to," Hartley says.

"Can you build a bomb?" It's a stupid question. I hold up my hand to stop him from answering before I'm even finished. "What do you need? And how long will it take?"

"Lucky for us it's not that hard. Foer and I can rig that thing in under an hour. The real question is, when should I set it to go off? We're not anywhere near ready to go."

Soon after, the meeting breaks up. Once I relay our day-and-a-half time frame and the need to create a way for Sarka and Jordan to gain access to the ship, I dismiss everyone to get started. The way Hartley put it, we have three weeks' worth of work to do in thirty-six hours. I've broken the crew into three groups. The first is in charge of getting the *Persephone* up and running. Their priority is to get her spaceworthy. We don't need everything at a hundred percent; we just need to get her out of the bay and away from the resulting conflict.

Hartley's group is in charge of building the bomb and planting it in the waste-management system. He says one bomb in the system won't be enough to take this ship out. Not like the *Persephone*. So they're working on a three-part plan to cripple the ship. His group is the smallest since it won't take much time or resources. Once he completes that mission, he'll be in charge of the first group.

And my group is in charge of finding a way to get Jordan and Sarka on board. We need to make it obvious, since we have no way to communicate with them. Our task is also the most dangerous, since we'll have to do a little reconnaissance on the *Kudo* to learn what weaknesses, if any, they have. Yakovich and Ito are on my team. I've also asked the doctor to join us because I find he has interesting solutions to hard problems. And that's what it feels like, a puzzle we need to solve on a deadline. I used to love these as a kid. It's less fun when people's lives are at stake.

The four of us are standing on the track. This is my place to think, plus it gives us a good view of the *Kudo*'s ship bay.

"What if we found a way to open the main doors to the bay?" Yakovich asks. "I mean, we're going to have to eventually anyway, to get the *Persephone* out."

"Eventually, but shouldn't that be the last thing we do? We'll be escaping. I highly doubt the illya will let us go once we detonate a bomb on their ship." Ito is lying on the track with her feet propped on the windows. Every so often she taps them in a rhythm only she can hear.

My forehead is pressed to the glass. From this angle I can see all the way to the bottom of the bay. It's dark and not much is going on. "And we don't know if they've got some mechanism in place to keep us here. Our biggest problem is our ignorance." So far the illya have been nothing but kind and welcoming. But after learning their real motives, it's obvious they must have some sort of system to keep an eye on us. They wouldn't let us run around their ship without knowing what we were up to. We don't know what the illya are capable of, not fully.

"What about the venting system?" Ito asks. "When we have an emergency on the *Persephone*, we automatically dump all gray water into space."

Yakovich laughs. "Sort of like shitting your pants when you're scared?" She's sitting crossed-legged on the track next to the doctor.

Ito giggles. "Yeah, I guess. But those vents would be open at that point. Why can't they use those?"

"Would they be big enough?" Yakovich asks.

"I think so. This ship is massive. The system they use for heating is a meter wide. Of course, we don't know what kind of ship the captain will be on. It's too bad they couldn't enter in enviro-suits."

Yakovich perks up. "Hey, that's not a bad idea."

I clap my hands together before they get away with themselves. "Guys, this is all great, but we have no way to relay this information to the captain. It has to be obvious." I walk around to the other side of the track, the side where we can see the door that opens out into space. It's huge and most certainly guarded with a million security features that we couldn't hope to elude. We can't set a bomb because that'll tip off the illya. This problem doesn't appear to have a solution.

"Why can't we let them know the plan?" It's the first time the doctor's said anything since we got to the track. "If Sarka can send a message to you, then why can't we send a message to him? It shouldn't be very hard to figure out how."

I didn't like the first invasion. The idea of doing it again sounds horrible. "I'm not sure I want to do that."

He spreads his hands. I know he's leaving it up to me.

"What other choice do we have? We could do a million things to help the captain get on this ship, but how will they know which it is? The idea that they'll just know is ridiculous. Besides opening the bay doors here and throwing out a giant sign that says, 'this way, guys,' there's no other way," Yakovich says.

She's right, of course. There isn't any other way. I nod. "Okay. But we still need to find a foolproof plan to get them on the ship."

I leave it to the doctor to work out how to communicate with Sarka's mind knot while Ito, Yakovich, and I work out the kinks of getting them through the gray water vents. We just need to hurry. If this is going to work, we need to give them enough advance warning of our plan.

The next day I find the doctor in the med center. He says he's figured out a way to send a message to Sarka through the mind knot. Now we just have to hope that what we've come up with will work.

CHAPTER TWENTY-SIX

Jordan

I'm clinging to the side of the illya's ship with only one arm as the gray water spurts past, crystallizing as soon as it hits the vacuum of space. I shouldn't be hanging onto the ship in an oversized enviro-suit. This isn't the first time I've been in this situation in the past month. They try to prepare you for everything in the academy, and not once did we have a class that trained us how to break into a ship. There isn't a lot of call for that sort of thing in the Milky Way, but here, wherever the hell here is, it's popular.

On reflection, I shouldn't have left the ship. This is so out of character for me. There's always a better way, always a less rash way to get things done. And here I am, again, making a stupid decision instead of finding a more reasonable course of action. I swear if I get through this, I'm hiding in my cabin for a week. I won't even come out for food. I'll just have it passed in on a tray. I'm sick of all this daredevil shit.

Sarka and Tup have taken off. Tup declined our offer of asylum on the *Posterus*. I don't blame him. How could our tiny ship keep him safe? In a way I'm relieved. No way Sarka was coming back with me. If he does, he'll face charges, a slapdash trial, and imprisonment. No one trusts him enough to let him do anything, so he's useless.

And here I am, alone again. I've spent the majority of my life alone. Not that I wanted Sarka to come. This is a relief. And it's not like I'm some twelve-year-old who needs her hand held. But being out here, with my back to the vast emptiness of space, I can't help but wonder if given the chance I would do it the same way again. Since meeting Ash I've almost died more times than I care to think about, but I've also lived more. Being around her I feel more alive. It's the only way I can explain why I'm hanging off the side of a giant ship watching piss crystallize in the vacuum of space. I'm a captain in the Union fleet. It's not like I signed on hoping for an easy life. If I'd wanted that, I would've stayed back on Delta and taken over Kate's farm. But there's exciting and then there's shit-your-pants terrifying. I could use a little less of that.

The water flow lessens, which is my cue. I can't wait for it to finish, or I risk the hatches closing and trapping me in the tube. I'm thankful I'm in an enviro-suit, because I'm wading through sewage to make it onto the ship. I'm sure there are worse ways to gain access, but I'm stumped to think of one right now.

I swing around and straddle the opening. The flow is slow enough that I can crawl into the tube. Almost as soon as I do, the hatch closes and I'm left in complete darkness. I switch on my helmet light, and a strong beam illuminates the tunnel. It stretches in front of me, an unwavering line into the depth of the ship. The tunnel is broad at this end. I can crawl with room to spare above my head.

As I crawl, I can't get Sarka's last expression out of my mind. He had this strange look, like he couldn't believe I was actually going through with the plan. I think he figured that when it came down to it, I'd abandon Ash and go with them. Not that their way doesn't have its share of dangers. Those pilot ships don't have much range. Still, I would've hoped he knew better than to think I could leave my crew behind. Even if Ash wasn't on this ship, I wouldn't desert them.

I make it twenty-five meters in and find the rest of my way blocked by a hatch. I pull out the small torch Tup gave me. I was worried something like this might happen. I fire it up and start burning a hole through the hatch doors. The red-and-blue flame throws off a strange light. It hits the water droplets on the damp tunnel walls, and sparkles dance along the way I came. As soon as I've broken through, I reach in and pull the door open manually. It takes minimal effort for it to release and open.

It's possible I've set off certain alarms, but I refuse to worry about that until it becomes an actual problem. In the message Ash sent Sarka, they said to push through, and I should end up in a service corridor. That's if Sarka's telling the truth. Although at this point, I'm not sure why he'd lie. He only lies when it benefits him. And since he's gone, it doesn't matter to him what I do. It's not like we'd go after him. We have more important things to worry about.

As I move farther into the ship, the tube gets smaller as it meets several others. I'm no longer able to crawl on my hands and knees. I have to pull myself through on my stomach. I'm not sure what I'm going to do if I reach a point where it branches off and becomes any smaller. I'm not claustrophobic, but a small bubble of anxiety is forming in the pit of my stomach. If I get stuck, there's no way to turn around, which means I'll have to push myself back through on my stomach. The enviro-suit isn't helping much. It's not my size and is a little bulkier than I'm used to, but still a hundred times better than the one from the *Roebuck* when Ash and I retook the *Persephone*.

At the next junction I find I can't go any farther. My air tank hits on a ledge and won't budge. It's likely this area of the ship isn't pressurized, so I don't want to risk removing my tank and suffocating. I stare down the long tunnel as it curves out of sight. I know what I have to do, yet I just don't want to admit defeat. I'm going to have to crawl backward on my stomach through twenty meters of tube, which will take forever.

I count to ten and breathe in and out, willing my frustration to stay buried. This isn't the time to fall apart. I manage—barely—to keep it together and slowly push myself backward. It takes forty-five minutes to struggle to the place where the tunnel gets bigger.

I lean my head back and reassess my situation. It's possible these tubes won't lead me anywhere useful, although I doubt Ash would've suggested it unless she checked that this would get me onto the ship. I've evidently taken a wrong turn somewhere. Where I'm sitting, the tube curves around to a fork. I'll just have to try another direction. Of course, it may lead into the ship, but they might not have checked the width of the tubes. I don't want to believe that's true. There has to be a way onto this ship.

As I'm about to start again, I hear a grunt coming from around the bend. Shit. I must have set off an alarm, and a security detail is coming to apprehend me. I flick my headlight off and tighten my grip on the torch, ready to ignite it the second they come around the corner. There's a loud bang and another grunt. I raise the torch, my finger on the switch. When the lone silhouette appears, I flick it on. Sarka looks surprised by my greeting.

"Holy shit. What are you doing here?" I turn off the torch and switch my headlamp back on. He squints into the light.

"Rescuing you. What the hell do you think?" He's cradling his injured leg. The knife is missing from his thigh. The noise and effort make sense now. Without medical attention he's going to bleed out quickly.

"I don't need rescuing."

"No? You're going the wrong way. The turnoff is this way."

I narrow my eyes. "How would you know I'm going the wrong way?"

He shrugs in his heavy enviro-suit but doesn't say anything, just turns around and begins heading back the way he came.

I grit my teeth. I don't need him to rescue me. I was already on my way back when he showed up. And why the hell did he even come back?

He looks over his shoulder. "You gonna sit there and sulk? Or do you want to get the fuck out of here before we run out of air?"

"What are you doing here?" I start toward him on my hands and knees. "I'm capable of looking after myself. Have been for years now."

"No one said you weren't."

"Then why'd you come?"

He doesn't answer and I let it drop. The more I talk, the more air I use. We reach the fork where I veered left. Without stopping, he turns down the right tunnel and keeps up a steady pace.

"How do you know this was the right way?"

"I just do. There was probably a map included in the information sent. When that happens, it usually translates into knowing where to go rather than a visual representation."

"So you came back out of the kindness of your heart?"

"I came back because I couldn't leave it like that."

"Leave what like that?"

He stops and huffs. When he turns to me, his face is frozen in a pained expression. It's the first time I've ever seen him with creases on his brow. "I know what everyone thinks about us, and I don't blame them. But I always thought you knew better. But you don't, do you? You see us as the monsters they do. Even though you've seen how we live. Do you think I like living ostracized? After the years I've spent serving my country? My planet? And the thanks I got was to become a pariah? To have to steal to feed myself and my family? I don't deny that some of the things I've done are atrocious. It's not like I ever wanted to end up like this." He raises his hands and lets them drop at his side in defeat. "Do you think when I signed up to serve my country, to protect my mom and dad and brothers, I was doing it because I thought one day, hey, wouldn't it be cool to become some freak of nature my own people don't want anything to do with?" His voice is deep and gruff, reverberating through the glass of his helmet. It echoes down the tunnel, along the walls, invading every speck of space. It reminds me of when I was younger and he'd sit on my bed and tell me stories before bedtime. That voice was once comforting. Now it sounds like failure.

"When you were born, I thought, here's a chance. This is my chance to finally do something right for the first time. To create life instead of death. You know how many decades of my life have revolved around death? Too many."

"Nobody made that choice for you."

He pauses but doesn't comment. He stares straight into my eyes. Even in the dim light they flash with intensity. "You may not believe me when I say your mom and I loved each other. That's fine. I won't try to convince you, but I loved her and you more than anything. The day you saw that man hung up in the mess I knew I had to find a way for you to have a normal life. As much as it killed me to admit, that life would never be with me. So I helped your mom and you escape. I wanted you to live without death in your life." He makes a circular gesture with his hand. "And here you are. When I learned you'd been selected for this mission, I knew I had to do everything in my power to stop you. I wasn't trying to kill you. I was trying to save you. I knew if the *Posterus* couldn't make it to the rendezvous site, they wouldn't be pulled into this galaxy to be poached. Do you have any idea how dangerous these people are? They abduct humans and use their bodies to create their young. They kill humans, and you were part of a payment so they'd leave the Belt alone. I couldn't let you go."

"Wait. Hold up." I pull back both physically and mentally. This is all too much. I don't want to believe a word of it, but what if? What if for once he's not lying? "Are you saying this was all planned? That the Commons built a generational ship so it could send 45,000 people to their deaths? That's insane." He's insane.

"You don't have to believe me about that, but if you don't believe me that the illya are dangerous, you'll regret it. Now let's move before we're discovered. I'm sure you've tripped a number of alarms."

My mouth's still open as he turns and continues down the tunnel. I can't move. A part of me believes him, and not a small part. A brash alarm is going off in my head. Too many things are falling into place now. His story explains a million decisions that, at the time, didn't make sense, but given this new information, suddenly do. It's why they insisted the mission was on a volunteer basis only. And why none of the members in the Commons volunteered for it. Or why Ash's dad was so set against her going that he would give the worst recommendation letter I've ever seen. And if Sarka was trying to sabotage the mission to keep me safe, then he was willing to sacrifice Ash and everyone in the engine room.

"Jordan, move it," Sarka calls from up ahead.

"You programmed a human being to explode so you could save me? What kind of a person does that? Why'd you even bother telling me all this? Did you think I'd—what?—be happy you were trying to save me? What is it you think I want from you? Love? It sure as shit isn't that."

He slows and eventually stops. When he turns to face me he's so far down the tunnel I can't see his expression. But by the look of his shoulders and the way he huffs at me, he's long done with this conversation. "I don't really know what you want from me, if anything. You don't need to want anything from me. But I'm here just the same." He chuckles, a deep throaty laugh that echoes through the tube. "What does it matter anyway?"

"Ash could've died. Doesn't anything matter to you?"

In a tone of voice I've never heard before, he says, "I didn't know you'd fall in love with her. She was convenient. I'm sorry if that hurts you, but I didn't know her. It was you I needed to save." He turns back and continues crawling. "Now come on," he says gruffly.

I fall in behind him because I have no other choice. I'm ready to get the hell out of these damn tunnels. Sarka leads us to a large hatch at the end of a tunnel. It's locked, so I hand him my torch. The light from it illuminates the tension in his face. Is he worried I'm going to bolt as soon as I get out of here?

It takes only a few moments for the lock to give, and we're in. The tube fills with light from the service corridor we've entered. It's deserted as we step down. I remove my helmet and suit as soon as possible and dump it in a service hatch. An eerie feeling washes over me as we step into the main corridor. My feet sink into the ground. It's malleable, as are the walls. When I run my hands along them, it's like running my hand over someone's skin. The smell is sterile, like most ships, but there's something else. An unfamiliar smell that has me on edge.

Sarka and I exchange a look. We're both of the same mind. The sooner we find the others, the better. As soon as we round the corner I hear my name. When I turn, Ash is striding toward us. I don't think I've seen a more beautiful, more welcome sight in my entire life. I rush into her arms just as alarms start blaring all around us.

CHAPTER TWENTY-SEVEN

Ash

The moment I see Jordan all my anxiety and worry evaporate. She's alive. And I have proof because she's right in front of me. I stop from kissing her senseless only because as soon as I wrap my arms around her, the alarms go off. Hartley's started the process.

I step back to grab Jordan's hand and notice she's covered in blood. She has a messy bandage on her right forearm.

"Why are you covered in blood? Are you okay?" I ask.

She waves me off. "It's nothing."

I decide not to press it and pull her toward the lifts. "Come on. We don't have much time now."

"Where are we going?" She follows without hesitation, and that's when I notice Sarka lurking in the background. I ignore him. Why'd he even come back? Does he think this'll buy him some favor?

"Their bridge. The only way to open the bay doors to fly the *Persephone* out is from the bridge. We've created a diversion of sorts to clear it, but we need to hurry."

She stops and pulls me back. "The *Persephone*'s okay?" Relief and disbelief fight for prominence on her face.

I nod. More or less. "She's spaceworthy." And right now that's all that matters. The basic repairs are done. Anything else can wait until we get the hell out of here. "I don't have time to tell you everything, but we need to get the fuck out of here as soon as possible. These people—"

Jordan looks back at Sarka. "I know. They're dangerous." I'm not sure how she knows, but I'm guessing it has something to do with Sarka. The bastard probably intercepted some encrypted communique from the Commons and knew the whole plan. Hell, it could've been years ago. Twenty years of lies and deceit to intercept.

The noise of the alarms penetrates my brain. We don't have time for this. I tug Jordan's hand, and we take off for the lifts, Sarka close behind.

As soon as we're in the lift ascending to the bridge, Jordan asks, "How did you manage to create a diversion that will evacuate everyone from the bridge?"

I know what she's thinking. No force in the galaxy would make her abandon her bridge. "I had Hartley suck all the air out. Ito is meeting us on the deck below with our enviro-suits." Jordan nods. Something unsettling about the way she keeps glancing over at Sarka. She's unsure of something, but I have no idea what.

I can't keep my eyes off her. She's wearing some strange black uniform that looks perfectly tailored for her. It's dangerous and powerful. Just standing next to her, I feel those same energies radiating off her. I have a million questions, but they'll have to wait. She's alive. And she's here. That's enough for now.

The lift stops on our floor and we exit into darkness. Another of Hartley's precautions. We didn't want to risk bumping into anyone, so I had him cut the lights as well as the emergency lights on this whole deck. I raise the flashlight I brought and aim it down the corridor. It's empty.

We're halfway from midship and the bow and still have about a five-minute run until we're below the bridge. Hartley says the ship's so big it would take a good half an hour to get from one end to the other.

I see Ito a minute or so before we meet her. At this end of the ship the corridors are straight. She's carting two enviro-suits she brought from the *Persephone*.

"Captain. It's so great to have you back." Her voice falters when she sees Sarka. "I only brought two. I didn't know I'd need a third."

"It's okay. He's not coming with us," Jordan says.

"You're just going to leave me here in the dark?"

"What? Don't tell me you're afraid of the dark? I have no problem bringing you up on the bridge with no breathable air. None whatsoever," I say.

He scowls but doesn't say anything, which isn't like him. Has someone finally managed to reprogram him?

"Ash will leave her flashlight for you." Before I can protest, she grabs it and hands it to him. "Now let's suit up," she says. God, it feels good to have her back in command. She takes her enviro-suit from Ito and almost sighs with pleasure as she slips into it. "I never thought I'd be happy to get into one of these, but I forgot how much better they are when they're made to fit."

I check our time. We have two minutes until go time. I lift my helmet over my head and seal it. The noise of the alarms dulls, and it feels like I've entered a cocoon. Like those pillow forts you used to make as a kid. I switch on my comm unit and headlamp. "Testing, can you hear me?"

Jordan gives a firm yes. Now we wait. There's an awkward moment as we all stand around, the alarms the only sound. Nobody wants to make eye contact, so we have nothing to do but stare at our feet. Finally my alarm goes off.

"Time to go."

On this last deck we'll take the service chute up to the next floor. It's less likely we'll meet anyone.

Halfway up I ask, "Aren't you afraid Sarka will take off?"

"Let him." Jordan's voice sounds loud in my headpiece. "If he sticks around, he's going to be nothing but trouble."

"You're just going to let him go free? Instead of paying for what he's done?"

She sighs. "I don't have a good answer for you. But I don't want to have any part of his trial or punishment."

"You wash your hands of it?"

"This isn't the time to discuss this. Let's focus on the mission ahead of us. We'll worry about Sarka later."

I have some choice words for that statement but keep them to myself. Sometimes I forget she's his daughter. Most of the time I forget that. It can't be easy being in that position. If I were back on Alpha, would I be able to condemn my father for what he's done? He knew we were being sent to our death, and he did nothing. A half-assed communique doesn't make up for his actions. I grip the rung of the ladder tight and stop, my breathing erratic. The heat of my anger begins to boil low in my stomach. This is all his fault. He could've stopped this. Jordan interrupts my thoughts with a gentle nudge to my thigh to prompt me to keep moving.

We reach the bridge and pry open the main doors. It's silent and empty. And dark. Hartley's turned the lights off here as well. He's turned off all the consoles except the one we need. The only light comes from the large window in front, and even that light is dull and muted. We aren't very close to any suns.

"Where did they all go, do you think?" I ask in hushed tones. It feels wrong to talk at full volume. I imagine the illya standing behind the closed doors, listening in, waiting to surprise us if we make too much noise.

"A ship this big? They'll have a secondary command post for emergencies like this. Let's hurry. It's likely they'll be able to monitor everything that happens on this bridge. Or worse, they've gone to get their own enviro-suits." Jordan walks to the window and looks up at the second deck of the bridge. "What's up there?"

"Their main command post. That's where the captain sits."

She turns back to the enormous window in front. "Nice view."

"It is, isn't it?" says a hollow voice from above. I nearly jump out of my skin. On the above deck is Bragga, his mouth and nose encased in a breathing apparatus. He's leaning on the rail watching us. He pulls out a blaster and aims it at Jordan. "And who is this? Your captain, perhaps? The one you've been searching for?" He walks over to a platform along the side, steps on, and descends to our floor, his eyes and aim never wavering.

"And you are?" Jordan asks.

"Who I am really isn't important, is it? All that matters is what happens next." He reaches the bottom of the lift and steps off.

I wish we'd thought to arm ourselves. Breaking and entering isn't something we do often, but I'm guessing having a gun helps in these situations.

"So what is going to happen next?" asks Jordan.

"As soon as we secure the *Posterus*, you and your people will be returned to the planet."

"And what happens on the planet?"

"You live out your lives."

I push Jordan behind me. If he shoots one of us, it'll be me first. "As what? Containers for your offspring?"

He smiles. "Ah, so you've learned of your fate. I'm not surprised. Humans have always been resourceful beings. They have a tendency to muck things up. Yes, you are here to help us procreate. But we've ensured that the climate will be suitable for your needs. And we won't need all of you at once. Most of you have many, many years ahead of you." So it's true. All of it's true. The slow simmer of anger begins to boil over.

I look back at Jordan, and I can guess what she's thinking. Our time on that planet will not be pleasant. We'll spend most of it fleeing the natives and local wildlife. Not exactly the future any of us had in mind when we embarked on this mission.

"And what about the species that already lives there? They won't take kindly to sharing," Jordan says.

"They won't be around much longer. We've had scientists studying the effects of some germ-line editing we did. It makes them sterile."

"Scientists? Like that dead guy we found in the pyramid?" I ask.

"An unfortunate accident."

Jordan crosses her arms. "You'd be willing to eradicate a whole species just so you can survive?"

"Why not? They owe their existence to us. If we hadn't abandoned the planet thousands of years ago in search of a cure for our plague, they'd never have evolved into the creatures they are now. Our absence left a gap in nature, and they filled it. How fitting we're the ones to cause their extinction."

I can think of another word besides fitting.

"And the ship on the planet? The one with the humans?" Jordan asks.

There's movement from the far end of the bridge. I glance up and see Sarka moving through the room, holding a canister of air to his lips.

"An early experiment. We'd hoped to be able to keep bodies in stasis and use them when needed, but it only works if they're kept alive. We keep hoping. After all, wouldn't it be better if you didn't know your fate?"

"So you've been doing this a while? Killing humans? If you had the ability to travel to our solar system—"

"Yeah, how did you do that?" I take a step to the left, focusing his attention away from Sarka. "How did we get here to this system?"

Bragga smiles graciously, like I've given him a compliment on a nice table arrangement. "We have the technology to fold space." He mimics folding something in half with his hands. "As you travel from one side to the other, your body breaks up into base elements. When it remerges on the other side it's complete again."

"Complete but different," I say.

Bragga shakes his head. "No. Nothing changes. You are exactly the same."

"I came out different. I was in the process of—" I stop for a moment. It sounds so strange to say that I was in the middle of exploding. "I had been altered to explode."

"Altered how? Humans aren't combustible."

"Someone," I throw a glance at Sarka, who has moved to the lit-up console, "injected me with nanotechnology—"

"Your body would've been purged of any and all foreign objects not essential for living." Bragga interrupts and waves his gun as if to erase this conversation. He's growing impatient. And frankly so am I. What the hell is Sarka doing over there? "What does it matter now?" Bragga asks. "Why does it matter why you're here? If you're hoping this information will help you, it won't. We have you outnumbered, and our technology is far superior. What can a bunch of primates do to us? You've barely begun to explore space. You thought it was an accomplishment to land on your moon." He sneers like this is a task similar to learning to chew with your mouth closed. "We first reached space before you even left the trees. We have every advantage over you."

Except surprise. I smile as Sarka rounds the console and leaps onto his back. Both Jordan and I duck and roll out of the way. I hear but don't see the blaster discharge. It strikes a monitor to the right of us. While Sarka has him distracted, Jordan and I circle around. With one gesture, Jordan lets me know she'll go high while I go low. I run at his legs to unbalance him, and Jordan reaches for the blaster, wrenching it out of his hand. He howls as he crashes on top of Sarka.

Jordan aims the gun at him. He sweeps her legs out and kicks the blaster out of the way. At the same moment he smashes an elbow into Sarka's gut. Sarka groans and lets go of his neck. Bragga rolls off him and scrambles for the gun. I reach for his ankle, but I'm too far away. His fingers grasp at the handle, inching it forward.

I look over at Jordan, who's dazed. She must have hit her head on the ground hard. She sits up as I crawl closer to Bragga. His hand closes over the blaster. He spins and aims right for my head. A second later,

Sarka tackles him from behind just as the lights and all the consoles on the bridge come back to life. The canister of air he was using falls and rolls back toward the entrance of the bridge.

He doesn't stand a chance in this atmosphere. He'll suffocate in a matter of minutes. Jordan staggers to her feet to help. Her balance is way off, and she over-compensates, crashing forward onto the front console. A shrill beeping begins emitting from the panel. She scrambles to undo her mistake but loses hold of the console. As she swings her legs back to correct her move, the momentum pushes her to the ceiling.

I reach for Jordan, who manages to hook her foot under the console. We're rooted by this tenuous string to the ship. Sarka takes advantage of the moment to slam his fist into Bragga, and the blaster spins away, ricocheting off the front glass.

The great thing about our enviro-suits is that they have air thrusters so we can maneuver in space. But they also work in zero-gravity situations. I push off from Jordan and introduce the slightest thrust from my enviro-suit. My fingers wrap around the grip of the blaster, and I aim for Bragga. The shot goes wide and hits the floor of the lift.

We're all in this strange twirling dance, floating as if we were underwater. Sarka's face is hard and mean as he concentrates on neutralizing Bragga. Sarka wrenches Bragga's breathing apparatus off his face. He repositions himself to hook his legs around Bragga's midsection, then squeezes while securing the mask on his own face. The second he has it on, the hard mean is replaced by a wide grin that's all teeth.

I take aim again, but Jordan shouts for me to stop. "It's too dangerous."

Bragga boxes Sarka's ears, squeezes out from between his legs, and glides toward the upper floor of the bridge.

"Now," Jordan yells. But it's too late. By the time I take aim, Bragga is hidden from view.

Sarka shoots up toward the second floor of the bridge, gliding through the air as if he'd done it a million times before. He somersaults over the rail and disappears from view. From here I can see a blinking light on the console; the ship's bay doors have opened. We have only a few minutes before we're out of time. I look over to Jordan to see if we should wait or leave, but she's focused on the top deck.

Below me I hear the whoosh of the main doors opening. Crew members are streaming back onto the bridge. As soon as they enter, they begin to float. We've officially run out of time.

"Jordan, we need to leave." I point below us.

She nods. "We'll have to exit through the top floor and hope they haven't blocked our escape."

I adjust my thrusters and propel upward. As I rise to the level of the top floor, the artificial gravity comes back on, and Jordan and I fall to the ground. I slam into one of the crew and knock my head on the front console. Jordan lands a few feet away on her side.

I hear a crash from above and look up as Sarka throws Bragga against the rail. "Now," he shouts.

I aim the gun at Bragga's head and pull the trigger. It glances off his shoulder, but it's enough to subdue him. Sarka grabs his head and wrenches it to the right, breaking his neck. He drops him over the edge without a second thought.

"Let's go."

I untangle myself from the stunned crew member I landed on and run for the lift. Jordan slams into me as I hit the control to raise us to the second floor.

Outside the bridge, I pull my helmet off and fall to the ground panting, still shocked by the final expression on Bragga's face. "Are you crazy?" I stand and slam into Sarka. He's stunned enough that I actually manage to push him back a foot. "You didn't have to kill him." I smack my fist into his chest. It doesn't do much good. It's like punching concrete. But it feels good to unleash my anger.

CHAPTER TWENTY-EIGHT

Jordan

I pull Ash off Sarka. Her face is contorted in rage, and tears are streaming down her face. As soon as I touch her it's like a balm, and she collapses at my feet.

"We don't have time for this." I pull her up and push her down the hall. "We need to get moving. Now."

She looks back at the bridge and then to me. "The doors."

"I got 'em open," Sarka says. He brushes at the front of his uniform, as if Ash's fists marred it.

"They're on the bridge, you idiot." She points to the closed doors. "They'll just close them again."

"Gonna be kinda hard to do. I cut power to that console."

Ash's face contorts in disbelief. I pick up her helmet and push her away from the bridge. We need to get the hell out of here before the rest of the crew come after us. A dead leader will only delay them so long.

I shove her helmet at her. She huffs but moves, finally.

I follow Ash down the never-ending corridor with Sarka close behind.

"You're sure they're open?"

"Yes," Sarka grunts.

According to Ash, it's not far now. I feel as if she's been saying that for the last ten minutes. It's like a mantra in my head. *Almost there. Almost there. Almost there.* My feet and heart pound to the rhythm of it.

Ash pulls up sharply and I run into her. "Detour," she says, and points to several illya filing into the corridor up ahead. We dash into a side corridor. I'm sure Ash has no idea where we're going. But it's better than staying where we were.

Ash stops in front of a lift. "We're about a thousand decks above where we need to be."

"A thousand? Let's not be overly dramatic here." Sarka begins to examine the lift control panel.

"Yes, a thousand. We're on deck one, and the ship-bay entrance is on deck one thousand and fifty-six."

I put a hand on Sarka's arm, stopping him. "If they already have security teams after us, the lifts will be monitored as well. We'll have to find another way."

Ash's eyes widen. "Jordan, it's a thousand decks down. We can't climb down that many decks. They'll discover us. Besides, we don't have that much time left. Hartley gave me an hour to get the doors open." She checks her time. "We've got less than fifteen minutes before he blows the last bomb and they take off. We have to risk the lift."

My insides crumple, but I nod. What other choice do we have? I motion for her to lead the way. For someone who says she doesn't like being in charge, she's better at leading than she gives herself credit for. Before she can press the button to summon the lift, the doors open, and three guards draw their weapons on us.

"Run," she yells and yanks me by the wrist down a separate hallway. We're still in our enviro-suits, which makes running hard. My breath fogs the screen. I slam my hand on the release, and the screen retracts. We dodge down corridors trying to lose both teams, but it's only a matter of time before more converge on us.

"We need to find another way," I say. "We won't be able to keep this up long." And that has nothing to do with the number of people after us. My lungs are burning. I have a stitch in my side, and the only thing I want to do is collapse and puke. You'd think with all the training I've done over the last few weeks, I'd be better suited to this. Something about running for your life must tire you out faster.

Ash checks our time. "We'll never make it before he sets off the last bomb."

"Where's it supposed to go off?" As I ask this question, we spot another set of guards heading down our current corridor. We duck into a service bay. Ash guides us to a small chute that leads down to the next deck.

"The main kitchen. The ship is heated by the runoff from their—I guess you'd call it a stove? But he said that the entire ship is connected through that tube system. If he sets off a strong enough bomb, it'll carry it throughout the ship."

"So when it goes off, we need to be off the ship," I say.

When we exit the service bay, the corridors are free of guards. "It would be in our best interest, yes."

"Do they have escape pods?"

Ash nods. "Every deck. But how would we know how to activate or fly them?"

"If they're anything like ours, all you have to do is hit a button and the pod does the rest."

Ash grabs my arm and yanks me in another direction. "This way, then."

"Do you have any way of communicating with Hartley?"

She pulls up and crouches in a doorway. "He may have gotten the comms working. We can try with the suits." She activates her comm. "*Persephone*, this is Ash. Come in. *Persephone*, this is Ash. Do you read me?" She shakes her head. I guess not. "I told him to get the crew out whether I was back or not."

I motion for Ash and Sarka to follow me. We need to keep moving. "But will he do it?"

Ash doesn't hesitate. "Yeah, he'll do it. He knows it's more important to get everyone out alive. Like you always say, don't play the hero."

We jog down the corridor. We must be close by now. "I always say?"

She shrugs. "You've said it a few times."

"Yet you never listen."

She turns back and grins at me. Out of the corner of my eye, I see three guards appear at the end of the hall. Sarka slams into Ash and me, knocking us to the ground. As we fall, I wrench the blaster out of Ash's hand and aim for the guard in front. The shot hits him in the stomach. I crouch next to Ash and take aim again. This shot goes wide. We crab-walk into a doorway and try to make ourselves small targets. That first guard is still down, and I momentarily wonder if he's dead. I have little time to dwell on this, though, because we're showered in return fire.

I wish we had more than one blaster, but then I notice the model. It's one of the weapons the Varbaja had me train on.

"How far are we from an escape pod?"

Ash points down the hall. "They're standing in front of one."

I look back the way we came. There's little chance we'll make it out of sight before we get hit by blaster fire. And it's only a matter of time before more teams join.

"Okay," I say. "I'm going to set this to overload and use it as a grenade. Hopefully it's enough to disable them without harming the escape-pod hatch." I'm about to punch in the command when Sarka grabs it from me.

"That's stupid. This thing will damage everything within three or four decks." He motions for us to get behind him. "I'll get you to the escape pod. Get inside and leave as soon as the door shuts."

I shake my head. "No. We're not leaving you behind."

"Why not? What good am I in your world? I'm better off dead." He stares hard at me as he says this. More shouts come from behind us.

We're out of time. Time is strange like that. For the first time since I was a kid I actually want more time with my father. I'm not going to pretend that our relationship would ever inspire others, but the fact that I'll never get to try saddens me. He reaches out and touches my cheek with the tips of his fingers. And in the second it takes for me to feel the chill of them on my skin, I can imagine a world where he loved my mother and she loved him and just possibly he wanted a better life for me. But then the second is gone.

I take a steady breath and slap him on the shoulder. "Fuck 'em up."

He grins. "I always do." He races off toward the security team positioned down the corridor, taking aim and firing off several shots that wound at least two. He screams as he gets closer, and they take off.

Ash stops at the pod door. Something's on the middle of it, like a large lock box.

"What is that?" But a loud piercing sound drowns out my question. Ash and I cover our ears, and then the hallway explodes. The force of the blast knocks us several meters back. Christ.

"What the fuck was that?" Ash asks.

My ears are buzzing. I can't hear anything except a loud, incessant ringing.

I stumble up, using the wall for support. Debris is everywhere. I jog down the hall and find the security team. They're all dead. I avert my eyes and focus on Ash, whose face has gone pale. Her eyes stand out dark and fearful.

I cup Ash's helmet and stare straight into those eyes. "We need to go, love." She focuses on me, nods, but doesn't move. I rest my forehead on the hard glass inches from her face. "We can't stay here." I take her hand and pull her through the aftermath.

When we get back to the door, my heart sinks. The force of the explosion bent the doors to the pod inward. No way will they open now. And even if we could pry them apart, the pod's doors are more than likely trashed as well. Fuck.

"Where's another pod?" My hearing is starting to come back. Loud shouting is coming from behind us. I shake Ash's hand to get her to snap out of it. "Where?" She looks behind us, slow and deliberate. I tug her away, hoping we're heading in the right direction.

In the end it isn't me who snaps her out of it. It's the loud explosion that sounds like it's coming from everywhere at once. We both fall as the floor quakes underneath us. We're out of time.

Ash gets up first. "This way." She drags me to my feet.

I've never run so fast, not even when that beast on the planet was chasing us. We are literally in a race for our lives. If we can't find a pod before the ship implodes, well, we won't have anything more to say.

The ceiling behind us collapses in flames, and the ship lists to port. I slam my helmet screen down and reactivate my air. I'm okay with a little fog. The heat from the fire is enough to bubble the finish on the walls.

"Here," Ash yells. She stops in front of a pod and slaps the panel to open the door. We list again, this time toward the bow. Toward the fire. I fall and roll. My foot stops me from going too far, but it gets wedged in a broken wall panel about to catch fire. I yank as hard as I can. The fire creeps closer. Ash crawls toward me, she grabs both my arms and pulls.

"Stop. My foot's stuck," I yell.

Another explosion rocks the ship. This one is closer. Ash and I work to pry my foot loose. The wall panel next to us catches fire. It jumps onto my enviro-suit leg. These suits are meant to repel almost anything, even radiation, but fire is one of those things that will only stay out for so long. Ash kicks the wall panel with a fury I've never seen. She picks up a mangled metal brace and swings it with all her force. It works. She pulls me free and whacks my leg, smothering the fire.

We clamber toward the open pod door. Ash slams her hand down on the initiate-launch button. It's the only control in the whole pod. The doors hiss shut, and in less than ten seconds we're jettisoned from the ship. We lie breathing on the floor, and then we're lifted into the air. The farther away we get from the ship, the less gravity there is in the pod until there's none, and we're left floating. The pod is round and clear, giving us a perfect view of the destruction we've left behind.

The illya's ship is now a rotating fireball. Or perhaps giant mass is a better description. Very little is left of the actual hull, only arms and legs set askew as the flames engulf what's left.

In the far distance are the *Avokaado* and the *Posterus*. I don't see any sign of the *Persephone*, but then Ash points it out among the giants. My heart soars. She's fared well for everything she's gone through.

A few other pods are drifting beyond the wreckage, tiny dots in the great expanse of space. Again I'm amazed at the fragility of life. Somehow we manage to survive every catastrophe, and I attribute this to Ash's win factor. She always comes out on top. The pod spins in a slow arc, affording us a view of the entire galaxy. If I'd thought I'd be here two months ago, I wouldn't have believed it.

We really are starting new. Even if we could go back to our own galaxy, who would want to? Not after they learn what we were. A payment. The Commons bartered with our lives like we were bars of gold. I don't even know if that was a good price. Forty-five thousand for a million. And for what? To live out the rest of their lives on the Belt? What a waste.

Ash opens her helmet screen and breathes deep. "There's air. Not sure how much, but I think someone will pick us up before we run out." She unhooks her helmet and lets go. It drifts around the pod, twirling until it bumps into a side.

I follow her lead. I float to the edge of the pod and pull off my gloves. I press my fingertips to the cool glass. We are truly alone now.

Ash spins me to face her. "Hey." Her smile is tinged with sadness. "We made it."

I nod. I'm embarrassed to say I'm on the verge of tears. It all seems so pointless. To make it this far and for nothing. No planet is waiting for us. Our descendants have no future.

"Hey." Ash pulls off her own gloves and cups my face. "We made it. All that other shit can come later. Right now let's just be happy we're here and not back there." She cocks her head toward the burning ship. "It's over. We may not have a plan, but at least no one else has plans for us." She kisses me. Her lips sink into mine, and in that moment I have no more thoughts of what will happen to us. I'm happy to just exist in this tiny world with Ash.

She unzips my enviro-suit and slides her hands inside. Her eyes dip to my cleavage and my internal temperature spikes. I shrug out of my suit, and Ash helps slide it down my body. Her hands glide along my skin, setting fires as she goes. She quickly discards her own suit, and we spin in a tight embrace around the pod. Her lips dance down my neck to my collarbone, and I grab tight, keeping her close. When all barriers have been removed, I pull back and stare.

The ambient light from the pod makes her skin look luminescent. It also highlights every scar, cut, and bruise on her body. There's a scar from the mess incident right above her left breast. I bend and kiss it, then move on to a small bruise on her shoulder. I soothe each cut, each scar. My hands run along her arms, stomach, legs. Ash's breathing comes in short gasps.

"We might run out of air sooner than I thought," she says.

I grin and take a nipple in my mouth, tempted to test her limits. She grasps my shoulders and arches her back. I ache to speed things up. I have an unexplainable need to hear her come. I run my fingers through her folds and slip inside. Her nails dig into my shoulders. I hook one of my legs around hers, and we slowly spin around and around as she builds toward her own explosion. Her breath hitches and a low moan escapes as she tightens around my fingers. We're pressed together so tightly I can feel her heart hammering in the same rhythm as mine. And that's when I realize we have our whole future to worry about what happens next. In this moment nothing but us exists.

EPILOGUE

Jordan

I wake to an empty bed. Ash hasn't gone far, because I can hear humming in the other room. This is just one of the many things I love about her. You'd never imagine she's the type to hum, but she does. All the time. It took me years to discover that about her. She'll do it only when she thinks she's alone.

I turn over and shield my eyes from the sun. I can picture Ash moving around the kitchen, preparing coffee for us to take out onto our back deck and watch the sun rise over the mountains. We call it coffee. It isn't really. It's similar and still gives you a jolt in the morning. And after years of getting used to the bitter aftertaste, I can pretend I like it.

Ash tiptoes into the room, afraid she'll wake me. Her robe sash has slipped open, revealing the small curve of her belly. She's only just started showing, even though she's already five months along. I close my eyes and pretend to be sleeping as she moves around the room getting dressed.

The bed dips as she sits. She runs the tip of her finger down my nose. "Hey, you're missing the sunrise." She kisses me on the lips. I open my eyes and am treated to a pleasant view. She hasn't put a shirt on yet.

I pull her into bed with me and throw all the covers over us. It's warm and cozy, and I debate trying to convince Ash to stay in bed for the rest of the day. She'll refuse. Especially today. It's a big day. I make a big effort to convince her with only my hands and mouth. I run my hand down her belly, about to start closing arguments, when she wraps her hand around my wrist and gently pulls it up.

"Not today." She gives me one last chaste kiss and throws the covers off. "Your coffee's on the counter." She throws a shirt over her head.

Dressed with coffee in hand, I step onto our back deck. It overlooks a huge valley, which dips to meet the mountains in the distance. It's so early mist still obscures the river at the bottom of the valley. I take a seat next to Ash as our second sun rises above the tallest peak.

It's been two years, and I still can't get over how beautiful it is here. The air is humid and fresh with the scent of flowers from the fields drifting through our yard.

It's been two years since we found New Earth. We don't have an official name for it yet, but that's what everyone calls it. Hartley says it's not good enough or, in his exact words, "pathetic." I agree. From what I remember, Earth was a parched yellow sphere. We need something that describes paradise. And as I do on most days, I wonder if this is what it was like to watch the sunrise on Earth. Is this what Sarka saw? I think about him sometimes, more than I used to. When I was younger I rarely thought about him. It was a conscious effort to get over that part of my life. But after getting to know him as an adult, I think about him now, especially about what he said in the tunnel about choices. Will I make those same choices for our child?

It's been twelve years since that day. Over a decade and he's still in my thoughts. Ash says it must be because I believe him and forgive him. It surprises me that she can talk about that like it's okay—that day when I pulled her away from trying to rip him apart, I'm not sure if she was trying to hurt Sarka or her own father for what he did.

I know she'll never forgive him for what he did to her, but she's made her peace with it. Ash doesn't like to dwell on the past. I try not to.

After the destruction of the *Kudo*, I was worried the Varbaja would find a new prey, maybe us. It's hard to change direction after you've been going the same way for so long. Hundreds of years and dozens of generations were lost in that war. Once it was over, I thought they'd feel bereft. Many didn't have homes to go back to, or they were so far back in their memories there was no point to returning. But as soon as the war was over, they did take on a new purpose. Us. They helped us fix our ships, even sharing some of their technology. Those who wanted to join were invited to come along with us on our journey to find a new home. It was decided unanimously that we would continue from where we were.

We never did tell the others the true nature of our mission. Those of us who knew decided it was best that the others remember home with fondness instead of bitterness. It hasn't been as hard as I thought. Shortly after we rendezvoused with the *Posterus*, Vasa took his own life. I think the guilt was too much for him. It's one thing to agree to something when it's only an abstract mission. But when he saw the results of his decisions, he couldn't live with himself. I wish I'd had a chance to talk to him before he made that choice. He was just a pawn. They would've found someone else if he'd refused. But that's what life is, a series of choices, and it's how we decide to live with those choices that defines what kind of life we'll lead. I haven't always made the best ones, but I feel I've come to terms with the ones I'm not so proud of.

Gladwell was given an opportunity to either lose his rank and position or leave the ship and join the Varbaja. Since it was agreed we would hide why we ended up in that system, it was hard to punish him as a traitor. Even stripping him of his rank would be risky; we had no guarantee he'd stay quiet. But he chose the latter and left the *Posterus*. Who knows where he is now, and frankly, who cares?

If the Commons hadn't bargained our lives for theirs, we'd still be stuck on the Belt with them. Instead we're here. And it wasn't just our species we helped; the Varbaja and every species the illya preyed on are now free. That wouldn't have happened if the Commons had made different choices.

I drain the last of my coffee and set the mug on the table between us. It hasn't all been great. There have been sacrifices and hardships. The *Brimley* and her crew never made it back from their mission. They just stopped reporting back one day. We waited for as long as we could. The Varbaja sent out probes and scout ships, but we never did learn what happened to them. Ash says it's a new mystery to replace the one we solved on the planet. That's where Hartley says they probably ended up. They found the planet and decided to settle. As much as I disliked Harrios, I don't think he'd do that. Not because he was a selfless person deep down. The joy of gloating that he'd found a planet for everyone to settle on would outweigh any urge to keep it for themselves.

We'll never know what happened to them, but whatever it was, it wasn't good. Space is never easy. No matter how much we think we've conquered it, there's always something to smack you in the face and prove you know nothing.

Tup decided to stay with us after all. Living on a large ship was the only life he'd ever known, and as he put it, "I'd grown to like a lot of human customs." He especially liked scrambled eggs with hot sauce. But when we settled on New Earth, Tup decided to keep going. We helped him upgrade his ship for long journeys, gave him as much liquid egg solution as he could fit in his cargo hold, and said our good-byes.

For the first year or so we got long-range probes from him. But soon those stopped. I like to think it's because he found a natural wormhole and is exploring a whole new solar system.

Ash stands and I groan. I'm not ready to start the day. I pull her into my lap. "Just a few more minutes."

"Are you kidding? We have so much to do." She pecks me on the forehead and stands. "If you're still here when I'm done showering, you're in trouble."

"Hey, you can't boss me around. I still outrank you."

She smirks at me from the door. "On the *Persephone* that's true. But when we're at home," she chucks a thumb at herself, "I'm in charge."

"Says who?"

She looks around like I'm crazy, then points to herself again. "Me. Of course."

It wasn't easy at first, and not because people objected. Sure, we'd broken Union fleet rules, but fuck the rules. Out here things are different. No one gave a shit or begrudged us our happiness. But those rules were there for a reason. It's not easy maintaining a relationship with your subordinate. Yet Ash has never wanted my command, which makes things easier. We made our own rules. Very early on we decided that when we were on duty, I was in charge. To make it fair, when we're not, she gets to be in charge. Sometimes. A lot of the times. But I have the power to veto. I've used it only twice. Once when we were deciding on colors for our walls. No way was red going to be the color of our bedroom. And when she wanted to name the baby Zuma if it was a girl. We have no idea what we'll name her, but it's not going to be Zuma.

Ash pops out of the door in a towel. "Did you remember to bring a case of tofuloaf from the *Persephone*?"

I roll me eyes. "Yes. It's in the back storage room. I still think it's a stupid wedding present."

"It's a joke. I got him something else as well." She ducks back inside.

Hartley's getting married today, and Ash is his best man, which means duties. I've not been to many weddings, but I do know it's best when you're not part of the wedding party. I like the idea of showing up, handing over a gift, enjoying the refreshments, and leaving. The wedding isn't until this afternoon, but we have to be at the hall before noon. I'm not sure who Yakovich's maid of honor is, but I'm happy to be surprised because it means I'm not in the wedding party. Not that it matters. I'm as good as in, according to Ash.

I hear the water from the shower turn on. The window is open, so Ash's humming floats out over the sound of the water spray. A tiny yellow bug with long wings lands on the edge of my coffee cup. A thin, forked tongue unfurls and laps up the liquid left in the bottom.

This planet is almost perfect. Atmospherically, very similar to Earth, and best of all, we have the whole thing to ourselves. As far as I know, no one on my crew has ever mentioned the planet and the avians to anyone. I hope as they evolve, they make better choices than we did. We're living proof of what happens when you don't care.

From what I've seen of this planet so far, and we've done extensive exploring of this continent, this planet is much better suited to us. It's in the goldilocks zone in a binary system, just like the one we were heading toward. Only this one didn't take us a lifetime to reach.

I spend a few more seconds watching the birds and insects wake up and begin their day before I head toward the shower.

Ash is still humming when I pull the curtain back. She's mildly shocked until she notices my nudity. Her eyes drop lower, running the length of my body.

"We have a few minutes before we need to start our day." I step into the shower and close the curtain behind me.

She grins. "Challenge accepted."

About the Author

CJ Birch is a video editor and digital artist based in Toronto. When not lost in a good book or working, CJ can be found writing or drinking serious coffee, or doing both at the same time. She doesn't have any pets, but she does have a rather vicious ficus that has a habit of shedding all over the hardwood, usually right before company comes. *False Horizons* is her fourth book. You can find CJ on social media @cjbirchwrites or www.cjbirchwrites.com.

Books Available From Bold Strokes Books

All She Wants by Larkin Rose. Marci Jones and Tessa Dalton get more than they bargained for when their plans for a one-night stand turn into an opportunity for love. (978-1-63555-476-2)

Beautiful Accidents by Erin Zak. Stevie Adams doesn't believe in fate, not after losing her parents in a car crash. But she's about to discover that sometimes the best things in life happen purely by accident. (978-1-63555-497-7)

Before Now by Joy Argento. The instant Delaney Peyton and Jade Taylor meet, they sense a connection neither can explain. Can they overcome a betrayal that spans the centuries to reignite a love that can't be broken? (978-1-63555-525-7)

Breathe by Cari Hunter. Paramedic Jemima Pardon's chronic bad luck seems to be improving when she meets police officer Rosie Jones. But they face a battle to survive before they can find love. (978-1-63555-523-3)

Double-Crossed by Ali Vali. Hired thief and killer Reed Gable finds something in her scope that will change her life forever when she gets a contract to end casino accountant Brinley Myers's life. (978-1-63555-302-4)

False Horizons by CJ Birch. Jordan and Ash struggle with different views on the alien agenda and must find their way back to each other before they're swallowed up by a centuries-old war. Third in the New Horizons series. (978-1-63555-519-6)

Legacy by Charlotte Greene. In this paranormal mystery, five women hike to a remote cabin deep inside a national park—and unsettling events suggest that they should have stayed home. (978-1-63555-490-8)

Somewhere Along the Way by Kathleen Knowles. When Maxine Cooper moves to San Francisco during the summer of 1981, she learns that wherever you run, you cannot escape yourself. (978-1-63555-383-3)

Blood of the Pack by Jenny Frame. When Alpha of the Scottish pack Kenrick Wulver visits the Wolfgangs, she falls for Zaria Lupa, a wolf on the run. (978-1-63555-431-1)

Cause of Death by Sheri Lewis Wohl. Medical student Vi Akiak and K9 Search and Rescue officer Kate Renard must work together to find a killer before they end up the next targets. In the race for survival, they discover that love may be the biggest risk of all. (978-1-63555-441-0)

Chasing Sunset by Missouri Vaun. Hijinks and mishaps ensue as Iris and Finn set off on a road trip adventure, chasing the sunset, and falling in love along the way. (978-1-63555-454-0)

Double Down by MB Austin. When an unlikely friendship with Spanish pop star Erlea turns deeper, Celeste, in-house physician for the hotel hosting Erlea's show, has a choice to make—run or double down on love. (978-1-63555-423-6)

Party of Three by Sandy Lowe. Three friends are in for a wild night at billionaire heiress Eleanor McGregor's twenty-fifth birthday party. Love, lust, and doing the right thing, even when it hurts, turn the evening into one that will change their lives forever. (978-1-63555-246-1)

Sit. Stay. Love. by Karis Walsh. City girl Alana Brendt and country vet Tegan Evans both know they don't belong together. Only problem is, they're falling in love. (978-1-63555-439-7)

Where the Lies Hide by Renee Roman. As P.I. Camdyn Stark gets closer to solving the case, will her dark secrets and the lies she's buried jeopardize her future with the quietly beautiful Sarah Peters? (978-1-63555-371-0)

Beautiful Dreamer by Melissa Brayden. With love on the line, can Devyn Winters find it in her heart to stay in the small town of Dreamer's Bay, the one place she swore she'd never remain? (978-1-63555-305-5)

Create a Life to Love by Erin Zak. When sixteen-year-old Beth shows up at her birth mother's door, three lives will change forever. (978-1-63555-425-0)